THE ALMOST ROMANTIC

LAUREN BLAKELY

ABOUT

Fake engagement. Real marriage. Both have an expiration date in this spicy marriage of convenience romantic comedy standalone!

"Marry me."

They were the last words I expected to say to my fake fiancé, but I'm the kind of guy who doesn't back down from a challenge.

Pretend I'm engaged to my gorgeous and talented business partner to secure a business deal?

No problem.

Agree to a no-touch rule even though she's been driving me wild since I met her?

Challenge accepted.

Resist grinning like a damn fool every time that same big-hearted, sunshine-y woman laughs with my little daughter?

Done.

So, yeah, when my fake fiancé's vindictive business

rival threatens to expose our make-believe romance, I can handle that too.

I'll prove our engagement isn't fake – by marrying her for real.

A marriage with an expiration date at the end of the year.

But that's when I run smack dab into the biggest challenge ever – not falling madly in love with **my wife.**

DID YOU KNOW?

By Lauren Blakely

To be the first to find out when all of my upcoming books go live click here!

PRO TIP: Add lauren@laurenblakely.com to your contacts before signing up to make sure the emails go to your inbox!

Did you know this book is also available in audio and paperback on all major retailers? Go to my website for links!

For content warnings for this title, go to my site.

1

THE BAD SEX CHALLENGE

Elodie

Pretty sure I shouldn't have come to a bar staffed by the world's most droolworthy bartender after hosting a *chocolate as an aphrodisiac* class.

After teaching all those oh-so-in-love couples at my shop tonight about the sensual powers of chocolate, I should have marched straight home and taken an antidote in the form of organizing the junk drawer or scrubbing the kitchen floor while thinking deep thoughts on how to adult better.

But the rosemary fries at Sticks and Stones lured me here, and as I wait for the kitchen to finish my to-go order, my libido takes the wheel.

That man mixing a mojito at the other end of the bar is seriously scorching. This place should come with a warning sign reading: Enter this establishment at your own risk.

I need to tap the brakes and stop staring at the ink on his arms, the scruff on his jaw, the sin in his dark eyes.

I pop in my earbuds and scroll through my podcasts for a distraction. I hit start on a new episode of my friend's dating show, and after the Heartbreakers and Matchmakers intro, a soprano-pitched guest host immediately begins: "Who wants to take the bad sex challenge? Tell us your sex troubles and we'll help you figure out how to do it...better."

Intrigued, I listen for another minute. But while the guest hosts—a disgustingly happy married couple— offer to tackle the between-the-sheets troubles of the single listeners by recreating the bad sex, off-air of course, my attention strays once more to Mister Drool-worthy. I've seen him here a few times when I've swung by. Exchanged a word here or there. And admired the view.

Right now, he's dropping a sprig of mint into a frosted glass. I'd let him fix my sex life. I'd let him fix it so hard. I bet he could fix it with those hands, those arms, that firm body...that's coming my way.

Ack!

He delivers the mint-sprigged drink to a woman behind me, then stops right by my side. I smile a little innocently then pop out my earbuds.

"Something amusing?" he asks when he reaches me, with a tease of a smile coasting over those lips. Why does he have to have a bedroom voice to match those bedroom eyes?

Because the universe likes to taunt me with things I can't have—like a mortgage and a hot-ass man.

"Very much so. It's the bad sex challenge," I tell him, after hitting stop on the podcast.

He frowns. "Who would take that?"

"Apparently lots of couples are taking it without even knowing it."

He wiggles his fingers, beckoning me to share more. "Details."

"I hate to break it to you, but there's a lot of bad sex out there in the world. People suffering from this condition are calling into this podcast with their sex woes, and then this happily horny couple are offering their fixes."

"*Sex* and *woe*. Two words that should not go together."

"You're probably right."

"I'm definitely right," he says, but he's clearly intrigued. He hasn't even asked me for a drink order. He tips his forehead toward my phone. "So do they fix them? These...sex woes?"

It's said with a shudder.

I make a seesaw gesture. "Sort of. They say they're going to try out the bad sex to diagnose what others are doing wrong. Then, they'll share tips to help make the sex lives of others great again."

"I did not know Good Sex Samaritans existed," he says, deadpanning amazement.

"You learn something new every day."

"I guess it's actually the great sex challenge then." He

takes a beat, his gaze lingering on me for several long, delicious seconds. "Right?"

Sign me up for that, I want to say. Right now. Right here. But even I'm not *that* impulsive. "That doesn't sound like such a terrible ordeal," I say with a bob of my shoulder.

"Challenge accepted then," he says, then clears his throat, and almost like it's hard for him, he shakes his head and shifts to business mode. "Need anything while we finish up your order?"

To sit on your face.

I smile like the superhero I am. Classy by day. Horny by night. "Just the food," I say, surprised he knows I'm here for a pickup rather than a drink since he wasn't behind the bar when I arrived earlier to place my order. "Margo said they should be ready soon. But how did you know what I was waiting for?"

"It's my job to know. I own the place." Bartenders are already unfairly sexy. Now I learn he runs it too? Responsible men are so hot. I'm not and have never been in a bad boy era, so my hormones are waving the white flag.

"And you own it well. It's one of my favorites."

"Good," he says with a smile that melts me even more. "Let me check on that order for you."

He turns to go, and I shamelessly watch as he strides to the end of the bar. He has an athlete's physique, and I'm not complaining. Except when he disappears out of sight.

I'm definitely going to take a long, hot shower this evening after my little sister goes to bed. Spend some quality time with a waterproof friend to forget about the day, and the swirl of upcoming decisions that have been chasing me.

Or, better idea. Maybe my favorite sex toy shop can deliver me a new one since you can never have enough chocolate or vibrators. I hop over to the website for Risqué Business and skim the new offerings, gliding my polished cherry-red nail against the screen until I reach…The Command Performance. I read all about its stimulating properties.

And I'm sold. I'm one of the store's platinum customers, so I hit order, then re-enter my address. A few seconds later, the "coming in one hour delivery" confirmation pops up.

With that dirty deed done, I act casual, smoothing a hand over my polka-dot skirt, fiddling with my rhinestone cocktail ring that I wear nearly every day, then adjusting the red paisley bandana that keeps my blonde hair in this retro style as I wait for the owner's return. I mean, my takeout.

Did I put on lipstick before I came?

Couldn't hurt to apply some more. I grab the tube from my handbag, slick some on, then purse my lips. There. I'm ready.

I replace my earbuds and tune back into the podcast, hoping Mister Droolworthy returns to finish the job— the job of asking me for my number.

One minute passes. More customers arrive. Another bartender comes behind the bar, a pale, petite woman with a silvery pixie cut.

Two minutes. Servers rush out from the kitchen,

lifting trays of burgers and sandwiches and scurrying to tables.

Three minutes. I check my phone, then groan privately over the new email. It's from The Chocolate Connoisseur, and the CEO's asking if I have reviewed his buyout offer. *Yes, I have, and it's seriously stressing me out so much I need fifty orders of fries.* The low-ball offer from the corporate giant's been weighing on me, but I can't drag my feet on it much longer, so I reply that I'll respond soon.

Four minutes, five, and then Margo emerges from the swinging door instead of the man who'd said he was checking on my order. Her crinkled eyes swing to me, and she nods, heading my way. She's carrying a brown paper bag with my name on it.

"Here you go, Elodie. The rosemary fries, a hummus sandwich, and a salad," she says in her grandmotherly voice, weathered but playful. Her gaze strays subtly, or not so subtly, toward the back of the house.

"Thanks. I think I'm addicted to the fries," I blurt out. I don't want her to think I was waiting around for the hot bartender to make a move. I'm here for the food. Just the food.

She leans closer, her gray eyes full of a wisdom I wonder if I'll ever possess as she says, "I get that. They're addictive, so you can just keep coming back. Need anything else, hun?"

To tell the owner that I'm sorry I misread him so badly.

He's a friendly bartender, that's all. I'm just a woman amped up from her chocolate class. A woman who should go home and focus on her sister, and her bills, and her bank notices.

I smile brightly, hoping it doesn't read as false. "I'm all good," I say, then grab my sweater, take the bag, and go.

It's fine. It's just fine. I'll go home, spend time with Amanda, then once she goes to bed, I'll have some *me time*. And I don't have to wonder what The Command Performance's intentions are whatsoever.

2

PRETTY IN PURPLE

Gage

I'm almost too busy at the bar to be annoyed that Rosie the Riveter, with the swingy skirts that show off her legs and the snug tops that make my brain scramble, took off before I could chat with her some more.

We're packed tonight at Sticks and Stones, so I barely have a second to stew on that missed opportunity—*again*—since I'm serving brews, mixing cocktails, and putting out fires.

It's the third time the blonde with the clever mouth has come here in the last month, but it's the first time I've flirted with her. And I never flirt with customers. That's just asking for trouble, and I've had enough of that in my life, thank you very much.

But there's just something about her that makes me want to break my rules. Hell, I was ready to head back out there and ask for her number. Right as I was about to return to the front of the house and throw caution to the wind, my eleven-year-old texted. She asked for my Webflix password so she could watch a new dragon flick at her friend's home, and I had to tease her that parents are supposed to forget the passwords, not kids, and then she said I forgot to bring her glove to her softball game last week, and I had to point out, too, that bringing her mitt is her job, not mine.

And well, Eliza's the priority and that's just the way it is. By the time I sent her a gif of a dog rolling his eyes and saying *yeah right*, the woman at the bar was long gone.

Probably a sign from the universe and all that now's not the time in my life to bend any rules.

Besides, as I pour a pale ale for one of my regular customers a half hour later, I've got expansion plans for Sticks and Stones on my mind. Maybe I'll hear back tomorrow about that lease I've been trying to get for a second location over in the Marina District.

That'd be sweet.

And, since I've got Friday night off, I could spend my time firming up my ideas. I usually take off one Friday night a month to work on marketing or admin.

I set the beer down in front of the guy who stops by a couple nights a week and likes to talk all things hockey while he nurses a brew. "Here you go, Russ. Did you see Armstrong's goal last night right after that line change?"

"Saw it. Called it. And then wondered why the Foxes don't hire me for their coaching staff."

"I ask myself the same damn thing," I say, and I'm

about to dive deep into strategy matters when Zoe strides right up to me, then tips her forehead toward the back of the bar. "Margo says she needs you. As in Gage Reginald Archer, *right now*."

I cower a bit at the use of my full name. "You man the bar," I say, then before she can correct me, I do it myself. "*Woman* the bar."

"And he can learn," says the spunky twenty-two-year-old with silvery hair and ears full of piercings. "But you can also just say *handle the bar*."

"Got it," I say, then hightail it to the back.

Right before I reach my office, my grandmother steps out, arches a brow, then says, "What did I tell you about sending private things to the restaurant?"

I rack my brain, trying to find a grandma-ism in there. What salty piece of life advice did she dispense about where to mail things? But I come up empty. "Nothing?"

"Then it's time we discussed it now, young man," she says, and at thirty-three I hardly feel young, but it's best not to argue with Grams.

"Yes, ma'am."

She beckons with her finger, and I follow her into my office, which is also her office, where she grabs a padded, pastel pink envelope from my desk. There's no store name on it so I've no idea where it came from, but judging by the shape of the bulge I have an idea.

"Is that the new rolling pin I ordered? The cook was looking for one."

"In a way," Grams says, but there's a smirk on her face as she thrusts the envelope at me.

I dip my hand inside and…that's not a rolling pin at all. That's a long, thick, purple dong.

In my hand.

I blink down at the thing that's got to be at least eight inches. The tag on it says The Command Performance.

"How did this get here? Is it yours?" I ask, then instantly want to eat my words. I don't want to know what Grams does with her alone time.

She's staring at me with amused eyes. Holding her phone. And recording me.

Ah, hell.

"What are you going to do with that?" I ask, shocked at her speed. "Post it on the restaurant's social media?"

"No. But I might show it to your brother. He'd find this entertaining too. So would your friends."

I groan. "You're not going to do that." I'm not weirded out by sex toys. I think they're awesome, and I'm glad women use them, and one of my biggest goals in life is to never discuss sex toys with my daughter. Ever. Like, in the history of forever.

But, all things being equal, I don't need to give my brother or buddies more ammo either.

Grams lowers her phone, then pats my shoulder. "Don't worry, hun. My generation had to deal with those desires too. And back then there wasn't even a thing about sex positivity."

"I swear, Grams. It's not mine."

"Whatever you say. I'm here when you're ready to talk," she says, then lets her gaze stray very purposefully to the envelope and the address on it. "Maybe you want to do the right thing."

My brow creases. "And that would be?"

"Well, if you found a wallet, what would you do?"

On that chestnut, she takes off, leaving me in my office with an envelope and a fake dick.

I flip over the label on the package, hunting for a clue. That's the address for Sticks and Stones right in the center of it, but the name above it is Elodie Starling.

Huh.

She's not one of my employees.

Instantly, I'm consumed with the need to know who she is. My gut is telling me something. I set the vibrating dual-density dildo on my desk, then google the name. In seconds, the search engine spits out some intel. Elodie Starling is a San Francisco native, lifelong chocolate devotee, and a believer that life's better when it's sweeter.

She's also the owner of Elodie's Chocolates, which is a mile from here. I click on the link, and hello, sex challenge.

There's her picture. The gorgeous, sassy blonde who sent a vibrator to herself at my bar tonight.

It's not quite like finding someone's wallet, but perhaps it's even better. And really, I should follow Grams' advice.

Even if it means I'm bending the rules a little. Or a lot.

3

THE DILDO THIEF

Elodie

Talk about a parenting trial by fire.

That's what the last two years have been. With no safety net or help from a partner, I've had to scramble to have the period talk, the *we need to change schools* convo, and the birds and the bees discussion with Amanda.

Parenting is so hard, especially when it comes to parenting your thirteen-year-old sister.

But *this* is uncharted terrain, and I don't even want to google *what to do when your kid sister steals your battery-operated-boyfriend*.

Since last night's disappearing dildo act, I've been practicing for just the right moment to ask Amanda if she nicked it, but I'm still flabbergasted the next day when I'm behind the counter in my chocolate shop, checking the time. Three-thirty. She should be here any minute.

My assistant manager, Kenji, catches me staring at the clock. "Please don't tell me you're already counting the minutes till quitting time. If so, there's no hope for the rest of us," he says, while tying bows on gift boxes.

As I delicately place salted caramels into paper cups on the counter, I peer out the glass door, past the pretty *Elodie's* script in robin's egg blue. No sign of Amanda yet.

There's a brief lull in customers. "Listen," I say quietly to Kenji, since I can't take the worry anymore. "I'm seriously worried that Amanda took my—" Dammit. It's hard to say, even to an adult who's a friend. Where is the handbook for all this hard stuff?

Kenji makes a rolling gesture with his hand. "Your flat iron? Your credit card? Your Webflix password? Or the Louis Roederer 2013 Cristal Rosé Brut that you got me as a surprise for my twenty-eighth birthday next month?"

Laughing, I whisper out of the side of my mouth, "My...Command Performance."

"Your Command Performance?" he repeats, at top volume.

"Shush," I say.

His brown eyes pop. "Oh! That must be one of your battery-operated friends."

A flush starts in my chest, spreads up my neck, and splashes across my cheeks. "How did you know that's what it was?"

He laugh-scoffs. "We don't call you the Queen of Toys for nothing. You've gifted sex toys to Rachel,

Hazel, Juliet, and Fable." He frowns. "But not me. So sad."

Shit. Is that crossing a line with an employee, to give him one? But he's a friend too. "Do you want one?"

"Nope. I want the champagne. But don't even try to turn this around. Tell me all about this missing Command Performance," he says, like he's eating this story up with a spoon.

At least this conversation has taken my mind off The Chocolate Connoisseur offer still sitting on my desk at home. It's too hard to think about the future of my shop and the right way to run it, when I have to deal with a missing dildo.

As I pluck the final caramel with a pair of tweezers, setting it delicately in the paper, I take a deep breath and explain more. "So last night while I was at Sticks and Stones, I ordered a new toy for one-hour delivery. An hour later I was home, putting on jammies when the *package delivered* notification from Risqué Business popped up on my phone. But when I left my room, Amanda had already disappeared into her bedroom, and there was no pink envelope from the shop waiting for me. Ergo..."

Kenji's eyes spark with pass-the-popcorn delight as he clears his throat and tips his head toward the door. "I think *that's* what happened to your order."

A bell chimes. Like I'm watching a traffic accident in slow-mo, I turn to the store's entrance.

Mister Droolworthy walks into my shop with easy confidence. He's wearing well-worn jeans, a dark blue Henley, and the most satisfied grin. Maybe because he's carrying a pink envelope as he holds open the door for a pack of other customers to go ahead of him because when it rains, it pours.

On the one hand, I'm relieved because I couldn't quite believe my sister would take it. But on the other hand, I'm looking for a portal to another dimension.

That casual smile never leaves his too-handsome face as he hangs back, letting the other customers head to the counter first.

I straighten my shoulders and smile for the customers, hoping they're fast and I can get this whole thing over with quickly. The first pair asks questions about my new line of bonbons in autumn colors, then the dark chocolate-covered blackberries in a rich purple shade from the Melt In Your Mouth line. Maybe I can talk to them the whole time and Mister D will get the message and drop off the dong, then be on his merry way without mocking me.

I spend the next few minutes bantering with them, as Kenji handles another customer.

Then they're gone.

And Kenji flashes the biggest smile in the world at Mister D. "It sure looks like you have something Elodie wants badly," he coos, grinning at the envelope.

I vow to kill him later.

Well, after he rearranges the schedule for the employees next week. And removes the peanut butter cups from their molds. And places our next Valrhona order since, as a chocolatier, our business is chocolate-to-confection, and Valrhona makes the best chocolate to use in all the recipes I've created.

Ugh. He's too valuable to eighty-six.

As another group of customers comes in, Kenji slides past me with a wink, moving to help them at the other end of the counter.

Which means I can't avoid Mister D anymore. He's standing across from me. "Elodie Starling." It's like he's having fun saying the name on the package. "I believe this is for you." He dangles the pink envelope as if it's a prize when really it's a billboard advertising *good girls with dirty desires.*

My face isn't just a flame. My whole body is red with embarrassment as I get a better look at the envelope at last. It's ripped all along the end. "You actually opened it?" It's not an accusation. It's a quiet question, spoken like a mouse.

Where has all my confidence gone? Oh, right. It whooshed out the door five minutes ago, right along with my dignity.

"Not me," he says with a shake of his head.

"Then who?"

"My grandma."

I didn't think this moment could get worse, but I was wrong. I close my eyes, deflated, then open them to say, "I'm...so sorry."

But then, wait. I replay those words in my head. Did I just apologize for ordering a vibrator? Who am I? Am I a mouse or a flamingo?

A flamingo, dammit.

An unabashed sex toy aficionado too. I have a platinum account at the finest shop in the city. I have great orgasms I give myself, and I *love* them.

They're the only sure thing in my life right now—a life that's teetering with bills and questions and decisions I don't want to face.

I lift my chin. "What I meant to say is thank you for returning this." Then with my head held high, I reach for the envelope with pride. "In fact, I was definitely missing it last night."

There. Not ashamed at all. Just to prove how not ashamed I am as I tuck the package under my arm, I add, "And I'm so glad to have it back. No idea why it wound up at your bar though."

"Me neither, but I definitely didn't mind," he says, but I barely register the words as I look closely at the address on the envelope. That's weird. That's not my address.

It's his.

Which means...

"Oh my god. I know what happened. I must have copied the Sticks and Stones address into my GPS on my way over to pick up my order. Then when I pasted in the address for *this*, I copied in yours, not mine."

"Too bad. I was hoping it was subliminal."

He was?

And wait. Did he just say he didn't mind that I'd sent this by mistake?

All that red-hot embarrassment slinks away, replaced only by curiosity. "You were hoping I'd sent you a toy?"

He leans closer, like he did last night at the bar. Immediately, I'm caught in his flirt bubble once again. "I did a little research on Risqué Business. They have one-hour delivery. This package arrived an hour after you left," he says, his green eyes glimmering, asking what his mouth won't—*did you order it while thinking of me?*

I don't answer. Instead, I ask a question of my own, whispering, "Are you a sex-toy detective?"

"Just got my license last night. And I'm enjoying this new line of work immensely," he says, sending a zing of desire down my chest. "But I'm a little concerned about something, and I'm hoping you can help me out."

"Sure," I say, going with it.

Brow creased with concern, he points to the package I'm now holding. "It arrived with lube. But no batteries. Are the batteries coming separately?"

"Yes, that's often how it works. Simultaneous deliveries aren't that common."

"They're overrated anyway," he says.

"You think so?"

"It's more important that ladies go first. And often."

It's official. I've met my soul mate. "Preach."

"Do you know what else I learned last night in my recon?"

"Dying to know."

He glances down at the counter where Kenji's tapping away on the tablet, ringing up an order. The man of my fantasies looks back to me. "That the dual density simulates the...real thing." He takes his time saying those last two words, and an electric charge pulses down my spine.

Partly because he did research the purchase. He didn't just laugh at the silicone schlong. He looked it up. Wanted to understand it. A man who tries to understand the properties of sex toys is my kind of man.

"Yes, that's why I ordered it," I say.

"Good to know. Plus, it has seven vibration modes. *Seven.*" He lets out a low whistle of admiration.

"Seven's my favorite number."

"And it has a remote control. For hands-free action."

"Well, they don't call it The Command Performance for nothing," I say.

"Why not just name it The Maestro?"

"You can give it that nickname if you'd like."

"Does this mean you're taking the great solo sex challenge?"

"Don't mock solo sex."

He lifts his hands, his smile disappearing, his eyes turning starkly serious. "I would never ever mock solo sex. It's some of the best."

The image of this man enjoying his shower time lodges in my brain and makes no plans to leave. I try to come up with some clever reply when he checks his watch, then the door before he shrugs, *fuck it* style. "I'm Gage Archer. Can I challenge you to go on a date with me tomorrow night?"

The bell tinkles above the door, and a whoosh of still-warm October air rushes through. Amanda walks in, baggy jeans on, AirPods in, and blonde hair already swept back in a paisley bandana.

There's not a second to weigh whether it's the right time in my life to go on a date with a man I've been crushing on this hard or not. Or to even consider when

I'll fit this date into my busy schedule. I don't think at all. I just *do*. "Yes, you can, Gage Archer," I say.

"Let me give you my number. But I'll need something to write it on." He taps his chin briefly as if in deep thought. I'm about to suggest—well, duh—that a simple exchange of digits via phone would do when he lifts his finger, his expression saying *aha*. "Yes, a receipt would be good to write on. I'll take ten Melt In Your Mouth boxes, five It Had to Be You chocolate bars, four of the You Make Me Feel salted caramels, three of those Lovin' Feeling boxes, a bag of chocolate-covered almonds, and the twenty-four-pack of Always Yours Decadent for my grandma."

My. Mouth.

I can't close it.

"Are you sure?" I ask, my jaw agape.

"When I want something…" He steps closer, and I raise my chin to look at him. "I do what I have to to get it."

Swoon.

Chocolate is the way to my heart—especially my chocolate.

That's our biggest order in ages. As Amanda heads to the back to drop off her bag and fasten on her apron, I quickly gather Gage's order, ring him up, and give him my number with a flourish on the receipt. When he leaves carrying two huge bags, I'm sure I've never seen anything sexier than *that man* carrying my chocolate.

As the shop clears, Amanda strolls behind the counter, AirPod-free, waving a hello to Kenji, then saying hi to me.

"Hey, bug," I say to my favorite person in the world. "How was school?"

But before she can answer, Kenji holds up a hand. "Wait a hot sec, cutie-pie. We need to get all the deets from your sister on what just went down."

Amanda tilts her head, blue eyes sparking with questions. "That dude with the big order?"

Kenji turns to me. "Yes. Tell us all about the dude with the big order. Who was *that*?"

"Who do you mean?" I ask innocently.

Kenji tilts his head, his sleek black hair flopping over his shrewd eyes. "He bought the shop. Wait. He better not be working for The Chocolate Connoisseur."

Amanda's nose crinkles. "Ew. I can't stand their chocolate. Ours is so much better."

"Gage owns a bar, not our rival chocolate shop," I say to them reassuringly.

Kenji snorts. "Rival chocolate shop? Euphemism. More like soulless chain with zero taste. Anyway, I suppose I don't have to hate your new suitor then." Kenji taps his Converse-clad foot. "So, I ask again, who is he?"

"I want to know too," Amanda says with a curious smile. That's nice to see. I didn't see a lot of her smiles, understandably, the first year we lived together. When our parents died in an accident two years ago, both our lives changed overnight. I became her guardian instead of just her sister. I'm thirty to her thirteen, so we only ever lived together as kids for one summer before I left home for college—which means everything I know about being a mom I've learned in a crash course in the last twenty-four months. One I'm pretty sure I'm failing.

Am I supposed to tell her I'm going on a date? Ask her if it's okay? I haven't dated much in the last two years.

"He's a guy I'd like to go on a date with. Would that bother you?" I ask my sister, deciding honesty is the best approach.

She rolls her light blue eyes. "You're such a weirdo."

I blink. "What? Why?"

"I can't believe you're asking my permission. Kenji, can you tell her how cringe she is?"

"So cringe," he seconds.

"How is that cringe?" I ask genuinely.

"If you have to ask," Amanda says, then bends, grabs some chocolate bars from the cabinet, and adds them to the display case.

I look at Kenji with question marks in my eyes.

He whispers *no idea*.

"Hey Els. I have to finish my application for art school next week. Can you look at it later?" Amanda asks, having already moved on.

"Of course," I say, relieved I know the answer to that question.

Then her smile is downright devilish. "Since I want to be done with most of it before tomorrow night and your much-needed date."

Kenji hoots. "Little sister knows best."

She does since I do need a date. Badly.

4

THE FASHION INTERVENTION

Gage

That was so unlike me.

Not the way I asked her—I wasn't kidding when I told her I go after what I want. I just haven't wanted to go on a date for a very long time.

Life is messy enough. I didn't need to make it messier by asking out a customer. Or, really, by tracking down that customer, going to *her* business, and buying up half the store to ask for a date for the next damn night.

There's just something about her though.

So, here I am, freshly showered and dressed in a T-shirt and jeans. I just let my brother into my little town-home in Russian Hill when he arrived a few minutes ago. But I need a better shirt to take out Elodie. Problem is, as I check out my uninspired closet now on a Friday evening, I'm not sure I have a style at all. As I'm staring at the sea of navy, black, and gray Henleys—all bartender gear—I mutter, "What the hell do I even wear?"

As if I've summoned a genie or two, Eliza and Zane stride into my bedroom from the living room.

"We heard your cry," Zane announces, towering over my little girl.

"Don't worry, Dad. We can help," my eleven-going-on-thirty-year-old declares as my little brother smooths a hand down his trim, purple button-down with tiny cacti illustrations on it. The dude knows how to dress snappy. "You should always come to me for fashion advice," he offers.

Zane's the first baseman for the San Francisco Dragons, which means he's busy nearly every day and night during the summer. But with the season over, he and his partner are taking off soon for a long European vacation, so he'd already offered to host Eliza at his place tonight before I even asked Elodie on a date.

"Then help me out," I say to him, eager for some fashion guidance.

Eliza sets a bossy hand on Zane's forearm, "My dad needs something to impress Elodie, okay? This is his first date in a year. Find something that says he's not wearing the *same boring* clothes he wears every night to work."

This kid knows me too well.

Zane smiles as they reach the closet. "I'll find something perfect for the man who bought five million chocolates from her already." He shoots me a curious stare. "What was that about? Are you already in love?"

I scoff. *Loudly.* "No. This is just a date."

"A date you must have really wanted," Zane adds as he flicks through my shirts with the confidence of a man who knows exactly what he's looking for.

Yeah, well. There's no point denying that. And I'll never live down the five million chocolates, but hell—I wanted Elodie to know I wasn't just some dude amused by a sex toy. I wanted her to know I meant it when I asked her out. I wanted to impress her.

For one date.

"But it can't go anywhere. I'm too busy with expansion plans. I heard back from the landlord this afternoon. Celeste said she wants to see my marketing plans before she finalizes the deal for the place in the Marina," I concede, but that also means I need to put something fantastic together to impress the woman, who's picky when it comes to who she'll do business with. These days, money isn't always the answer. Marketing often is the trump card.

"Not worried. You know how to bring in the customers," Zane says, then stops his clothing hunt to pat my cheek. "With that Archer charm."

I roll my eyes. "Charm doesn't pay the bills."

"I think you're charming," Eliza pipes in. Instinctively, I run a hand over her hair, styled in two soft brown braids.

"And you'll put that charm to good use," Zane says. "Just look at what you've done with Sticks and Stones in the last few years. You've made it a go-to destination. Ping-Pong, pool, and shuffleboard—you can't get bored there. Not to mention you've got good food and good service."

That's worked well for now. But you just never know. Will that be enough for Celeste to grant me the second spot? "I could add more bar games," I say, lasering in on the hoops I need to jump through. "We don't have room now to expand in Sticks and Stones. But there's an outdoor space in the Marina. I could convert it for bocce ball." I can already see it—string lights illuminating a court, picnic tables next to them.

Zane fixes me with a stern stare. "Dude. Chill. You've got a date tonight."

"I should write this down though. To share with Celeste next week when we have our meeting," I add, grabbing my phone from my pocket to dictate a note. But the instant it's in my hand, it's already gone.

Zane is barking into it. "Dear Reddit Forum for Hapless Men. I went on a date tonight, but she left after twenty minutes because all I talked about were bar plans. Any advice for me?" Then he shifts to a shrill masculine voice, adding, "Dude, here's my advice. Don't suck."

Eliza snickers, even though I doubt she gets how horrifyingly accurate Zane probably is when it comes to Reddit posts. I huff as I wiggle my fingers at the phone. "Point taken. But give a guy a break. I don't have much time to date," I add, taking the device back.

Meeting Zane's eyes, Eliza turns her hand into a puppet, making the mouth gab.

"You've heard him sing this *I don't have time* song

before too, haven't you?" Zane asks with such affection for her and such mockery for me.

"All the time," she says as she points at a shirt hanging in the closet. "Ooh, how about that one?"

Zane snags the midnight-blue shirt with a floral pattern on it. Wine-red artsy flowers crawl down the front next to curling vines. It doesn't look familiar.

"Yes. This one is perfect. Good job, Eliza," Zane says.

I stare at it like it's an alien artifact from a time capsule. "Where did that come from?"

Eliza smiles at me sympathetically. "I told you you're the forgetful one. You forgot we stopped at the clothing store after a game one day when you said you needed new shirts for work."

I scratch my jaw. "That is not ringing a bell at all," I say, and I smell a fashion intervention. I point from my brother to my daughter. "Did you two go shopping for me for my date?"

"I just got here, big bro. We didn't have time to shop," Zane says, then shoves the shirt at me. "Now go put this on. Let's see how you look."

His tone brooks no argument.

I comply, heading to the bathroom and putting on the shirt. I check out my reflection. It's a little snug, and definitely more vibrant than the clothes I usually wear. But I know nothing about fashion. I return to the bedroom, holding out my arms for an appraisal from the lifesavers. "This looks so—"

I'm about to say *not me*, when Eliza offers, "Handsome."

"And perfect for a man trying to impress his date," Zane puts in.

"Plus, it shows off your guns, Dad. Like you've been to the gun show," Eliza adds, flexing her little biceps too.

"How do you know that saying?"

"Duh. I hang out with athletes and former athletes," she says, gesturing to Zane, then me. "And you had guns, too, on your rookie card."

That was ten years ago—my one season in the majors. A lifetime ago, practically. The reminder of it doesn't sting as much as it used to, but it'll probably always make me feel wistful. I counter that uncomfortable feeling by flexing my right arm. "Still do," I say confidently.

Eliza spins around in a blur of girlish energy. "Let me go check." She runs off to her room, presumably.

When she's out of earshot, Zane pats me on the shoulder. "Listen, man. Just have a good time tonight. Everything will work out with the bar," he says with the optimism of a man who's been blessed with talent *and* luck. I'd never begrudge him for his good fortune, since that's all I've ever wanted for my little brother—to watch him soar. But facts are facts—Zane's led an injury-free life for nearly a decade in pro ball *and* he met his soul mate when he was just twenty-five. Luck shines bright on his side. "Tonight though? You just gotta be present," he adds.

I blow out a long breath, absorbing his last piece of advice. It's been a while. I never have the time to go out. I need to try to stay in the moment. "Yeah, you're right."

"Always am." He gestures to my shirt, giving me a

thumbs-up. "This looks good. It says you're the kind of man who asks her out by buying up her shop, yet you're cool enough to know not to propose to her tonight."

No clue if that's good or bad. "And that's the right look?" I'm still skeptical. Been burned before on the rules of dating.

"It is," Zane confirms. "Eliza and I looked her up. She's very fashionable and she dresses well. This is what you need to wear. One hundred percent."

"Done." I don't have time to question him more, especially if I'm going to make it to the date on time. We exit my bedroom, and I grab my wallet from the living room table right as Eliza rushes out of her room, waggling her phone. "Sent you a pic of your rookie card. You can show it to her."

Zane's eyes pop, and with Eliza behind him, he makes a slashing gesture across his throat, then mouths *don't*.

I laugh, then clap his shoulder. "I do know that." I also know that Elodie's easy to talk to and easy to flirt with, and that's all I need and want for one night.

I give Zane instructions on food and bedtime as I head to the door. He turns his big right paw into a hand puppet now. "You say this like my niece hasn't slept over before," he remarks.

Eliza grabs her bright yellow sleepover bag from the living room floor. "Dad, I have my own room there."

And it's nicer and bigger than the one she has here. "I'm glad you like it," I say, since I can't let myself get caught up in those kinds of comparisons. My brother's a millionaire athlete and I'm not, and that's just the way it goes.

Before we leave, I hand Zane one of the Melt In Your Mouth boxes. "For Maddox, since I know you don't eat sugar."

He grabs it like an alligator snatching dinner. "I'll make an exception."

Eliza bats her lashes. "I eat sugar!"

I laugh, then shake my head. "You already had a bar."

"But I have room for more," she says hopefully.

"Don't worry. We can share," Zane stage whispers to her.

"Yes!"

When we all reach the stoop outside the building, Eliza drops her bag and gives me a hug. I scoop her up and hold her close, sighing contentedly. This kid is my whole entire heart and has been since she was born. "You have fun tonight, but don't forget tomorrow afternoon we're doing the beach cleanup by Crissy Field."

"I know, and I have my work gloves with me so I can pick up all the plastic," Eliza says, sets a hand on my back, and firmly guides me toward the waiting Lyft I ordered.

"You have fun too," she calls out as I reach the sedan. "Maybe after the new bar opens, she can be your girlfriend!"

I groan. Zane laughs. I turn back to the troublemakers. "It's one date. I don't have time for a girlfriend."

"Everyone has time for love," my brother says. "You just have to make the time."

But tonight is not about love. Love isn't in the cards

for me. It hasn't been for a good long time. Love has a way of just not working out. But business? Family? Those are the things I can count on.

I pluck at the shirt. "Thanks for the shirt, Zane."

"Anytime."

As I slide into the car, my phone pings with a text from Grams.

> Grams: Favor!

> Gage: Sure. Hit me up.

> Grams: I need you to ask your date for a gift recommendation for a friend of mine.

Figuring it's for chocolate, I reply with a *sure.*

> Grams: Can you ask your date for her absolute favorite toy?

I groan. She's savage with her burns.

> Gage: Well played, Grams. But I will get you next time.

> Grams: Doubtful.

Then I set the phone down, but I linger on Eliza's parting comment. Have I left a hole in her life by avoiding romance? For ten years, it's been just Eliza and me. Since she was one and her mom died far too young. And a few times over that decade, I've tried again. But I flash back to the last time I was serious with a woman—

a little over a year ago—and how that turned out for both my daughter and me.

A dark cloud passes over me briefly. I refuse to think of my ex tonight. I refuse to think of the distant past too.

I also vow to set aside my obsession about the future. I'm going to do something I rarely do. I'll enjoy tonight for what it is—a moment in time. A brief respite from work and reality.

And that's all.

5

WALL ART

Elodie

As my black skirt swishes around my thighs, I head to the door, where my gaze strays to an unfortunate basket of custom-made bath bombs in all scents of the chocolate rainbow. Toffee, mint, cinnamon, milk.

My nose curls from the cloying smell of the woo-me gift that Sebastian Roberts at The Chocolate Connoisseur sent me this afternoon before I took Amanda to her friend Ally's house. Cocoa soap is not the way to my heart or into my business. I run a finger along the crinkly paper inside the basket but look the other way. I'll deal with them tomorrow.

Cute cropped cardigan and lucky ring on, I head out, leaving the bath bombs behind. I send Amanda a quick text as I go, letting her know my phone is on if she needs anything. She replies that Ally's mom is making homemade veggie burgers. That must be a relief for her.

She stresses hard if she thinks her food choices are inconveniencing anyone.

I walk down the street to meet my friend Juliet. She lives nearby and has a dinner meeting with one of her clients near the spot where Gage is meeting me, so we're walking together most of the way.

I spot her on the corner, her chestnut hair framing her cheekbones, her fair skin as dewy as always. "Hey you," I call out.

We hug like it's been ages, then head toward the Painted Ladies.

"Are you going into tonight's date armed with your favorite bad sex position to test with him? Because that'd be awesome for me." Her green eyes glint with podcast possibility. "You could come on *Heartbreakers and Matchmakers* and report back. We love real-world details."

I've listened to every episode religiously since she joined the podcast, sharing her optimistic perspective on both dating and moving on with her more pragmatic co-host, a well-known couples therapist. "While I love your show, I can't help you out. I don't plan to have had sex," I say with a *take that, world* lift of my chin.

Her brow knits. "Well, I don't think anyone *plans* to have it."

"True. Let me rephrase then. I've learned the best way to avoid it."

"I'm all ears."

"If a man isn't good at kissing, he's a DNF for me," I say as the light changes and we cross. "Kisses don't lie."

She hums thoughtfully, then says, "You know, I think

you're right. But can you train a man to be a better kisser?"

I shoot her a skeptical look. "I don't train men to become better in bed. And no woman should either."

I just wish I felt as certain about other things. Even as Juliet and I catch up on our days, those damn bath bombs nag at me. I'm worried they'll weigh me down all night. When there's a pause in the convo, I turn to Juliet and blurt out, "But I still don't know what to do about The Chocolate Connoisseur offer."

Juliet gives me a sympathetic smile, then rubs my arm as we stride up the hill. "They didn't up their counteroffer much, did they?"

A little embarrassed, I shake my head. I hired a business attorney to negotiate, and she's badass, but Sebastian wouldn't come up by much. The buyout offer is still lowball. And while I'd retain control of the brand and run the shop on a steady salary, technically he'd own my recipes. My precious IP. "The owner is trying to woo me with gifts instead. Last week he sent gift certificates to a spa. This afternoon, he sent me a basket of chocolate-flavored bath bombs, with a card saying this is what my life could be like if I say yes. *More relaxing,*" I say, then frown.

"Is that frown because it's weird that a guy who's not romancing you sent you bath bombs?"

I jerk my gaze to her. "Yes! I don't want to take a bath with his bath bombs. But still. I'm torn and I know I *should* take it seriously."

"The shop is so successful. Do you have to take it?"

"Elodie's Chocolates does well for a chocolate shop, but..."

I don't have to say it. My parents died with nothing. They squandered away their fortune when Amanda was younger. So a shop that funded my once-upon-a-time fun, flirty, very solo lifestyle—full of skirts and shoes, spa days and facials, manis and pedis—now must take care of me *and* a kid who's so talented with ceramics she wants to go to a special art school in the city.

Amanda *deserves* to go to art school. Art school *here*.

Who am I to destroy her dreams? I want to make sure my sister has everything she could need and want, and I had to take out a small business loan in the last year to cover increased rent since, well, my expenses went up. That's why the buyout is appealing. It's guaranteed money versus rolling the dice every day when I go into work. But I don't want to be impulsive in making the decision either. I'd give up a decade of work building my business as a chocolatier in this city. A decade of recipes. If I ever wanted to start over, I'd face a non-compete for a few years. Ergo, I'm stuck in limbo.

"It'd be a nice chunk of change," I admit. "A nest egg for her future. And isn't that what a good guardian would do? Take it?"

Juliet offers a sympathetic smile. "I wish I had the answer for you. We could talk to Rachel and Hazel." She says it with such problem-solving hope. That's her fix-it, make-things-better nature. "They're good at this stuff, too, even if none of us are parents."

"You're right. We need the brain trust. Maybe everyone should come to brunch tomorrow."

"I'll handle everything. I'll get a reservation and round up the crew for a morning session."

"And thanks. I needed this. I'm officially done thinking and worrying about the offer tonight. I'm going on a date with this hot tamale of a man, and I'm going to have a good time. Dammit."

"Because dates are awesome," she says as we near the Painted Ladies, their pretty pastels coming into view. "Every date is a new chance for love. This could be yours."

"But what would I even do with love?" I ask, though I adore her attitude. Juliet is a breakup party planner for the best of reasons. She sees every end as a new beginning. For a while I was like her, hunting for big, swoony, head-over-heels love. Now, I just can't imagine making it fit in my very messy life. "I can barely figure out how to send a sex toy to the right address," I say breezily.

"We all make mistakes. Maybe yours happened for a reason," she says as we hug goodbye, and I head off to meet Gage Archer a block away.

The sexy-as-sin bartender is waiting for me at the entrance to Alamo Square Park, next to the famous houses. His shirt is nice and snug, hugging those pecs and showing off some seriously strong arms. When I checked him out online, I learned he's a former major league pitcher, and he sure looks like he's still got a strong body. He strides up to me, all confident and assured, the kind of man who'd put me on my hands and knees then spank me into next year.

When he reaches me, he doesn't hesitate—doesn't shuffle his feet or awkwardly offer a hand to shake. A man who knows his mind, he sets a hand on my shoulder. "You look stunning, Elodie," he says, curling that palm over me as he drops a chaste kiss to my cheek.

I can't speak for a few floaty seconds, all thanks to a whisper of a kiss on my right cheek. A starter kiss that definitely didn't lie. "So do you. Nice shirt," I say. "I'd like to give thanks for how it shows off your arms."

He laughs, dipping his face in the slightest show of… shyness. "My brother got it for me."

"He buys you clothes?" That's unusual.

Gage shakes his head. "He bought it for me for tonight's date. Along with my daughter. Then they tried to pass it off like they hadn't joined forces."

That's a whole lot of intel dropped in three sentences. "You have a kid." I'm a little delighted.

"I do. She's eleven." He sounds so proud.

"Mine's thirteen. She's my sister, and I'm raising her solo," I say, but I *don't* get into the *our parents died* detail. Now is not the time to dive into grief or how I'm sometimes a mom and sometimes a sister. "She arrived at the shop right as you were leaving yesterday. She's at the age where she thinks she knows everything."

"Eliza's at the age where she thinks my clothes are boring." He pauses for a beat, giving me a warm look. "And I'm raising her solo too."

Well, then. We've declared enough. With a smile, I say, "Do tell her I approve of the shirt."

"I will," he says, and we both know he probably won't but it's sweet anyway that he says it. "And she approves, too, of your chocolates."

His big gesture was such a better gift than chocolate

bath bombs to get me to sign a deal. "What have you got next in that bag of tricks?"

Gage didn't tell me what was on the agenda tonight. Just that he wanted to show me an art installation he thought I'd enjoy then take me to dinner.

"Let me show you." He sets a hand on the small of my back as we walk along the edge of the park. I shiver a little under his firm touch as he says, "But I have a theory about dates."

"I have this theory about men who put their hands on the small of women's backs," I counter.

His eyes spark with interest. "This I want to hear."

"You'll have to earn that. Maybe I'll tell you later," I say with a playful lift of my eyebrow.

He shakes his head, smiling in admiration. "You are definitely making me work for it, Elodie," he says, then clears his throat. "My theory is this—if you over-plan a date, it takes away from the fun. But I think you'll like my plans."

When we turn the corner a few blocks past the Painted Ladies, we arrive on a street teeming with storefronts and murals a few buildings ahead. That must be the outdoor art installation—bright, bold graffiti art I can't quite make out yet. "I had a feeling you might like graffiti art," he says.

"Presumptuous," I tease.

"Only because I know a few things about you already."

"Like what?"

"You'll see," he says, walking me toward the first mural.

It's a huge mural of a proud, red rooster. My hand flies to my mouth, covering up peals of laughter. After a few seconds, I swat his chest. "You're mocking me."

I don't even see it coming, but he grabs my hand and holds it tight. Then he meets my gaze with the most playfully sincere look. "I would never mock your affection for roosters."

He takes his time, threading his fingers through mine, then he rubs the pad of his thumb along my palm. I stop laughing instantly. I stop smiling too. Because it feels so good. I'm quiet, caught in a hushed charge of electricity. His green eyes turn a dark shade of emerald as he holds my gaze with such intensity I can read his desires like they're a marquee above a theater at night.

My body aches a little for his touch. For those lips to crush mine and for his kiss to take me away.

But he doesn't make a move. He just strokes the place between my thumb and forefinger, which is officially a direct line to my panties right now.

So far, in the span of five minutes I've learned his chaste kisses don't lie, and nor do his hands. This man turns me on.

"Are you going to show me the others?" If he keeps touching me, I might melt. Best to at least move so I don't turn into a puddle.

"I am. But first…"

He leans in and dusts a kiss to my left cheek. When he lets go, he gives me a closed-mouth smile, then says, "When I kiss you for real…"

That's it. He doesn't finish the thought—just leaves it

hanging in the air between us. A sexy promise of more plans I'm sure I'll like.

He clasps my hand and we wander down the street full of graffiti art.

A rooster riding a bike.

A rooster sunbathing in a flower bed.

Then, a painting of three roosters and a chicken, titled *Her Posse*. Next, one that says *Wake Me Up*.

"Well, thank you for the cock art, Gage Archer. I can honestly say I've never had a tour of so much cock before."

"Good. Let's get something to eat then, Elodie." He takes a beat. "I'm very, very hungry."

I hope he says that to me in other ways later tonight.

6

THE WAY TO HER PANTIES

Gage

I already don't want this date to end, and there's so much left of it. We're heading to the restaurant, walking through Hayes Valley now and nearing a boutique hotel that's giving me all sorts of ideas about how I *do* want this date to end. The young and beautiful stream out of the hotel entrance as we check it out. This place has become the *it* hotel in the last year. Celebrities stay here, athletes frequent it—even a famous tennis player and her rock star beau spent the night at this spot. Five stories tall, The Escape has a sleek modern design with a silver facade and clean lines, but twinkling strings of lights cover the entryway, giving it a whimsical feel.

"Love those," she says, stopping to point to the lights.

Huh. This feels a little like kismet. "Funny, I was thinking about those kind of lights earlier," I begin, then…*Wait. No. Shut the fuck up.* I'm not ruining this date by talking about my vision for an outdoor bocce ball court, complete with string lights, for fuck's sake. Talk about a mood killer.

"You were thinking about…lighting?" she asks, seeming amused but a little befuddled.

Great. Now she's going to think I have nothing to discuss but the exterior design of my potential second bar.

This is why I don't deserve nice dates. "Just for a few seconds," I say, then do my damnedest to right this ship. "Then, I entertained deep thoughts about whether mojitos are better than martinis, the best cock art for a woman I very much wanted to impress, and if I had gloves for tomorrow's beach cleanup."

"Don't tease a girl. Tell me more about the lighting thoughts. I haven't met a man before who copped to thinking about lighting. Now, I need to know."

Dragging a hand down my face, I groan, thoroughly busted. "Fine," I say with a *you caught me* shrug. After a trio of men dressed more dapper than Zane pass us, chattering about the best sushi ever, I tip my forehead to the twinkling lights. "I thought those would look good with a little outdoor eating area at a potential second bar. You got it out of me, woman. You happy now?" I ask with narrowed eyes and a faux grumble.

"So very happy. Also, *do it!* I love fairy lights outdoors. They make everything feel like a secret garden. And gardens are sexy."

Maybe I do get to have nice dates. "Glad I have the Elodie seal of approval."

"Definitely. Also, are you opening a second location?" she asks, and she sounds fascinated by this topic, so maybe Zane was wrong. But then Elodie's attention catches on something else. She's pointing to the busy hotel entrance, and the evening crowds milling nearby. Well, to a little archway next to the entrance and then a storefront just beyond. "Is there a pop-up shop in the courtyard? Wasn't that one selling those must-have cakes in a jar recently?"

"No idea," I say.

Clasping my hand tight, she leads the way a few paces. The small courtyard is flanked by ivy-covered walls on one side. In the center sits a cobblestone fountain, the water sounding a little like chimes as it falls. A pack of girls who could be the cast of a Webflix ensemble show toss coins into it. Next to it is an empty storefront—formerly home of the jar cakes, I guess.

"Look at that," Elodie says in a whisper, a little awed. Well, clearly she gets off, too, on talking about leases and retail space.

"Let's see it."

Her smile is magic. "Don't you just know the right words to say to a girlie-girl business owner."

I brush a few strands of her lush blonde hair from her ear, then whisper, "Don't worry. I've got lots of other words I want to say to you later." I keep my hand in hers as we bound up the steps to the courtyard. Beyond the fountain, an older man with a trim dark brown beard, warm bronze skin, and curious eyes sweeps the cobblestones. Looking our way, he gives a chin nod. "Good evening."

"Don't mind us. We're just admiring the shop. This place is stunning," Elodie says immediately.

"Want to check it out? It's available next week," he offers, an eager salesman it seems.

I'm not at all in the market for a pop-up shop, but maybe she is. "Sure," she says, then looks to me with mischief in her eyes. "Let's check it out...*honey.*"

I roll with the affectionate nickname, giving her one of my own. "After you, *cupcake.*"

The man chuckles to himself as he swings open the door for us. The space is tiny but clean. The inside looks like something out of a fashion magazine—one exposed brick wall, a sleek modern chandelier, and a clean, white bar.

Another wall is painted a warm yellow color. The chandelier illuminates some of the art on the wall—caricatures of San Francisco and Hayes Valley. "It's sexy and fun," she says as she drinks in the space, running a hand along the counter. "I could test out new flavors here. Tropical chocolates. Tea-infused squares. An extra spicy line." It sounds more dreamy than real. But it's a dream she's enjoying, it seems. Sparking with ideas, her eyes meet mine. "What about you? Oh, I know! You could offer cocktail taste tests! *Find out the answer to whether mojitos are better than martinis on Friday night.*"

"Martinis," I say decisively.

"Mojitos," she declares with a bob of her shoulder.

I shake my head in dirty, flirty admiration of this woman. "That's it. I have no choice."

Her brow furrows. "You actually have two choices—martinis or mojitos?"

I close the distance between us and cup her chin. "I mean…I have no choice but to kiss you."

"Oh," she says, her voice feathery. She sounds and looks a little flustered. But the glimmer in her blue eyes says this is the good kind of flustered. "And why does that give you no choice?"

I don't look away from those gorgeous eyes or her beautiful face. My focus is solely on her. "Because mojitos are sexy. Just like you. And I can't wait any longer to kiss you, Elodie."

Her pretty red lips part, and I'm dying, just dying, to taste her. "Then stop waiting," she says.

I don't rush in and crush her lips. I don't slam my mouth to hers. I come in slowly, so we can both feel the tease, so we can climb the stairs up to this kiss together, savoring the anticipation, the final seconds till a kiss becomes more than a wish. Then, when she's inches away from me, I drop my lips to hers, in a soft, slow kiss that lingers for several tempting seconds.

Seconds that could become all night long. That could become my kisses on her thighs, my hands on her ankles, our bodies tangled together. I finish the kiss with a bite, nipping on her lower lip, a little fiery, a little rough. Letting her know that I might start sweet, but I'll finish hard, full of passion.

When I let go with a brush of my stubble against her cheek, she wobbles.

I catch her, a hand on her hip in seconds. I steady her as she blinks, breathes out hard, then whispers, "That was…"

I feel the same.

I kiss the corner of her lips, catching her unfinished sentence with my mouth, then I pull back. "We should go."

"We should." She looks around once more, maybe getting her bearings before she shifts and says, "This is going to go in seconds."

"Let's get you out of here before I do bad things to you in this pop-up shop."

We leave and out in the courtyard the man gives us a curious look as he rests the broom against the window. "Nice, isn't it?" he asks, nodding to the space.

"It's perfection," she says.

"It'll be available on Monday," he says, then his phone rings, and he brandishes it with an apologetic "I should take this."

"Have a good night," I say, and we take off, passing the packs at the fountain, then a handful of couples meandering out into Hayes Valley. We dart around them, turning the corner toward the restaurant.

"So let me get this straight. Kisses and retail spaces are the way to your heart?"

She shakes her head. "They're the way to my panties."

Then she strides ahead of me, and I want dinner to end before it even starts.

* * *

"And I was truly shocked when we won the championship," I say an hour later, after I take a drink of my wine at a small booth in the corner of the restaurant.

"Humble brag," Elodie says with a faux cough as she sets down her fork and napkin.

We're nearly done with the meal at a Mediterranean-fusion café. The deep blue tiled walls feature colorful photographs of cities in Morocco, Egypt, and Lebanon. Golden overhead lighting makes everything glimmer.

"Hey! *You* asked about my softball coaching," I point out.

"And you made sure to tell me exactly how you did," she says then sets her chin in her hand. "Maybe you want to tell me more about your stats as a coach. I'd love to know. How many softball championships *did* the elementary girls win?"

I hold up my hands in surrender. "You win."

Elodie gives me a saucy look then licks her lips. "But you can definitely tell me more about the time when you played in the majors."

I tense, my shoulders hard like rocks. She can't know she's hit a sore spot, but oh hell, has she ever.

"Oh shoot," she says, her hand flying to her mouth. I guess my body language made my feelings clear. When she drops her hand, she says with a wince, "I shouldn't have mentioned that."

But it's understandable she'd bring up my one season after I went on and on about coaching girls' softball. "It's okay. I swear."

"Are you sure? You seem annoyed."

She's too astute, but I can't let her feel bad. I reach

across the table for her hand, softening. "It was one season, and it was a long time ago. Which you probably learned when you looked me up."

"Well, I think it's a wise idea to look up guys who deliver me sex toys then ask me out."

"Words to live by. And I looked you up too. So did my brother and my daughter, which is why they made sure I dressed extra nice for you. Eliza said you dressed well in your pics so I had to do the same. It's been a while since I went on a date," I admit.

"Me too."

"Yeah?" This delights me too much.

"Nearly a year, if you must know," she adds.

Can't help it. Pure, masculine pride suffuses my chest. "Same for me." Then hell, fuck it. She deserves to know she's special. "I don't usually date customers. Hell, I don't *flirt* with customers. I'm friendly, but that's all." I pause. "But then you came in. And there was something about you."

If I'm not careful, this date is going to turn into something riskier. But I know better than to believe one fantastic night means anything more than that. Still, she made herself vulnerable to me. She opened up, so I give her something more than she could learn online about my far too short stint in the majors. "And yes, I was drafted right after college. Played in the minors for one season. Then I played for the Los Angeles Bandits. It was a decade ago. I blew out my elbow after eighteen wins in one season and it was...*devastating*," I say, and I leave it at that. Don't need to get into what it did to me.

How it affected my head and my heart. The hell I experienced after.

"I'm sorry, Gage. That must have been so hard," she says with genuine sympathy.

Hard doesn't begin to cover the death of my dreams. "It sure was," I say evenly, but it wasn't even the hardest thing to happen that year. "But life happens, and you move on."

"I hear you," she says, and there's soul-deep understanding in her voice. I want to ask what she's grappling with in the *life happens* department. But I don't want this date to get too heavy. Even though Zane warned me, I go against his advice because we need some levity, and we need it, stat. "My daughter said I should show you my rookie card," I say, like I'm dangling a carrot.

Elodie brightens, her smile spreading to her eyes as she beckons with her fingers. I grab my phone, and find the pic in my texts from Eliza. I spin the phone around to show Elodie.

She takes a beat to check it out. The serious game face I'm wearing. The uniform I didn't get to wear nearly enough. And, of course, the pitcher's scowl, designed to terrify batters. It worked. My cut fastball was a thing of legend. When I was on, it was nearly impossible to hit.

After she studies the picture of the faded card, she declares, "You were hot."

I arch a brow, then ask in a stern tone, "*Were?*"

She leans closer and lowers her voice. But again, she doesn't answer directly. "I have a secret."

And I'm hanging on her every word. "Tell me," I say and it's a demand.

"I thought of you when I ordered The Command Performance."

I'd wanted to believe the timing of the order meant something. But hearing her say it, sends the temperature in me soaring. I get up, move around the table, and sit next to her in the booth where I wrap an arm around her shoulder. "Want to hear a secret?"

"I do."

"I wanted to ask for your number every time you came into the bar."

"What stopped you?"

"Life. It's busy. The whole kid thing. I don't go out much," I admit.

Her eyes sparkle with some relief, telling me she's on the same page. "I hear you. Same here. This was my only free night in ages. Amanda happened to have a sleep-over so it worked out," she says, a little pensive, but understanding too.

"Same. Eliza's with Zane, that is. My brother."

She pauses, then asks, "So why now?"

"Couldn't get you out of my head," I tell her, because fuck the rules of dating. Fuck holding back. We both have busy lives. No time for bullshit. "That's why I bought all those chocolates. I wanted to impress you."

"Mission accomplished," she says.

Pride floods my chest. Then I slide my hand down her back, resting it right above the swell of her sweet ass. "Now, I believe you said earlier you had a theory about men who put their hands on the small of women's backs."

"I do," she says, as I spread my fingers over the thin fabric of her shirt.

"Tell me."

"That they kiss in my favorite way."

My chest is a furnace as I run my knuckles along her jawline. "And what way is that?"

She takes her time, holding the cards, holding my gaze, holding all my desire in the palm of her hand as she studies my face, my mouth, my eyes. "Hard and passionate. Just like how they fuck."

That word.

On her lips.

I'm on fire. It's blazing in me as I thread my fingers through her lush locks. "Want to get out of here?"

"I do. Because I have a theory about dates too."

Her theories are my undoing. This I have to hear. "What is it?"

"The best ones end unplanned in a hotel."

There's no way The Escape has a room free on a Friday night. But there are other hotels if they don't. Not quite as close, but still, I'll find one. Dammit, I'll fucking find one.

Ten minutes later, thanks to the serendipity of a last-minute cancellation, I've got a key card to a room at the most sought-after hotel in town.

7

IT'S AN ORDER

Elodie

There will be no DNFing.

I want the opposite. I want to finish him. I want him to finish me. Over and over, again and again. In all the ways.

The second the brass doors to the hotel elevator shut, I back up to the corner of the lift. He stalks over to me, prowling, eyes hard, dark with desire. He cages me in, grabs my face, and crushes his lips to mine.

It's aggressive in the way I fantasize about. A man in control. A man who'll hold me down, pin my wrists, fuck me hard.

He kisses like he knows precisely what he'll do to me tonight. I'm outrageously wet in seconds. I loop my arms around his neck, trying to tug him closer when he stops abruptly.

He breaks the hard kiss and pulls back, but doesn't

quite end it. Instead, Gage downshifts with his lips still on me. His kiss turns slow, seductive, a long tease of a kiss.

That throws me off in a brand new—and not at all unwelcome—way.

Maybe he's not *only* a rough, hard man in bed. Maybe he's many things in bed. Perhaps he can play many parts. He's kissing me now like a man who'll take his sweet time, draw it out deliciously, fuck me slowly.

Make me beg for every inch of his hard cock.

And my god, is it hard and thick against my hip.

My head goes woozy as the reel of possibilities plays out.

Then the car slows at the fifth floor, and he breaks the kiss. I can barely think from the most thorough, mind-bending kiss of my life. I'm shocked it only lasted five floors. I feel a little lost in time and space with him as he takes my hand and leads me down the hall. We reach the room, and he slides the key over the door.

Once it's open, he says dryly, "Want a tour of the room?"

I shake my head as the door shuts and the soft glow of a lamp lights the room.

I grab his face, running my fingers along his scruff, loving the feel of his stubbled jaw. "Not at all."

"Good. Because I don't give a fuck about the room. I care about one thing right now," he says, his voice rough, raspy, and full of heat.

"What's that?"

"Tasting you, cupcake. Because I bet you're as sweet as I've been imagining. Now, why don't I get on the bed, and you sit on my face? We can take a great sex challenge."

"Yes. Please. Now," I murmur as all the breath whooshes from my lungs.

Maybe fantasies do come true.

He hauls me up, tosses me over his shoulder, and carries me to the king-size bed, then sets me on my back.

The covers are dark blue.

Maybe.

Or navy. Or black.

Who cares?

Gage is taking off my low heels, pressing a kiss to one ankle, then the other. Murmuring sweet nothings against my calves. Pushing up my skirt, then climbing between my thighs, gazing wantonly at my soaked panties. "So fucking wet," he praises, then shakes his head. "But these really need to go."

I reach down to slide them off, but he's faster, a hungry man, determined to feast.

He presses a hot kiss to the panel of my damp panties, then unleashes a greedy groan. "Mmm. Yes," he says.

He kisses me through the slick panel once more, flicking his tongue against the soaked fabric. "Baby, how long have you been like this?"

"Since you kissed me in the shop," I admit, my voice pitching up with need, just like my hips.

I'm arching for him, eager for him.

No, I'm *dying*.

"Well that won't do," he says, then slides my white

lace panties down my thighs, his face lighting up in filthy delight as he stares savagely at my wet pussy.

"So beautiful. So fucking wet," he rumbles. Then he sits up, smacks the outside of my thigh, and unbuttons his shirt.

"Leave your clothes on. That skirt's been giving me unholy fantasies all night."

I push up on my elbows. "It has?"

"All through dinner, I thought about crawling under the table and eating you. Then I thought about you crawling up on me in a bed like this one, and demanding I eat you out."

Can I clone him and have him fuck me every night?

He's shrugging out of his shirt, and his chest is firm, toned, and I want to run my hands all over his torso, drag my nails through the dark, wiry chest hair, explore the ink along his arms.

Lick his abs.

Taste his cock.

But again, he's faster than I am. He flops to his back, settling into the pillows, patting his chest. "Fuck my face, baby. Do it now."

I obey. I climb over him, clothes on, straddling this gorgeous stranger who's hardly a stranger in some ways.

He grabs my hips, then tugs me down on his mouth. I brace my hands against the headboard. "Gage," I moan from that first tantalizing lick.

He goes down on me like he's French kissing me. It's luxurious. Sensual. Erotic.

The sounds he makes are filthy. The carnal noises

that come from his mouth send pulses of electricity from my core all the way to my fingertips. His hands curl tight around my hips as he pulls me closer, a man determined to devour me.

But I'm cautious. I don't quite move or rock. I'm a little afraid to. I'm five nine, have curvy hips and generous boobs.

He must sense my reticence since he stops licking and stares up at me with lust-glazed eyes. "You like this?"

"So much," I gasp.

"Then you want to fuck my face a little harder?"

"Are you sure?"

His lips quirk into a naughty grin as he glances down, nodding toward his body. "Yeah, but why don't you check?"

I turn around and gasp. His hard-on is making a serious dent in his jeans.

"Believe me now?"

I turn back. "Yes."

"Good. Use me as your toy. And do it now, woman."

Well, then. "Since it's an order," I say.

"It absolutely is."

With my black skirt rucked up and my thighs framing his face, I rock my hips back and forth.

The second I do, his fingers dig into the flesh of my ass. His moans against my pussy tell me how much he loves it.

And I let go.

Rocking, riding, and finding my pleasure. Using him like the best kind of sex toy. That's how he eats me too.

Like it's his one job. Like he read all the instructions from Risqué Business. Like he's learned exactly why I'd buy a toy that simulates oral.

And he gives it to me like that.

Greedy, focused, determined. And full of so much passion. His tongue is an eager explorer. His lips are hungry.

He kisses deeply, then flicks his tongue against my clit, and soon I'm lit up, sparking everywhere. Pleasure's rising higher in me, spreading from my center through my whole being.

Grabbing the headboard harder, I ride his face with abandon. I use him. I take everything his tongue and mouth and lips have to give. I rely on his scruff. I enjoy everything about his face as I fuck him recklessly, seeking one thing and one thing only—an orgasm that'll obliterate my senses.

And it's barreling toward me. Heat roars through my body. Bliss knocks on my door.

And this man eats me like it's the Fourth of July carnival and he's entered a pie-eating contest.

He doesn't hold back.

He's all in, kissing and sucking and consuming my wetness till pleasure tightens, coils, then bursts.

"Oh god," I cry out, as an orgasm slams into me like a wave against the ocean shore, then crashes beautifully, powerfully, before it rolls out to sea.

I don't know how long it lasts, but a minute later, I'm panting, murmuring, lying next to him. "I'm going to need some new theories."

"That so?" he asks, stroking my hair.

"Yeah. Men who return sex toys and read all about them perform better than one."

"Better than a toy? That's high praise," he says.

"The highest," I say, then roll to my side, my hand exploring his firm abs. "Mmm. I think it's my turn now, Mister Cocktail."

And right as my fingertips reach his jeans, an idea pops, fully formed in my head. What if our idea that we played around with earlier turned into a business? "We should do a chocolate and cocktails pop-up shop."

He cracks up. "Did you just come up with a business idea before you're about to free my dick?"

"Well, your cock is very inspiring," I say as I run my hand along the ridge of his erection. "Mojitos and martinis."

"Truffles and toffee," he says, getting into it.

"We could do taste tests," I say.

"Theme nights. I can see the marketing now."

"Yes!" I rub a little harder. "They do go together."

"Like your hand on my cock," he says, then lets out a long groan.

But before I can finally unzip his jeans, my phone rings. Amanda's calling.

8

SPECIAL EDITION

Elodie

"I'm so sorry, Mrs. Navarro," Amanda says in the doorway of the pink duplex with artfully arranged plants lining the railing on the little porch of her friend's home.

Amanda's purple backpack is slung on her shoulder, a new friendship bracelet on her wrist with gold beads forming the words *make art.*

Ally's mom—Stella—shoots Amanda a sympathetic look from behind her trendy electric-blue glasses that frame wise brown eyes. "You don't have to apologize. Just be sure to drink plenty of water."

"And walk around if you need to," Ally chimes in from next to her mom, a little mini-me with matching glasses and equally good advice. "Don't forget what we read—it's totally normal the first time a vegetarian eats meat. So don't worry about it."

"You'll feel better soon. It's just that your body uses different digestive enzymes for meat, and you're not used to that," Stella offers, and dear god, she's a mom nurse now. "Take a digestive aid if you need to."

"Thank you for all this," I say, overwhelmed but grateful. My head pings with information. Stella's already researched the problem and is offering advice. Meanwhile, I've barely said a word since I arrived and I'd spent the ride over hoping my panties dried while I freaked out that Amanda would have to go to the ER to get her stomach pumped after accidentally eating meat for the first time in her life.

Amanda offers the superhero mom a weak smile. "I'm sure your veggie burgers are really, really good."

"Next time. You have an open invitation," Stella says.

"Thanks," Amanda says, then waves goodbye to her friend.

Ally offers a goodbye wave in return, her *make art* bracelet slipping down the tanned skin of her wrist.

"Thanks again for having her over," I say to Stella. "I'm really sorry it didn't work out. Ally's welcome at our house anytime." I *think* that's what you're supposed to say when a sleepover snafu happens.

"Text me? Let me know how she's feeling tomorrow," Stella adds.

Right, right. *That's* what you say. "Of course. Absolutely. Thanks again."

"Don't forget—a digestive aid if she needs one," the superhero calls out.

"On it!"

With a wince, Amanda sets her hand on her stomach. I walk her down the steps, wrapping an arm around her shoulders as we head to the waiting Lyft, the same one that brought me here in a flash, weaving expertly through Friday night traffic. From Lyft drivers to ultra moms, I'm surrounded by rock stars at their jobs.

"I only barfed once," Amanda says, trying hard to be strong.

"That's good," I say, then worry digs into me. "Do you need to throw up again?"

She shakes her head. "I feel *okay* now."

But okay isn't how you want to feel when you stay at a friend's house. "You'll be better soon."

"I just can't believe I took the wrong burger," she says, embarrassment thick in her voice as we reach the car while she explains again that it was a mix-up. The burgers on the plate all looked the same so she snagged a meat one rather than the special veggie one for the vegetarian, like our parents were after they had Amanda.

"Don't beat yourself up. Mistakes happen," I say.

I open the door for her and she slides into the car. Gage is long gone. The second I got the call that Amanda wasn't feeling well we scrambled and said hasty goodbyes. But I can't think about him right now.

As the driver pulls away from the pretty home in Lower Pacific Heights, I buckle in too. "So I guess you're not going to ask me to cook you a steak tomorrow?"

Amanda makes an exaggerated gagging sound in her

throat, then giggles. I'm glad she can laugh about it but her mirth doesn't last long.

"I feel so dumb." She slumps back against the seat.

She's not a sister now. She's a daughter. A girl trying to navigate the world. A girl raised by our parents who changed their ways with her and went farm-to-table as much as possible. Cooking all their own meals for her. Eating dinner with her.

Me? I was raised by those same people on whatever I wanted, eating alone most of the time.

"I didn't even realize it until it was a few bites in because I've never even tasted it," she says, still beating herself up. "How dumb am I?"

I want to snatch away all that unnecessary self-loathing. Squash it. Throw it in the trash so she never has to face it again. "No, bug," I say emphatically, trying to impart some of my certainty. "You've never had it in your whole life. It was an easy mistake to make." I pause for a few seconds. "How do you feel now?"

"Stupid. I couldn't make it through a sleepover. What am I? Nine?"

"You are not stupid. It happens."

"I just didn't want to stay there and keep barfing," she says, staring out the window as the driver cruises down Scott Street into the night, past Alamo Square Park where tonight's doomed date began just a few hours ago. Feels like many days ago.

"Of course you don't. Even if you're feeling better, you just don't want to take that chance."

"I guess I'd rather just barf with you, Els," she says, then sets her head on my shoulder. After a few quiet seconds, she seems to have found the end of her frustration since she says, "What are sisters for?"

I pet her hair. "More than I ever imagined."

She sighs. "Sorry about that too."

"Nope. Do not say that. Do not ever say that," I say fiercely.

"Yeah?" She looks up at me, eyes full of questions, heart needing reassurance.

"Yes. Just yes. I'm exactly where I want to be," I say. *Even if I have no clue how to do this thing most of the time.*

She seems relieved, and I'm glad I can give her that. But as the driver steers his way down the bustling streets, I worry away at my cuticles. Did I handle this right? Did I say the right thing when she called? Was I supposed to research the issue immediately like Stella or say it's no big deal? Instead, I simply reacted like I always do, saying *I'm on my way* then flying out the hotel room door. I didn't ask what she wanted. "Was it okay that I came to pick you up before even asking?"

She nods. "Yeah. I wanted you to. And Ally's mom is cool, but I don't think she wanted me there."

"I get that. I mean *I* want you around though," I quickly correct.

The car slows at a light while a pack of women my age in slouchy tops revealing their shoulders stream out of a neon-lit bar on the corner. Amanda glances at them, then me. "But I ruined your date, didn't I?"

I'm certainly not about to tell her that it'd be impossible to ruin a date when I already rode a guy's face like he was a wild Mustang. "We had a nice time and I think it ended exactly when it was supposed to end," I say.

"Do you believe that? That things happen for a reason?"

An ache digs into my breastbone. I know where this is going. She still wonders if our parents died for a reason. What the meaning is behind that loss. What the meaning is behind...anything.

"I don't know. I wish I did," I say.

Some days I feel like the only thing I really know the meaning of is chocolate. I guess that's why I keep going back to it. It's the one thing in my life that feels consistent. The only thing in my life that has always been there. That promises exactly what it delivers—comfort, sweetness, and escape.

"Me neither," she says. "I don't think so though."

"It would be hard to think it happened for a reason," I say, especially considering *how* it happened.

As we turn onto our block, she looks me in the eyes again, her blue irises thoughtful and sad. "One time I was at a sleepover and I wanted to say goodnight, but I couldn't reach Mom and Dad. I thought they were drinking again." My throat tightens with too many emotions. Of course she knows about their past. They talked about their alcoholism openly with anyone and everyone. They'd stopped before my mom got pregnant with her. They'd become sober coaches, running sobriety retreats, ones they poured all their own money into, going into debt to try to help others. Ironic, in a terrible way, that they were killed by a drunk driver. That can't possibly have been for a reason.

Amanda finishes with a shrug. "I think it turned out they were just busy in other ways."

Like I was earlier. But at least I had my phone on. Maybe I deserve a badge for that?

When we reach our home, the one I moved into when my little one-bedroom was no longer enough after a late night when my parents didn't make it home, and I took on their roles, I thank the Lyft driver, then go.

As I'm walking up the steps to our building, waiting for the notification about leaving a tip, a text blinks up at me from Gage.

> Gage: I took care of your Lyft, including the tip. Hope your sister is OK. Thanks for a fantastic night.

Oh, right. Everything happened so quickly, I'd forgotten he'd ordered the Lyft from his phone in the first place. I'd just rushed downstairs with him, and he'd held open the car door for me.

A rush of warmth fills my chest at the reminder.

I unlock the door, then return to something Amanda said earlier. "Hey, don't feel bad about the mistake. Mix-ups happen. I'm the girl who has sent packages to the wrong address."

She doesn't know the details of *what* was in the package, but she doesn't need to. She smiles my way regardless. "I guess mix-ups run in the family."

"Maybe they do," I say, then rub her back.

Once she's had a glass of water and is settled into her bed, feeling better, I head to the kitchen and take a deep breath in the dark. I turn to the cupboard, grab a bar of dark chocolate with almonds and sea salt—it's not even one of mine. It's Lulu's, the brand I saved all my allowances for when I was younger—and break off a small square.

I bite into it, letting the flavors flood my tongue and fill my mind. Smooth, a little salty, a tiny bit nutty. A reassurance in a storm of uncertainty.

I feel reassurance in a strange new way too. I might not have known exactly what to do with my emotions when I got that call, but right now, right here, I'm exactly where I'm supposed to be. Somehow, I've figured out what to say to Amanda, how to help her, how to be there for her when she needed me to be.

That's what matters.

But a romance with Gage?

Do I have the skills to balance that *and* everything else? In one night, he's already sprinted miles ahead of other men I've dated, and I don't even mean in the bedroom. Or not *only* in the bedroom, anyway.

I break off another small chunk of chocolate, then hold it in my cheek, letting it melt slowly as I flash back over dates and the short-lived romances of my twenties. There was Charles, the venture capitalist, who loved to play blackjack and took me to Vegas, where we went and lounged by the pool, then dined on fancy small plates at famous chefs' restaurants. It felt romantic, but he never truly opened up, never told me about his family, never shared his fears. Before him was Jean-

Pierre, my dashing French-Canadian lover who opened a wine shop here in San Francisco, and whisked me away on Wine Country weekends, where everything felt like falling in love. Except for the fact that I never knew what excited him, what drove him on, what made him who he was. I'm not sure he was capable of loving a person like he was a vintage Bordeaux.

Then, there's Gage. A guy who plans a great date, executes it, and then actually shares some of his heart and soul with me. Telling me a little about his daughter, a little about himself, and a little about asking me out.

That's rare for a first date. I want that. I crave that. But do I even know what to do with it right now in my chaotic life?

I don't have the answer. Instead, I open my texts and reply to Gage, thanking him profusely.

Gage: Anytime. By the way, we should call it Special Edition.

It's not until I get into bed that I realize what he means. And I can't stop thinking about it all weekend long.

9

PILLOW TALK

Elodie

Elodie: Is this too crazy?

> Gage: Yes. But I'm pretty sure crazy is good.

Elodie: You sure? I feel like you're the responsible one.

> Gage: And that makes you…the fun one?

Elodie: Yes, of course I'm the fun one. That's why I'm asking YOU!

> Gage: I think you meant to say responsible is hot.

Elodie: You just want me to call you the hot one. And we agreed we can't do that anymore if we're going into business.

> Gage: Hold on. Pretty sure we agreed if we're going into business that we're hands off. Not that I can't flirt with you.

Elodie: So is that your loophole to the hands-off rule?

> Gage: Yes, I believe it is.

Elodie: You're bad.

> Gage: And you had no complaints Friday night.

Elodie: Or last night when I replayed it.

> Gage: With The Command Performance?

Elodie: Of course.

> Gage: Did you name it after me?

Elodie: If your name is oh god.

> Gage: Now who's enjoying the loophole?

Elodie: I guess I'm bad too. But seriously, is it crazy trying to pull off this new venture?

Gage: No, it's a good idea. Trust me. It's such a good idea that I'm willing to keep my hands off you. And don't think for a second I don't want to fuck you. I do. Badly. I want to take you out on another date and then put you on your hands and knees and give you ten more screaming orgasms, but I also really want to make sure my daughter never winds up in the financial holes I've been in. And oh, yeah, I'd like to pay health insurance for my employees for a long, long time to come. And I think this is the way.

Elodie: Yup, responsible is hot.

On Sunday night as I'm wiping down tables in the back of the shop, I steal a moment to read our recent text exchange one more time. Nearly forty-eight hours and several brainstorm calls later, during which we also talked about our weekends—he did a beach cleanup with Eliza, and I took Amanda to check out a new ceramics shop in Noe Valley, then she insisted I learn to play a new trivia game with her since she's obsessed with trivia games—and Gage and I have a plan and an appointment at The Escape in the morning.

It feels a little crazy, but it feels right too.

I had the weekend to weigh mojitos and martinis, truffles and toffee. What started as pillow talk turned into something even sexier—a bold idea for a new business that can solve both our problems, even if it means setting aside the spark I felt for him. There's so much more at stake than sparks. The shared space can drive business to our existing businesses—and that's what we both need. I can potentially gain more customers for my chocolates at the shop, pay off the loan, and keep growing Elodie's Chocolates. And Gage can use the pop-up to get customers excited for the higher-end bar in a more cocktail-centric location that he wants to open. It's a win-win.

I even talked to my friends about Special Edition over our pancake brunch, during which they teased me for *locking it up* with Gage.

But the reality is this—banging your new business partner is a bad idea, so Gage and I agreed to put our attraction on ice. Something about Special Edition feels right. Right in a way The Chocolate Connoisseur offer never did. I return to the counter, so Kenji and I can finish cleaning up the shop on Sunday night. When we're done, my second-in-command shoots me an expectant look as he undoes his apron and hangs it up. "So, did you decide, mama?"

Nerves rush through me, chased by excitement. He's got a lot at stake here too. A first generation Japanese American, he helps pay the bills for his family, who all moved and live here in the Bay Area too. If I took The Chocolate Connoisseur offer, I'm not sure there'd be a job for him.

"I did," I say, then add a smile. "Wish me luck saying no."

He mimes putting a tiara on me. "Queen."

"Get out of here," I say, and he leaves first.

When I lock up a few minutes later, I gaze at the sign above the shop feeling something like certainty when I see my name. That's something I don't always feel, but right now I cherish it, I clutch it.

And I *need* it.

Amanda's at home, making a salad for us, since she swears she's only eating salads for the rest of her life, and that's that. I take out my phone to call Sebastian on the way, passing the perfume shop next to my store right as the owner steps out for the night too.

Samira Haddid also owns the retail space itself for my shop, her shop, and for the lingerie store next door to Scents & Sensibility. A real estate investor and a perfumier, I like to say. She's older than me, probably in her sixties, with warm brown skin, weathered from the years. Her voice is melodic. "Elodie, it's trading time soon. I have new scents for you. Do you have some salted caramels for me?"

"Always, and they're on the house. But why won't you ever let me buy your perfumes, Samira? I'd happily do that."

She shakes her head adamantly. "It's best to be fair."

"If you insist."

"I do," she says, then waves and heads the other way.

As I walk home, I dial Sebastian's number.

He answers on the first ring. "To what do I owe the pleasure of a Sunday night call? I hope it's a yes."

My stomach dips. It won't be the first time I've turned him down. "I want to thank you for the offer. Truly, it's amazing," I tell him even though it wasn't amazing. *He* doesn't need to know that though.

"I hear a *but*," he says, his voice full of a little too much charm. "Sort of like when I asked you out."

It'd been foolish to hope he wouldn't bring that up. A few months ago, the chocolate magnate—the man who bought The Chocolate Connoisseur and turned it into a national chain with fantastic low prices—had visited my booth at the San Francisco Chocolate Show several times. First, he'd talked about how he built his company as a bean-to-bar business—meaning he makes his chocolates straight from cocoa beans, making him the *biggest small-batch* chocolate maker.

Then he'd tested the milk chocolate bar I'd crafted from Valrhona, the dark chocolate with hints of orange, and the semi-sweet with just the right amount of coconut and almonds. Some of the best from a chocolatier, he'd said, then asked me out to a fancy dinner.

While I'd appreciated both his effort and his chocolate compliments, I didn't feel the chemistry. I don't believe, either, that chemistry comes later—you either feel it or you don't. And fine, maybe the ultra-romantic in me had rushed headfirst into romances in my twenties with the wrong men, but I also know that I need chemistry. I need flutters. I need to feel that special something. But I'd listened to enough of Juliet's podcasts so I'd turned him down politely with a kind *thank you but I don't think I feel the same way.*

Gentle honesty is better than saying you're busy. They can tell when you're not busy, she'd said on an episode.

A few weeks ago, he asked to buy my shop, and I was this close to accepting the offer.

A buyout felt like the safe answer. A way to pay off the loan. To avoid my parents' pitfalls with money. But perhaps it's not the only answer. I don't want to give up what I've dreamed of my whole life. What my parents never really achieved—independence. Maybe this is foolish. Maybe this is risky. But I'm doing it anyway.

"It's a great offer, but I want to keep growing Elodie's," I say, and I'm bouncing with new hope over how to do that thanks to an idea born over pillow talk.

Because chocolate? That's been my one constant in my chaotic life. It's the one thing that's never let me down. The one thing I could always depend on when my parents weren't dependable at all. Maybe a future with Elodie's Chocolates can make Amanda's dreams possible. More than a buyout.

Sebastian's quiet for a long beat, a kind of icy silence. I don't breathe until he sighs ruefully, then says, "All right. I'll just have to continue competing with you from down the street."

It's said jovially, but is there a warning shot in it? "There's room for both of us," I say, because really, there is. Can't he see that? It's just chocolate. You can never have too much of it.

"Of course there is. But enjoy the bath bombs."

"I will," I say, feeling only a little guilty about that lie.

I return home, excited and hopeful about tomorrow. I made a decision and it feels like a damn good one. I'm such an adult.

I can't even say my parents would be proud. They never adulted this well.

* * *

"Your outfit of the day is ready," Amanda declares as she leaves my closet on Monday morning. "Today you're the...candymaker."

I laugh. "Isn't that my outfit of the day every day?"

"Work with me here. Today you need to be *extra*. Extra candymaker," she says. "It's all hanging up for you."

I gesture to my sweats and hoodie. "And what's this?"

"Walking your sister to school outfit," she says.

Along the way, we catch up on how she's doing with her application to art school (great!), the next level in Valorant, the video game she plays (so close), and the inscribed decorative plate she's working on in ceramics (so hard).

It's like Friday night's burger fiasco never happened, especially when she takes off to meet up with Ally outside their middle school with barely a goodbye.

But that's for the best.

I return home and strip out of my casual clothes and into the candymaker costume.

I put on my best *I'm going to look really fucking good on social media* dress. It's a red-and-white checked skirt, swingy and playful. It hits at the knees. A belt cinches at the waist with a buckle made in the shape of a heart. I pair it with the white tank top Amanda picked and a matching three-quarter-length red cardigan with buttons shaped like cherries.

Damn, Amanda did good with her picks.

I curl my hair in my best retro do. I check my reflection. Yep. That girl in the mirror can sell the hell out of chocolate. I slick on some lipstick, then some gloss, then spritz on the tiniest bit of perfume—the same cherry kind I wore on Friday night, courtesy of a Samira trade for salted caramels. I put on my lucky jewelry too, just like I wore that evening.

I leave and head over to the place where I sat on my business partner's face seconds before our date ended.

He's impossible to look away from, leaning casually against the entrance to the hotel courtyard. Gage looks the part too. Dark jeans, motorcycle boots, a tight, and a trim black short-sleeve Henley that shows off the lotus flower on his arm, and the swirls of black ink climbing up his skin. His tattoos are all black, fine linework and intricately drawn.

He whistles when he sees me, shaking his head in admiration as he walks over to me like a lover, even though he can't be anymore. "Damn, woman. I don't think I'm good enough to be seen with you," he says with an approving hum.

I jut out a hip, enjoying the compliment. "Amanda picked it out. She's into the whole outfit-of-the-day thing. Do I look the part?"

"You look like a piece of chocolate, and I want to eat you."

"Good. Because we're selling an image. We're selling a partnership. The tattooed bar owner and the va-va-voom chocolatier."

"We are. But I'm going to need to steal one last touch," he whispers, then he runs a hand down my arm, warm under the October sun. That's San Francisco for you. Sometimes it's freezing here in October. Sometimes it's summer.

His touch makes me shudder. He groans too. "Fuck, am I really giving this up for business?"

It's rhetorical. It's for the universe. Still, I answer for the universe and me. "Yes, because there's one rule of business—don't screw your business partner."

"Amen," he says, letting go of my arm. "So basically it was special edition sex we had."

"But did we even have sex?"

"You came on my face. I'm counting that as sex."

"Well, aren't you just an evolved male," I say.

"I don't have to whip my dick out to have sex. You know what counts as sex?"

"Do tell."

"If you come, we had sex. That's all that matters."

"I guess there's a whole new meaning to if a tree falls in the forest. I'm just really sorry that a tree didn't get to fall in your forest," I say.

He laughs, then his laughter burns off as he nods toward the courtyard. "But that's just the way it goes."

I have a feeling it's not the first time he's said those words. I have a feeling that Gage Archer has become accustomed to life hitting him in unexpected ways. I have a feeling he doesn't even think he can have it all.

I suppose he's right.

Who really can? You simply have to pick what you can handle at any given moment in time. There's no way I can handle more than this.

I march into the meeting, leaving sex behind me.

10

JUST A LITTLE COMMITTED

Gage

Felix waits in the courtyard for us with a look in his eyes that says this is practically a done deal. At least I sure hope that's the look. "I had a feeling this place would be too hard for the two of you to resist," he says with the confidence of a seasoned businessman. I feel *some* of that confidence. I crave *all* of it.

"You were right," Elodie says to him, then follows as he leads us into the hotel lobby, down a hall, and into his office.

Turns out Felix isn't simply the guy sweeping the courtyard. He's the owner of The Escape and the coveted retail space it leases.

His office is unassuming. A simple oak desk. Some blue chairs. A vase of fresh flowers in fall colors. A couple framed photos on the desk, including a shot of three women on the deck of the San Francisco Ferry with crinkles in the corner of their eyes and bright smiles. "My daughters," he says, proudly. "My grand-daughter took the shot."

"It's lovely," I say.

"You have a beautiful family," Elodie adds.

"Thank you."

Felix gestures to the two chairs waiting for us. We sit and he moves behind his desk. He sits back in his chair, strokes his beard, those eyes twinkling again like they did on Friday night. There's something about this man that's almost magical. Swap that dark brown beard out for a white one and he'd play Santa Claus in every Webflix holiday special. But instead he's playing the part of the savvy businessman, since he wastes no time. "I looked over your pitch. It's promising. I wasn't expecting to have this space available in the evenings till next year. Starting in a few weeks we'll be selling branded merch during the day, but at night it can easily be used for other things. In fact I had leased it through the end of the year for weekend nights. But it didn't work out," he says, a hint of irritation in his tone that he quickly dismisses, as if he considers irritation rude. "Their loss. Potentially your gain. And mine as well."

"And all the future happy customers' too," Elodie adds, and damn, she is good with her saleswomanship.

"That's the goal, isn't it?"

Yes, yes it is.

He pauses for a moment, clearly thinking, then he says, "There's no point beating around the bush. I'm quite intrigued by Special Edition. I think it could be the perfect business to delight my guests as we head into the holiday season. And I'd been looking for something in the dessert world for weekend nights. But to have two of my favorite things? Cocktails and chocolate?" He makes a chef's kiss gesture.

Briefly I consider hiding a smile, but what'd be the point? I'm fucking excited. "They go well together," I say.

"So well, I can see the crowds now," he says, then sighs like he's really enjoying the image. He shakes it off though, his gaze intense and lasered in on us. "You must have been working on this idea for some time."

Two days, give or take.

I steal a glance at Elodie and she shoots me a grin that I suspect says *go with it*. What's the harm in stretching the truth a bit? "We've been talking for a while and we really thought it would be great. Then we happened upon your space when we were out," I say casually.

"Kismet." He picks up a pair of horn-rimmed glasses on his desk and peers at the screen, presumably checking out the info we sent him over the weekend for our concept for the Friday and Saturday night pop-up shop. *"It'll be intimate. We'll encourage people to take pics, then put their phones down. Our offerings will be highly curated with playlists and themes,"* he says, reading back what we wrote. Then he turns back to look at us. "We have a lot of foot traffic already with the hotel and our other retail shops. Our guest list is highly desirable, but we also attract plenty of locals. For the pop-up space, my goal is to have both a place that my guests will frequent, but one that'll draw traffic to my hotel and the other retail spaces too. You'll market the hotel, and the hotel can help your shop," he says and those are the magic words that I need to impress Celeste. Running this pop-up shop here has the potential to bring buzz to my name and the Sticks and Stones brand to help me seal the deal for the second location.

Not to mention the money.

That's why I enlisted Zoe to help out more. I trust her immensely and she's game to handle running Sticks and Stones on those busy weekend nights that are usually mine if we can pull off this pop-up shop.

"Yes, and I'm already active on social with the bar. My accounts are very engaged," I say, then gesture to my business partner. "Elodie's, too, for her shop. So we're ready to hit the ground running on that front," I say. I want this badly. I can practically taste security on my tongue.

"That's great. That's one of my key criteria in leasing the space. I want partners who, frankly, already have somewhat of a following."

"Some people post the outfit of the day. I do the chocolate of the day," Elodie says with that smile that knocked me on my ass.

"Excellent. I checked out both your socials, so that's all good. And you bring other things to the table too. Because it takes a load off my mind to know that you two are committed," he says.

"We're definitely committed," I say, and he really seems stuck on that idea. But it's no big deal to let him think this is a passion project we've been cooking up for some time rather than an idea that came together after we came together. Well, *she did.*

"Good. Good," Felix repeats, then takes off his glasses, gives me a grandfatherly stare, then her. "The last couple I rented this space to?"

"The cake-in-a-jar shop?" Elodie asks.

"Yes. Their treats were mouthwatering and it should have been a slam dunk. But when they broke up, they broke their lease. Which is why I'm pleased the two of you are interested."

Hold the fuck on.

Time slows.

My brain goes sluggish, then speeds up all at once.

"Wait," I sputter. "They…what?"

"That's why the space is, unfortunately, available when I'd hoped it wouldn't be," he says, sounding not quite bitter but a little irked. "I detest drama. I don't have the time or patience for relationship this and that. *She loves me, she loves me not. He loves me, he loves me not,*" he says, clearly parroting the prior tenants. "Life is short. I'm not a couples counselor. And I'm simply not in the mood to deal with that again." He points to Elodie's big sparkly cocktail ring. "I'm glad to know this is serious."

Holy fucking shit.

That's the commitment he's talking about?

He thinks we're *together together.* But why does he think that?

The answer comes instantly as I flash back to Friday night. We held hands the whole time we spoke to him. I kissed her like she was mine right there in the shop we're trying to lease. She's wearing the blingiest ring I've ever seen. And he's the hotel owner. He may somehow know we rented a room—together.

Hell, I ran a hand down her arm outside the shop when I just saw her minutes ago. We act like we're madly in...*gulp*...love. To top it off, we pitched a chocolate and cocktails concept, targeting it especially for date nights.

Adrenaline surges through me. I've got to handle this. I've got to fix this problem. I should tell him the truth. Really, I should, even if it means losing out on this space.

But would we for sure lose it? Do I actually have to lie? Maybe I could just let him think we're together without saying otherwise?

That's not technically a fib.

I steal a glance at Elodie, trying to read her like I would when I was on the mound back in the day. Like she's the catcher behind the plate. Is she giving me the sign that I'm throwing a curveball when she's expecting a fast one down the middle? Her blue eyes flash with something. But is that a sparkle or a warning?

Ah, hell. It's been a while since I read a catcher.

I take a chance and lob an easy pitch. "Who wouldn't commit to her?"

I'll just see if she catches it. If she's comfortable. How she reacts.

Elodie's still for a beat. Maybe contemplating. Her left hand is raised in the air, fingers fiddling with the ends of her hair. Ring glinting like a beacon guiding a plane to the runway at night.

Then she shrugs happily, smiles, and takes the flight in for a smooth landing when she says, "We're totally marrying the hell out of each other."

11

A FUNNY THING

Gage

Talk about swinging for the fences. I can't believe she leveled up like that.

And yet here I am, going along with it. That's the part I can't believe the most. I'm Mister Responsible. But right now, I'm Mister Keeping Up With This Woman. I am not going to be the weak link.

"Yup. We sure are," I say, reaching for her hand and squeezing it. Sending a message too. *What the hell*?

She simply squeezes back and shoots me an adoring look. So that's how she's playing it. Over the top in love. All right then.

"Wonderful," Felix says, beaming. "When's the wedding?"

I scratch my jaw, stalling, since we don't even have time to devise a single answer to any relationship question. Like…how did we meet?

Oh, the usual way. She accidentally sent an eight-inch dildo to me.

But Elodie jumps right in. "We're still working on picking a wedding date," she says, breezily. "Partly because we can't decide on a venue. Part of me wants to get married in the Conservatory of Flowers, but that's best during the end of summer. We were considering someplace in the Presidio because of the views. But there's also City Hall. The rotunda there is simply amazing. But so is Shakespeare Garden in Golden Gate Park."

What. The. Hell. She's rattling off dream venues for our fictional wedding?

"You can't go wrong with any of those," Felix says, then shrugs playfully and gestures around...indicating the hotel. "But The Escape is lovely too."

Elodie laughs, bright and golden. "As if we could get on the schedule here. I'm sure you're booked solid."

I fucking hope so.

"We are. But I might know a guy."

My brain screams. What is she doing? Keeping up with this sexy tornado isn't for the faint of heart. I squeeze her hand harder. "But it's nice being engaged too," I cut in. "We're enjoying the engagement so much, aren't we, cupcake?"

Translation: *slow the hell down.*

"We sure are," she says.

"Plus, we have kids, so we have to think about the best time for them," I say, since it's best to turn this fake romance into a long, long, long never-ending, will-not-see-the-light-at-the-end-of-the-tunnel   engagement.

"Mine's eleven. Busy with school and softball and all that."

"And mine's thirteen. She wants to pick my dress too. Make sure it fits right. She loves outfits of the day."

Felix leans back in his chair, seeming utterly charmed. "A family affair. How wonderful," he says, then glances fondly at the photos on his desk. "And where did you two meet?"

Of course he went there. It's a normal question. And I'm taking this one. I jump on the question before my *fiancée* can say a word. "Funny thing," I begin, patting her hand once again. "Elodie loves the French fries at Sticks and Stones. She would always come in and order them. And I just thought: I need to meet that woman. So I did."

There. It's simple and true. Probably the first true thing I've said in the last several minutes. And I sure hope it's enough.

"And you asked her out that night?"

"Well, sort of," Elodie says with a light laugh.

I clench my teeth. Seriously?

But Felix is leaning forward in his chair, enrapt as Elodie spins more fables. "He came by my shop to ask me out. You see, the real funny thing is I accidentally sent him—"

"A new showerhead," I supply.

She blinks. Once, twice. Then smiles widely. "Yes. A showerhead *and* a book of love poems."

Fuuuuck. She was going to say *book* not battery-operated-boyfriend. She's smoother than I am. "And he returned the book of love poems to my shop," she adds.

"I did. The showerhead too," I say tightly, white-knuckling my way through this. So much for keeping up with Elodie. She's way ahead of me, and I'm not sure I can ever match her pace.

Felix chuckles. "That is one of the best how-we-met stories I've ever heard. Perfect marketing, too, for Special Edition."

Ohhh.

That was the method to her madness.

She's genius.

"Huh," Elodie says, like she just realized that. The woman can act. "I hadn't thought of it that way, but you're probably right."

"It was kismet you stopped by the other night," Felix says, then taps his desk and rises. "I have a few more candidates coming by later today, but unless someone wows me, you're the front-runners." I want to both punch the sky and curse the moon. "I'll need to move on this right away. Holidays and all."

"Right, of course," I say.

No worries. You won't see us again. Because this is not what I signed up for.

"If the timing works out, we should do a photo shoot of the two of you," he says as he comes around the desk. "Put pictures on the hotel's social media."

"That would be great," Elodie says, all cheery and bright, like her dress. Her totally delicious-looking outfit that's not helping me stay mad at her, but I am mad at her. But I'm mad at me, too, for not having a better handle on the situation.

Felix shows us out and says goodbye in the lobby.

The two of us remain tight-lipped on the way through the courtyard, then down the steps. Finally, when we're walking along the block, a safe distance away, I hiss, "We need to talk."

"I know," she retorts, in a tone laced with vinegar.

She's mad at me? That only ticks me off more.

We march out to the square in the center of Hayes Valley, where a man with a mustache rides a unicycle while moms and dads with toddlers drop bills into his hat. Nearby, a violinist tunes her instrument. Elodie gazes briefly at the buskers, then dips her hand into her pocket and tosses some bills for each. Once done, she turns to me, *I'm waiting* written in those blue eyes.

Shaking my head, I grasp her hand. "Not here."

I tug her across the street, dragging her behind a food truck making Cuban sandwiches and playing a tune in Spanish. I cross my arms. "Talk. Why did you just up the ante like that? He might have rented to us because he *thought* we were together. Then you went and told him we were getting married. And you listed all those locations. What the hell?"

"Because you said we were committed," she fires back, taking no shit.

"I was feeling you out," I say, just as fast, just as furious. Doesn't she get it?

Her eyes pop open wider, and she stares at me like I've lost it. "In a meeting? You were feeling me out in a meeting?"

"I was trying to read you like a pitcher reads a catcher."

She scoffs, her brow creasing. "It's not a baseball

game. We don't have signs. It's a business negotiation. How could I possibly have known when you said *who wouldn't be committed* that you meant you were feeling me out?"

But I'm not letting this go. I'm pissed for reasons I don't even fully understand. "How would I think you'd jump ten steps ahead to tell him about the Conservatory of Flowers? The rotunda? He's practically offered us space here to get hitched," I say, gesturing wildly to the hotel in the distance, frustration rising high inside me. I stab my chest. "I've been married. I don't need to do that again."

She freezes. Then takes a beat, probably to process the truth bomb I just dropped. One I didn't expect to blurt out. "Noted," she says evenly, but in a way that's clear I've hurt her.

Shit. "I didn't mean it like that."

She holds up both hands, shaking her head. "I get it."

"I don't have anything against marriage. I just...I don't—"

"It's fine. You don't need to explain yourself."

But I do. Because now I do understand why I was angry at first. She'd hit a sore spot back there.

That's all. "Eliza's mom died when Eliza was one," I say, heavily. "We'd been married for a year and a half. It was...hard."

Her face softens, sympathy flooding her eyes. "Oh, Gage. I'm so sorry. For you and for your little girl and her mom."

There's so much more to the story though, but now's not the time to tell her my marriage to Hailey was already on the rocks. Hell, it started on the rocks. I asked her to marry me when I learned she was pregnant. A few days later, we walked out of city hall as Mr. and Mrs. But that's not the hard part. Yes, our marriage was tough. I'm not sure we were ever really right for each other. The real hard part is how it ended, and it's pretty much never the time to tell anyone that terrible tale.

I drag a hand over my stubble, trying to reset my mind, my heart, the whole damn morning. "Anyway, my point is that I was just trying to figure out how to handle it with Felix. Maybe play along with him without promising him anything," I say, and perhaps I'm grasping at straws, but they're all I can find to hold on to.

"Just string him along?" she asks gently.

"Maybe," I mutter, but for a guy who prides himself on being responsible that was pretty irresponsible. "I was hoping he'd just think we were together. And we wouldn't have to…lie then."

"Is that what you were trying to do? Just string him along and let him think we're life partners?"

When she puts it like that it sounds pretty stupid. But, yeah. "I guess I thought we'd just sort of roll with it without ever actually having to say it or having to lie," I grumble.

"Like we're *sort of* engaged?"

I shrug, feeling foolish but digging my heels in. "Maybe."

"Sure. We're half engaged. It happens all the time. Actually there's this new trend. It's called partial engagement," she says lightly, teasing me now. "If it works out really well, you open it up to mostly engaged. Only then do you decide you want to be all-the-way engaged. And if neither of those work out you just change your status to otherwise engaged."

I meet her blue eyes, glad they're playful again because I've run out of steam. "Fine. Point taken. The reality is I thought I could kind of have it all. To say we're engaged without lying about it—that's what I meant. I don't want to lie."

"I understand and I'm sorry, Gage," she says with genuine remorse. "I was reading you too, and I must have read you wrong. I thought you wanted me to go along with it, so I went all in."

I bark out a laugh. "You sure did. And that story, woman? About how we met?" I whistle in admiration.

"Hey, it was better than the showerhead!"

"I know! Love poems? Damn. I should have sent you love poems. Fictional Me is going to have a word with Real Me about doing better."

She smiles softly. "I think taking care of my Lyft was better than love poems."

I smile now too. "I was happy to help Friday night. And I'm glad Amanda was all good. And listen, I get that you were trying to help. But we clearly took it too far." One more glance at the hotel across the street, then I shrug like I'm letting it go.

Her gaze drifts down to her big ring. "Funny thing. I picked this up at my friend Rachel's jewelry shop when she first opened it a year or so ago. Bought it as a show of support for a friend. I suppose it does look *a little* like an engagement ring." She shrugs, with a rueful smile. "But I guess Special Edition's not in the cards." She frowns. "None of this with us is."

I sigh, wishing she weren't so damn right. Every step of the way we were thwarted. "Neither dating nor business?"

"Seems that way."

She's resigned, and I suppose I am too. I still don't have time for a relationship, and while it'd have been fun to date before, now things are...almost awkward between us. "It was fun while it lasted. Like...a tornado."

She tilts her head, studying me skeptically. "Tornados are fun?"

"The tornado of you," I say.

She smiles, then drops a chaste kiss to my cheek. "Bye, Gage."

"Bye, Elodie."

As she walks away, I can't entirely believe we went from the greatest date ever to...nothing.

Well, more than nothing.

We went to a fantastic business idea that won't see the light of day.

I watch the tornado retreat then go on my way.

12

THE OUTFIT OF THE DAY IS...

Elodie

"Then you put your hands right here, like this?" I ask Amanda that evening as I wrap my palms around clay like I'm holding a teacup, but it's really, well, a lump.

She gives me the look that says *I'm not trying hard enough*. "No, you have to pinch it, like I told you last time," she says, then shows me again how to make a pinch pot, which is allegedly the easiest thing to make in ceramics, but as far as I'm concerned it's ten times harder than mixing chocolate.

She rolls her eyes my way. "How can you make a cinnamon and cayenne pepper chocolate bar taste amazing and not make a pot for a tiny little plant?"

"They are different skills," I say, defending my shapeless, formless mass of clay in the face of her crafts-womanship. She's putting the finishing touches on a vase that's worthy of Instagram adoration. "But also, in my defense, I'm having flashbacks to *Ghost*. It's distracting."

"What's *Ghost*?"

I gasp. "I'm going to pretend you didn't say that."

After she humors me through clay-making at her favorite pottery studio, she heads to the sink to wipe down her tools, tossing me a glance as she says, "So, what happened with your meeting with the hotel guy?"

My shoulders sag. I give her a smile—the kind that's really a frown. "It's not going to work out."

"What? Why? Your idea was so good. Not that I would know personally. Cocktails are gross. But chocolate is awesome. How did he not like it? What is wrong with him?"

"Nothing. Felix loved it. He *chef's kissed* it. But he thought we were engaged, and he ideally wants to lease the space to a couple that's...committed," I say, sketching air quotes.

"What's the problem then?" It's asked with genuine curiosity as she lines up her tools on a towel on the counter.

Isn't it obvious? "Well, we're not really engaged."

"Put on a ring and say you are," she says easily as she moves back to her station to gather her unused clay in a bag.

I grab some coils and drop them into the plastic. "But that's sort of lying, isn't it?" Actually, it's not *sort of*. *It is*. But I'm curious about her take.

"Sure. But he's being seriously patriarchal," she says with the certainty of a thirteen-year-old feminist.

Hmm. I could use some of her spunk. "How do you figure?"

"Who cares if you're in a relationship? What does that have to do with business? That's a sign of the patriarchy." She sets down the bag on the counter with a defiant *thunk*.

And there's nothing worse to this thirteen-year-old than the patriarchy. Well, except climate change and a lack of Wi-Fi.

"He *is* kind of paternal. Like a grandpa. But a good grandpa," I say, defending Felix, since, as a businesswoman, I understand his point. He wants to avoid potholes and pitfalls. "He just doesn't want to rent to somebody who's going to break up and cause problems," I say, trying to do a better job explaining where he's coming from.

"But you're not going to break up because you're not, duh, together. Just make a deal with each other that you're doing this cool shop, and you won't be jerks." She lifts her forearm, showing off her friendship bracelet, then shooting me a playful look. "Make friendship bracelets with your bar friend."

I'd like to make more than friendship bracelets with Gage. She makes it sound so easy that I believe her. "But Gage and I would have to act like we're in a relationship," I say, and isn't that the fly in the ointment.

She arches a blonde brow then looks me up and down. "Like you do every day at work? With the whole candymaker look. The dresses, the lipstick, the hair. What's the big deal if you pretend you're engaged for a few months? It's not like Grandpa is going to follow you around. *Oh, I have to make sure Elodie is having dinner with that guy. Let me make sure he kisses Elodie when he leaves the shop.*"

I wouldn't mind if Gage did. But I don't say that. "True. All true."

Amanda grabs her backpack and slings it on. "All you have to do is be flirty and friendly with Gage, and that'll make Grandpa happy. The rest is none of his business. It's just like wearing an outfit of the day for a few months. And your OOTD is engaged."

On that mic drop, she heads to the door. "I'm hungry. Can we get an acai bowl?"

"An acai bowl is practically dessert."

"It has peanut butter in it. Peanut butter is dinner. Also, I just gave you good advice. I earned dessert for dinner."

Dammit. She has me there too.

As we leave, I start working on how to convince Gage to be as cool as Amanda.

13

THREE STRIKES

Gage

At the start of happy hour that evening, I do my best to put the disappointment behind me as I set down a beer for Carter and a scotch for Monroe. "And then to sell it to the judge and the jury, she said she accidentally sent me a book of love poems. She just came up with this romantic story on the fly," I say, still downright impressed with Elodie even as I wish the tale had a different ending.

Carter smacks a big palm on the bar approvingly. "Dude, she is *good*."

I flash back to Elodie's finesse there in Felix's office as I recount the tale for my audience of two—Carter's the star receiver for the San Francisco Renegades. Monroe is a shrink and podcaster, and we've been friends for a long time. I've only gotten to know Carter recently, but he's a good guy too and plays a mean game of golf.

"She sure is," I say, a little regretful. I'm not sure what I'm missing most—another chance with her or the shot at the once-in-a-lifetime opportunity. Both, really.

Monroe clears his throat, all dry and deadpan as he lifts his tumbler. "But let's get back to the part where you cock-blocked yourself with the first great date you've had in years. Tell me more about that."

I groan in annoyance. "What choice did I have? You can't bang a business partner. That's just a fact."

"Or your best friend," Carter adds with a sly grin. He fell in mad love with his best friend and now they're getting married soon.

I point at him. "You're the exception. Not the rule."

"And you ruled against your dick," Carter adds.

"Yup. You put your dick on ice so you could go into business with her, and now you're not in business with her. *You* should be drinking," Monroe says, then toasts in obvious mock sympathy.

Carter clinks his glass to Monroe's, then looks to me. With less ribbing in his tone now, he says, "You really should. But since the deal didn't work out, does this mean you're going to see her again?"

I blow out a breath, shaking my head. "I don't think so." And that's a damn shame.

"But you're not going to go into business with her?" Monroe asks, sounding perplexed.

"Yup," I say, drying a glass from behind the counter.

Carter hoots. "You didn't just get cock-blocked. You got sacked in the end zone."

"Yes, and I lost the game too," I say dryly to the too-amused football player. "It's called *Nothing Works Out. Story of my life.*"

"Hey now." Monroe fixes me with a look that says *you're a pessimist and always have been*. "Things can work out if you work on them."

"Like muscles," I say. "Relationships, though? Different story." I lift my index finger. "Exhibit one. My marriage to Hailey." Another finger. "Exhibit two. My major league career." One more finger. "Exhibit three. My relationship with Kylie."

She was my first and only serious girlfriend after Hailey's death. A few years ago, I fell for the software designer, she fell for me, and Eliza fell for her too. Kylie came to Eliza's softball games, made dinner with me, and stayed over and watched movies since Eliza's obsessed with movies, like many kids her age. We air-popped popcorn and watched animated flicks on the couch. I was finally feeling like romance as a single dad was possible. But when Kylie was offered a job in New York and she moved two weeks later, that was that. A little more than a year after it started, the relationship was over with barely a second thought. Eliza asked why Kylie didn't love her enough to stay. It broke my heart all over again.

"But on the other hand," Carter begins, "you have Sticks and Stones. And your daughter. Those worked out just fine."

"All true," I concede.

Monroe lifts his glass. "Be a glass-half-full guy."

"I'm a moving on guy," I say with a full-speed-ahead attitude. Monroe's right in that I shouldn't dwell on the past and the things that didn't happen. Sour grapes and all. "We had one great date. She was incredible. Captivating. Gorgeous. Kept me on my toes like no one ever had. The chemistry was out of this world. And then…it was cut short. Our business thing isn't going to happen. That's two strikes. Which is more than enough."

Carter sets down his glass with a thunk. "I think you're getting your sports metaphors wrong. Sounds like it's time to take a third swing and fucking mean it when you do."

I love baseball analogies, but I'm not following his. "What pitch do you want me to swing at?"

Carter stabs the counter with his finger, adorned with one of his Big Game rings, bright and gleaming, a shining sign of the ultimate triumph on the gridiron. "You've got this goal of opening this other bar. Literally the only thing standing between you and this other bar is an engagement ring."

"But it's a ring that got us in this messed-up situation in the first place. She wears this gigantic cocktail ring, and that's why he thought we were engaged."

"Maybe that's kismet," Carter says, "Maybe she ought to wear yours for a few months."

"You're saying I should do this?"

"Take a swing. Take a big swing, man."

"It can't be that easy," I point out.

"Or maybe it can't be that hard," Monroe puts in.

I check the clock on the wall. I don't have time to hash this out right now. I set down the cloth. "And on that note, I need to go take this meeting with Celeste."

I say goodbye, leaving the bar in Zoe's capable

hands, then head to the most coveted block in the Marina to see Celeste. Her building is right next to the location I want for my upscale Sticks and Stones and I stare longingly at the brick facade, the bright green door, the windows that invite passersby to come on in, put up their feet, let the day go.

I snap my focus to the office building, then head inside. Celeste's waiting for me. She wears a black pantsuit and a slicked-back bun and barely offers a hello. "I appreciate you coming down here, and I like the ideas you laid out for the location, but I'd still need to know how you're going to market it. I need to know you have a name and a brand and some buzz. I need to see that and I don't right now, Mr. Archer."

Talk about a punch in the gut. But I don't show an ounce of emotion. Just resolve as I say, "I understand."

Three strikes and you're out.

* * *

Deflated, I head to my home in Russian Hill, trying but failing to shake off my funk as I bound up the steps of the sky-blue building. My grandma helps out both with the bar and with Eliza, so she picked her up from school today.

Time to focus on them, and only them.

"Hey, my favorite ladies," I say as I kick off my boots, then set my phone on the table in the foyer.

"It's mac and cheese and cauliflower night, and I'm not mad about that," Eliza calls out from the kitchen.

"Me neither. Grams makes the best mac and cheese."

"Grams makes the best everything," Eliza says, and when I reach the kitchen I give her a hug.

Right here, I have everything I need. I'd do well to remember that.

"Including chocolate chip cookies," I point out, then wink at Grams.

"Are you trying to steal my recipe again?" Grams asks.

I scoff. "Steal? I developed that with you when I was...what? Ten? I suggested we add the—"

"Shh. Enough about my secret recipe."

"*Our*," I mutter.

She pats my head, then winks at me, whispering, "*Maybe* ours."

I smile, but it disappears too soon. Today just didn't go the way I wanted. At the dinner table, Grams shoots me a curious look. "All right, what did you mess up today?"

"Why do you assume I messed something up?"

With her fork midair, Eliza says, "Because you're in a funk, Daddy."

And maybe I didn't shake off my mood. With a sigh, I set down the utensil and tell them about the meeting this morning and the one a little while ago. "But we're not going to get the pop-up. Shame because it would have helped with the second bar."

"But pretending you're engaged sounds like fun," Eliza says as her fork dives into the cheesy goodness. "Like a game of make-believe. What's the big deal?"

"That's an excellent question. What *is* the big deal?"

Grams asks, meeting my gaze with a serious one of hers.

One that says I'm being a stick in the mud. And the fact is, they're probably right, too, like my friends.

After dinner, as I take the trash to the street, I click open my text app to send a note to Elodie when I find one from her.

Elodie: So, I have this idea…

Gage: Yeah. Me too.

Elodie: You go first.

Gage: It's been brought to my attention it's NBD to pretend we're engaged.

Elodie: What do you know? Same here!

Gage: Yeah? Who told you?

Elodie: Amanda. She basically said it's so patriarchal if we don't pretend we're engaged.

Gage: Explain.

Elodie: Apparently wanting two people to be involved is patriarchal, so faking an engagement is an act of defiance along the lines of fuck the patriarchy, which is something Amanda is big on, and I suspect Eliza will be too.

Gage: It's a new world. We're just living in it.

. . .

And the thing is, I want to do more than live in it. I want to thrive. I don't want to be the *nothing works out* guy. I want things to work for me. As I close the lid on the trash, I kick the last remnants of my funk to the curb, sending her another text.

> Gage: Want to be my fake fiancée for the next three months to get the shop?

> Elodie: Is this your proposal? Because if so, let me put down the dishes and squeal.

> Gage: You're doing dishes? I was taking out trash. That is kismet.

> Elodie: Then, I'm not even stopping doing these dishes as I say yes to your temporary fake fiancée-ship.

A smile tugs at my lips as I write back, glad we're on the same page with the plan and the timeline.

> Gage: Let's call it a Special Edition Engagement. Same rules?

> Elodie: Same, sad rules. But alas, they're for our own good.

.   .   .

She's right there too. It's a bad idea to mess around with your business partner, especially when you already like her. Keeping this attraction on ice is the wise thing to do. It's the adult decision. The mature choice.

> Gage: They are. By the way, what was your idea?

> Elodie: Same as yours.

> Gage: Kismet.

The real kismet comes when I go back inside to email Felix and see how his other meetings went, and he tells me the place is ours if we want it.

I say yes so fast. When I tell Grams the details as I clean the kitchen, she says, "That cocktail ring she wears might fool a man, but I knew it was costume jewelry when I saw her at the bar. She needs a real ring."

"Yeah. She will. What'll that set me back?"

Her eyes flicker with mischief. "It's free."

14

THE HAPPY COUPLE

Elodie

There's a slight October breeze. The morning's a little warm and a little chilly at the same time. That's the Bay Area for you. I'm standing on the Embarcadero in Rincon Park, the bay glittering to the right, the Bay Bridge behind us.

Next to us is none other than one of the most social media-worthy sites in the city—Cupid's Span, a sculpture of a partial bow and a piece of an arrow. Late last night, Gage asked me to meet him here before work and to wear my favorite color. He said his grandmother wants to take pics of the happy couple.

Right now, my temporary fiancé is about thirty feet away, chatting on the phone, his back to me. I kind of want him to turn around, but he's been busy since I arrived a few minutes ago.

But Margo's here, decked out in khakis and a

lavender oxford cloth shirt, looking grandma chic and no-nonsense as she peers at my outfit. I'm dressed in one of my favorite dresses. Yellow with white polka dots and a halter top that ties at the neck. I have a matching little white sweater on. Well, they did say they wanted photos.

"Just fluff your hair up a little bit right there," Margo tells me.

I flick the ends.

"Perfect."

Margo steps away, phone in hand, then stops in her tracks and swivels around. "Wait, doll. Your lipstick needs a touch-up."

I click open my purse, check my reflection in my phone, and slick some more on, so my lips are nice and cherry red.

"Perfect. Be sure to smack a big kiss on his cheek at just the right moment," she says then winks and steps back.

"Easy enough," I say.

Don't think about how tempted you were when Gage first kissed your cheek on that date.

As I tuck the silver tube back in my purse, Gage turns around, then heads toward me, striding across the grass. The only info he gave me about today was to *look fantastic, but that won't be hard because you always do.* Now, I'm waiting for my temporary fiancé to, I don't know, sweep me into his arms and plant a sailor's kiss on me.

A girl can dream.

In jeans and a trim black shirt that shows off his ink,

the man is hot in a *bad boy is a daddy* kind of way. Is that a thing? If not, it should be. When he reaches me, his lips crook up. "Elodie, yesterday you said there's this new thing called being half engaged," he says, skipping small talk and diving straight in.

I'm all ears, especially since his tone is serious. "I did."

"But if we're doing this, we're going to be all-the-way engaged," he says with new passion in his tone. "No otherwise, no partial, no halfway about it."

Out of nowhere, he drops down to one knee. I gasp. My hand flies to my chest. My heart is beating so fast.

He reaches for my other hand. I'm shaking.

"Ever since I met you at the bar, I've been captivated by you. You came in and all I could think about was when you would show up again. I knew I had to ask you out. I had to see you," he says, and that feels all true. "And when you accidentally sent me those love poems, it was like a sign."

Oddly enough, that feels true, too, even though it's not. But the way he gazes at me with utter adoration makes my heart stutter. I'm only vaguely aware that from ten feet away his grandmother is taking pictures of us.

"It was a sign for you to ask me out," I whisper, as if talking louder could break this magic spell.

"I'm so glad I did. Because these last two months with you have been fantastic," he says.

Wow. He's doing all the work, crafting the backstory of this fake romance, and I am here for his effort.

"Getting to know you. Taking you around the city.

Falling for you," he says and my romance-loving soul does a little dance. "That time we went on the ferry ride and had our first kiss."

"What a kiss," I say, mesmerized by this tale. By his hand on mine, too, the warmth of his palm, the gentle stroke of his fingers.

"I'll never forget it," he says, eyes locked on me with heat and, perhaps, genuine affection.

"Then there was the date at the art museum when you showed me your favorite artist."

Oh! It's my turn. "Roy Lichtenstein."

His grin widens. "Yes. That guy. I love the way you love him."

"His style enchants me."

Gage's mesmerizing eyes hold my gaze like he doesn't want to let go. "You enchant me."

For a few dangerous seconds, I believe in this fairy tale. I want to believe in it so badly. "That time we went to the tea gardens was magical."

"I can't stop thinking about that day either," he says, and it's like we're swaying in the kitchen to a slow love song. We're moving seamlessly with each other through this make-believe romance. "I could have listened to your stories all day."

"I liked hearing yours when you took me to the game," I say.

"And I learned you're a hardcore football fan," he says, getting it right on the first guess.

"I sure am."

"But I think you should like baseball better."

"I like it so much better now, especially that time we

went to the park late at night with a softball and you set me up at home plate."

"Then ran out to the mound and showed off my best pitch."

"It was a softball," I tease.

"And you hit it right to me." He runs his thumb along the outside of my hand, his touch like electricity, sending sparks through my whole body. "Then, you ran to the pitcher's mound and I scooped you up in my arms and kissed you and told you I'd never had such a wonderful time with a woman."

His touch melts me. His words make me feel tingly. The look in his eyes, the commitment, the way he's willing to make this *business engagement* work makes my heart pound.

Gage reaches into his pocket, and I tremble with excitement. From several feet away, Margo takes another photo, then moves closer, snapping more.

My smile takes over my face. My eyes turn a little wet.

Gage opens a box. It's cream, faded, a little worn. It looks like the kind you'd find at a vintage shop. The kind of box that has seen lives and stories.

"My grandmother gave me the ring."

My throat catches. "She did?"

"Yes. She's held on to it since my grandfather passed more than thirty years ago," he says, and even though the loss was long ago, my heart aches for her. I send her a look of sympathy, of love too, then turn my attention back to the man on one knee. "She wants you to have it. I want you to have it," he says, and he sounds so earnest, so vulnerable, I barely know what to do with this wonder in my chest. This hope in my heart. None of this is real, but it's all so deliciously surreal.

"Would you do me the honor of being my wife?"

"Yes!" I say, shouting it, feeling the exhilaration of an engagement in this moment, which is ridiculous. Utterly ridiculous. And yet, I'm thrilled.

Even when he adds, "And for the next three months, my"—he stops, clears his throat, gives a tilt of his head that says we're in on this ruse—"fiancée."

It's a *no big deal* business deal. It's an outfit of the day. It's an act.

But when he slides the ring on my finger, the overflow of emotions is too real. I don't think you're supposed to feel achy or hopeful over a fake engagement. I gaze at the vintage ring, a tiny diamond set in a gold filigree band that was worn by someone in his family, someone who loves him, someone who already cares for me.

Gage stands, cups my cheek, and drops a quick but possessive kiss to my lips. It's a tasteful kiss, but it's a kiss that says to the world *she's mine.*

It's a claim.

I grip his shirt to hold on. His heart beats steady, loud, like a drum. His breath shudders. His stubble tickles me as he gives me a kiss for the camera.

When he breaks the kiss, he asks with a shrug, "Our last kiss?"

It sounds like that prospect devastates him as much as it devastates me. "Yes."

A few seconds later, Margo is by my side, saying, "I

guess I didn't need that cheek kiss after all. These were great and you're both naturals. But I'm a damn good photographer too." She waggles the phone like it's a treasure. "We've got these for whenever you need social proof of your official engagement. We can say these were taken last week."

Like that, the romantic moment unspools. It's time for business. As she wanders away, giving us space, I try to clear my thoughts. I rewind to a few minutes ago when I arrived. Something's sticking with me.

"Were you on the phone at all?" I ask. "When I arrived?"

Smiling, he shakes his head. "No. I wanted to surprise you."

"Well, you did."

He drops a kiss to my cheek. "Get used to it, cupcake. Your fiancé is full of surprises."

He sure is.

15

MY DARLING FIANCÉ

Elodie

There's no time to linger in this fizzy feeling over the next few days. We've got a pop-up shop to open. Kenji's handling Elodie's Chocolates in the mornings so Gage and I can deal with all the things from our business license to glassware and plates, to décor, and now to signage.

We've been spending Thursday afternoon in Loretta's Signs off Webster Street, picking out option after endless option to adorn the glass facade.

"I think you'll like this one. I'm pretty damn pleased with it," Loretta says in a gravelly voice like a country singer that fits her name. She fits the vibe too, all big hair and a checked boobalicious shirt with rhinestone buttons. She spins the tablet screen around, showing us a Special Edition: Cocktails & Chocolate mock-up in bright, vibrant neon pink. "Looks like neon. But made with LED. Perfect, since neon's making a comeback. Something I can never say about my ex-husband."

I laugh. Yup, pure country. "Well, neon deserves it. I am obsessed with neon and *this*," I say, then turn to Gage. "What about you?"

He studies the screen with an unreadable expression. "I like it," he says, but he couldn't have less emotion if he tried.

I swat his arm, like a fiancée would do. "You don't have to be obsessed with it but you can't deny it's amazing." Where is his exuberance? This script, this color, this look. "It's sexy and inviting. It's fun and pretty. It's beckoning."

Could I pitch him any harder?

"Sure." It's not as if he doesn't care. It's as if he won't give an inch.

Perhaps sensing she needs to give us space, Loretta offers a professional smile. "Why don't you two lovebirds talk about it? You let me know if there are any problems."

She slips into the back of the store, creaking the door shut, and I tug him away from the counter. Maybe this is a negotiation tactic, this whole overthinking side of him. "Are you playing hardball?"

He shakes his head. "I don't think it's perfect," he says, and I don't hear worry in his tone. I hear drive. A relentless desire to make something the best.

"What would make it more perfect?"

He scratches his stubble, then blows out a breath. "That's what I'm trying to figure out. My gut says we can do better, Elodie. This whole shop has got to be not just a home run but a grand slam. I'm not getting that second location from Celeste unless this is a grand slam."

Ohhhh.

Sure, I have a lot riding on this shop too. But I feel like I'm running a marathon, and perhaps he feels like he has only one shot in a sprint. I do my best to keep my voice open-minded, welcoming. I don't want to be the difficult business partner. "What do you think we should do differently?"

"It's too bright. The pink is just too bright."

I smile. That's easy. "We'll make it a little less pink. A touch of subtlety."

All at once, his shoulders relax. His jaw seems less tight. "That's a good idea."

We call Loretta back and give her a few tweaks. A minute later, she swivels the screen around, showing us the new mock-up. Her eyes say *it's a beaut*, but her mouth is silent since she's letting Gage lead. A business-woman who knows how to read a room.

He nods a few times, seemingly satisfied. "Perfect," he says, a smile finally tipping his lips.

I'm so relieved.

"We'll deliver the sign next week. And I can't wait to come to your opening. I can't think of anything better than cocktails and chocolate. Are you gonna have swag though?"

A line digs into Gage's forehead. "Good question. Let me give that some thought."

Great. Something new for him to obsess over when I want him to enjoy this pop-up shop like I am. "Maybe!

Thanks again for the hard work," I say to her brightly as I guide him out of the store.

"Do we need swag? I hate swag," he mutters once the door clicks shut.

"Of course you hate swag," I say, as we head toward Fillmore.

"Why do you say of course I hate it?"

"Because swag is usually made of plastic. You said you were doing a beach cleanup with your kid over the weekend. I assume you picked up a lot of plastic."

"I did. I hate things."

I laugh. "You have a little bit of grumpy bartender in you too."

He arches a brow my way. "And you're the upbeat, sassy chocolatier."

I give a half-twirl, my skirt swinging playfully, Marilyn Monroe style. "Deal with it," I say, then poke him in the side. "You've got yourself an exuberant business partner."

"I sure do," he says.

A sliver of doubt digs into me as we near a *romance is in the air* window display of pink and red and purple paperbacks with cartoon couples at An Open Book. Is he saying my go-for-it attitude is a bad thing? I kind of hoped he'd balance me out. "Look, I've always been excited about things, chances, opportunities. But are you worried that we're being too impulsive?"

"I am definitely worried, but I'm doing it anyway." His tone is surprisingly raw and I appreciate the honesty so much.

I curl a hand around his biceps, nice and sturdy.

"*We're* doing it. And I am going to do everything I can to make it work," I say, wanting him to feel some of my optimism.

His eyes meet mine. "I can tell you want it to work. That means a lot to me," he says, holding my gaze and speaking from the heart. Both make my stomach flip. Both make my chest tingle too.

This man and all his little moments of raw honesty, sexy compliments, and big gestures...I don't know what I'd do if our romance was real. I'd probably melt into a puddle. It's good we're not actually together. I'd get nothing done but swooning.

Instead, I tip my forehead to the coffee shop on the next block. "Let me buy you a cup of coffee, my darling fiancé. You take it straight up black, no sugar, I bet?"

"And you take yours in latte form, with two shots of vanilla and extra foam," he says, playful once more.

"Life is short," I say, a declaration. No, it's a rallying cry.

"It sure is," he says as we reach Doctor Insomnia's, the chalkboard sign with the cup of coffee inviting us in.

A few minutes later, we're settling into a table at the back and my own words echo in my mind—*life is short*.

So is this engagement. But there's no reason I can't get to know my fake fiancé better. "Back at the sign shop, I was thinking you're an overthinker, but now I suspect you go with your gut. And your gut was telling you the sign was wrong. But here's what I want to know —is that from your parents or your grandma?"

He blinks, perhaps taken aback.

Maybe I am too.

Normally, on a second date, I wouldn't ask such a personal question. I have a propensity for falling too hard, too fast, too foolishly. But this isn't a real second date. It's a chance to get to know my business partner and my fake fiancé, so I'm taking it.

16

OUR PREDICAMENT

Gage

Elodie just goes for it. I shouldn't be surprised. She's always been bold. Upfront. Gutsy.

I appreciate that in a woman. In a person. It's worlds better than the style of living I saw growing up—with the jabs, and the pokes, and the prods from my father.

I take a thoughtful sip of coffee and give her an honest answer since she deserves to know who she's getting into business with. "My dad's a hard-ass. He was always really hard on Zane and me. Try harder, get better grades, throw faster, hit better. But he did that to our mom too. He got on her case about everything from how she folded laundry, to how she stacked the dishwasher, to how she brushed her teeth."

"I take it they're not together?"

I shake my head, so damn grateful Mom got out of that situation. "Nope. She finally left him after I graduated from high school. Wish it were sooner, but thank fuck she did it." I take a sip of my coffee—black, as she'd suspected. "It took her a while to meet someone new. She married again recently and now she's traveling the world with her new guy. Zane's traveling, too, with his partner. They're both ridiculously happy," I say with a smile I feel deep in my soul. I'm truly happy for my brother and for my mom. "They deserve all the good things."

She smiles softly. "They do." For a second, I fear she's about to ask *but do you*, and I'm not sure I want to answer that. After a pause, she says, "But you're hard on yourself, aren't you?"

The caring tone unlocks a part of me. The part that doesn't always share. That hasn't really shared since I was in therapy several years ago. "Sure. I guess I'm always asking myself if I've done enough—at work, with Eliza, with coaching, with friends." I force out a laugh at my own expense. "Probably the only time I don't is when I'm making soap."

"You make soap?"

"Handmade."

She shakes her head with a big smile on her face. "That's too much."

"Why?"

"You have tattoos. You go all out. You're gallant and pay for Lyfts even when a date ends. You return a damsel's vibrator. And…you make soap."

I'm not sure why she likes that, but I'll take it. "It's good soap. But it could be better."

She laughs now. "That's my point exactly."

Owning my flaw, I shrug, then take a sip. "A lot of times I feel like I haven't tried hard enough."

She takes a drink too, then sets down the latte mug. "Do you have trouble sleeping?"

That's an odd question. "Why are you asking me that?"

"Because I just wonder if all these questions you ask yourself—have you done enough—keep you up late at night."

I sink back in the chair, feeling seen, feeling too seen. But not entirely minding. There's something about Elodie's easy intuitiveness that soothes me. There's no judgment in how she reads a situation. Just curiosity. It feels different than Kylie, who was harder to get to know, who held pieces of herself back. "Yes. It takes me a long time to fall asleep. What about you?"

"I do worry about a lot of things, but honestly, I let them go at night."

"Jealous. How the hell do you pull that off?" I ask, leaning closer, feeling a bit like we're all alone in the back of the coffee shop as "Unforgettable" plays faintly overhead. Reminds me of the names of her chocolates, the old standards.

But I'm too interested in the convo to go off on that tangent, especially when she says, "Don't laugh" like a warning.

"That's almost a guarantee that I will."

She wags a finger, the red polish on her nails gleaming. But my ring on her finger shines even brighter. "No teasing either."

"Now I have to know. What's the trick?"

With a smile like she has a secret, she lifts two fingers together and moves them in a come-hither motion.

Oh, fuck me. That's hot. I'm pretty sure the temperature in this coffee shop shot through the roof. "Seriously? You're going to be the death of me."

"Self-care," she says, smugly. Then earnestly, she adds, "Look, it works. It takes the edge off the day."

"Now I want to watch you go to bed. Grab a chair in the corner of your bedroom. Enjoy the show," I tell her, painting the picture I'm dying to see.

"You want that? Tickets to the show?"

"I want the *only* ticket," I say.

She leans closer now, her hair falling and hiding the side of her face, adding to the privacy. "I'd do that. For you."

I tug at my shirt collar. "Elodie," I warn.

"Gage," she fires back.

"Stupid fucking rules," I mumble, wanting nothing more right now than to grab her beautiful face and kiss those lush lips, hard. "You're making me want to finish what we started."

"I've finished it a few times already," she whispers. Her voice is feathery, full of lust.

"Same here."

"Yeah?" I swear her dirty brain lights up. Her blue eyes flicker. "How? Do I suck you off? Or do you bend me over the bed? Or do you reach into my nightstand and take out one of my toys, then use it on me?"

My skin crackles. My cells burn. My muscles are strung tight with restraint. "You get on your knees, but I don't finish that way. I haul you up in my arms, kiss those sexy lips, and then spin you around. And use one of your toys on you while I fuck you to countless orgasms."

"You use my toys," she says with filthy awe in her voice.

"Cupcake, we went on a date because of a toy. You better believe I'd make you come the way you want—with toys. Lots and lots of toys."

She shudders and it's a sight to behold, the way her desire moves like a wave through her body. Her eyes flutter closed. For a few heady seconds, she seems to be watching a filthy movie in her mind—the one we just wrote together.

Then, she opens her eyes. "I'll sleep well tonight." She blows out a long breath and flaps a hand in front of her face. "All right. We need a different topic. Something that won't make me want to sit on your lap right now."

I laugh, leaning back in my chair. "We could discuss the menu for our first night at Special Edition."

She scoffs. "Right. Because cocktails and chocolate *don't* turn me on."

"Woman, you picked our business over pillow talk. You picked it because it's sexy."

"My point exactly. I can't talk business with you to get rid of my hard nips."

A laugh bursts from me. I've never heard someone speak so directly.

She gestures to her fantastic chest and goddammit,

to the outline of her nipples in her red short-sleeve sweater. "Well, it's your fault."

I groan, a little in misery, a little in admiration. "I accept full responsibility. And damn, I do approve. And I'd really like to show them some well-deserved attention."

She growls at me. "Not helping."

I gesture to my hard-on, practically punching its way out of my jeans. "You're not helping here either!"

Then, we burst into laughter over, clearly, our predicament.

Soon though, we collect ourselves, and we do discuss the offerings for our first night, devising a plan, and, miraculously, steering the ship out of *I want to watch you get off* waters.

Once we're back on chaste shores, I return to the topic we never finished, because I genuinely want to understand her. "You said you worry but you let it go. What stresses you out?"

She draws a deep breath, perhaps a fortifying one. "It wasn't easy for me to suddenly become a mom out of nowhere." Then, like it's hard for her to say, but important too, she adds, "Amanda's seventeen years younger and our parents died in a car crash two years ago. I'm her guardian. Her mom. Her sister. It's complicated. Sometimes I feel like both. Sometimes I feel like a failure. It's extra hard because they were very different with me than they were with her."

"How so?"

"They were...uninvolved with me. They were too interested in drinking, partying, going out, having a good time. I was left to my own devices. Which seemed fun at the time, but wasn't really."

My heart squeezes painfully. "I get that. Kids might say they want to be left alone, but they really don't. They want us. They need us."

"They do." She nods sadly, then hesitates some before she adds, "We grieved them in very different ways. It was…much harder for her. I didn't feel as close to them." There's some guilt in her tone but not for long. It's mostly replaced by relief when she says, "With Amanda, they'd stopped drinking. Become sobriety coaches. Put all their money into that new line of work —sober houses and so on. They were walking the walk and talking the talk and helping others and being super parents. And I'm truly glad she had that. Really, I am. I'm glad she had the parents I never had. But maybe that's part of what makes me feel like a failure too."

"You're not a failure," I say instantly, reaching for her hand.

"How do you know?" she asks, quietly, taking my palm in hers.

"Because you're trying. Because I can tell how much she matters to you. Because I already know how important she is to you. You are not a failure, and I'm so sorry about your loss."

"Thank you. Every day feels like it has a new challenge. Every day I feel like I'm just making it up as I go along." She takes a sip of her latte—with extra foam, as I'd predicted. "I really want this shop to work, Gage. I had this offer from a chain," she says, then tells me more about The Chocolate Connoisseur and the low-ball deal she turned down.

"Good. I'm glad you turned it down. Elodie's is the best chocolate in the whole damn city, and I should know. I've eaten most of it."

She smiles. "Big spender."

"Seriously. Your chocolate is amazing and your brand kills it. You don't need anyone else but you. We're going to make this work," I say, since it's so much easier to feel certain on her behalf than my own.

"I hope so. I want to take care of Amanda. Be there for her...in a way my parents weren't when I was young." A pang digs into my heart. It aches a little harder for her as she gives a one-shoulder shrug and adds, "Like chocolate was for me."

"What do you mean?" I'm careful because that could mean sweets were her comfort, her addiction, or something else entirely.

"Just that it was reliable. It was—don't laugh this time—like a lighthouse. It was steady, reliable, and *always* there. And since I was good at chemistry, it made sense to me. I started experimenting with making chocolate in the kitchen when my parents were out. And then it became...my companion." It's said with such affection, such fondness that it's clear chocolate isn't simply what she sells. It's part of who she is.

"It felt like home?"

She's wistful as she nods. "Yes. In a way, it was home. Maybe like baseball for you?"

That's a damn good assessment. Baseball was my

constant. Until it wasn't. "That sounds about right. But not as tasty as chocolate."

"Maybe Sticks and Stones is that for you now. Something steady and reliable. A ballast?"

"Yes. We're going to make this work," I say with more certainty than I feel, but I need to give this strength to her.

She smiles, full of a hope that matches mine.

The moment ends when her phone buzzes. She looks down at it, perplexed. "It's a video from your grandmother."

"It must be of the proposal. Open it," I say, and I wouldn't mind seeing it, truth be told. The other morning already feels like a blur. And I don't want to forget it.

She hits play and turns the phone for us both to see. But the video's not the proposal. It's me at the bar last week as I removed a purple dick from a pink envelope. "How did this get here? Is it yours?" I'm asking Grams, off-screen.

And Elodie is dying. She's laughing over the remains of her latte.

When the video ends, I shake my head in admiration. "Grandma two. Gage, zero."

"I'll say," Elodie says.

"She will never not get my goat."

"You two have quite the bond, don't you?"

"Yeah, we really do."

"I'm glad she's in on it then. I wouldn't want to lie to her. Or to your daughter," she says.

That means a lot to me. That she feels the same. "Me

too. I'm glad they are as well. I'm glad we agree a little bit on how to be honest within our false romance."

Somehow, that makes me feel a little closer to her.

* * *

When we leave, heading toward her store, we pass The Chocolate Connoisseur, not too far from her shop. It's black and silver, all sleek and modern, with a red *sale* sign on the window and a chocolate sculpture of a horse in the center of the store. It's teeming with customers.

She slows her pace, checking out the shop as she whispers to me. "That's him."

"The horse?"

"No, I'm sure the horse is the patriarchy. But that's Sebastian next to it. He likes to interact with customers when he's in his flagship store," she says, nodding subtly to a man in a newsboy hat chatting animatedly to a group checking out the horse. He has one of those vaguely charming faces. Fair skin, straight teeth, probably a one-time frat boy.

Without thinking twice, I wrap an arm around my fiancée. I get to touch her like this. Me. Just me. "He won't ever get his hands on your shop."

"Good."

Then, to prove my point, I drop a firm kiss to her cheek. Her perfume tickles my nose and fries my brain. "Cherries. You smell like cherries."

She gazes up at me with that clever smile I adore. "We should have chocolate-covered cherries at our opening."

"Yes, we should. And we should call it Unforgettable."

"Like a good chocolate should be."

We walk, but a second or two later, the door swings
open and a booming voice calls out, "Elodie!"

Her shoulders tense, then her whole body. Her
expression shifts quickly, as she rearranges her features
to false cheer while turning around. "Hello, Sebastian."

"You walk by and don't come in? I've got some
autumn-themed bonbons just for you."

My neck prickles. That sounds awfully familiar.
Didn't she have bonbons like that in her shop when I
asked her out? But I dismiss the thought quickly. They
must be a normal thing in the chocolate business.

"They sound wonderful. And of course I'd love to try
one," she says, and maybe it's me, but she sounds like
she's having a harder time with that falsehood than the
ones we spun about us. "Excuse my manners though.
This is my fiancé, Gage Archer. Gage, meet Sebastian
Roberts, the mastermind behind The Chocolate
Connoisseur."

He hardly seems worthy of the title. But I go with it
as I extend a hand. "Nice to meet you. Great shop. Love
the horse," I add, though I don't, but any man who puts
a horse sculpture in the middle of his store clearly
wants everyone to admire his equine.

As we shake, his gray eyes darken with, perhaps,
confusion. Then, something else I can't quite read as
that inquisitive gaze strays to her hand while he shakes
mine, saying, "Nice to meet the lucky man."

She waves, showing off the ring. "Yes, we're...

recently engaged," she says, and I wish this weren't uncomfortable for her. I wish I could save her. But maybe I can.

"Why don't we get those bonbons? I can take some home to my daughter. And Grandma. They'll love them," I say.

"Yes! They're on the house." Sebastian gestures grandly to the shopfront.

That seems to defuse the strange tension. Men like him like commerce. After we go inside, I pick up more boxes than I want, then we say goodbye and leave, with the unwanted chocolates in hand.

Once we're outside, she rolls her shoulders like she's getting the scent of him off her.

"You okay?" I ask, wrapping an arm around her again.

She hesitates before she answers with a firm nod. "I'm fine. I just feel...oily."

"For lying to *him*?"

"Just the whole thing," she says, then draws a deep breath, like she needs it to clean away the encounter.

"Do you want to talk about it?"

She shakes her head. "No, but thank you for saving the day."

"Hardly," I say because I don't want to take credit. I'm just glad I helped her when she needed it.

We keep walking and I don't let go of her. Not when we reach the next block, or the next one, or the next one.

"By the way, the sign looks really good," I say.

"Good enough?" she asks.

"More than enough."

Then, because I can't help myself, rules or no rules, I say, "Text me tonight. Before you fall asleep."

"I will."

I want to say *send me a video*, but I don't. I'm so fucking behaved I can't stand it.

* * *

Later, when Eliza's gone to bed, I'm clutching my phone, pacing like a lion hungry for his meal.

I take a shower. Brush my teeth. Pull on sweatpants. Trudge to bed.

Finally, my phone buzzes.

> Elodie: Want to know what I pictured tonight?

> Gage: Like you wouldn't believe.

> Elodie: You were standing in front of me. And I was on my knees.

> Gage: Bet you'd look beautiful and filthy like that, those red lips parted.

> Elodie: Your hand in my hair.

> Gage: Your lipstick all over me.

> Elodie: You telling me what you liked.

> Gage: No, me telling you how fucking much I love it.

Elodie: All those dirty words driving me on.

Gage: Me turning into an inferno.

Elodie: Your groans, your grunts, your shudders.

Gage: Me throwing you on the bed and having you over and over.

Elodie: I'd be a very happy girl.

And I'm a very happy guy as I finish. Though, happy might not be the right word. I want her even more now.

I still can't have her.

17

MAGIC DICK

Elodie

"So how's it working out, keeping your hands off him?" Kenji asks several days later, ever so innocently, while presenting the damning evidence on his phone of a kiss between Gage and me. "Judging from this *engagement* photo, not well at all."

He gives me a *busted* smile. We're at the shop on Tuesday morning before it opens and my girls are here too, checking out the pics I posted from last week's staged proposal.

Keeping my hands off Gage is hard. Keeping my mouth shut about it is even harder as the other day, and night, proved.

But that's just for me to know.

"That was a staged photo," I say, deflecting, then I slide a tray of chocolates to my taste-test crew at a table in the back of the shop. It's been zero to sixty as we prep for our first night at Special Edition later this week. "Now, stop distracting me. And try this. The opening night sampler needs to be amazing."

"As amazing as this pic of the lovebirds," Rachel teases as she stares pointedly at my social feed.

Admittedly, it did feel a little weird to put our fake engagement photo on the feed for the store. Sure, I post plenty of other photos of myself serving chocolate, making chocolate, and setting out the chocolates for the day on the store's feed. I'm not camera shy, and I do play the role of the cheery chocolatier. But it's usually chocolate and me, not...*me*. These photos don't have that much to do with chocolate, but I understand the *romance* part of the image that we're selling for the pop-up. I shouldn't really feel bad that I'm not telling the truth on social media. No one does anyway.

But I do feel a layer of guilt roiling in the pit of my stomach.

Or maybe I feel bad knowing how much Felix likes our romance. He's already commented with several hearts.

I have a job to do though, so I laser in on it. "Be my guinea pigs," I say authoritatively to my friends, gesturing to the trays of chocolates. Time to focus on chocolate, not lust. I've assembled the brain trust for their palates. Rachel's here and she's my longtime bestie. I've known her since shortly after college—we've even shared the same shrink. Juliet's her sister, and she's here too. And our newest friend Fable's at the table as well. She used to work at Rachel's jewelry shop but recently landed a primo gig designing merch for the Renegades

—one of the city's football teams. She's brassy and bold, and I adore her. Hazel couldn't make it this morning since she had to shoot some promo videos for her next romance novel.

"I'll go first," Fable says, reaching for a dark chocolate square, then adopting a snooty pose and an erudite accent. "Now, dahling, do tell me all about this chocolate."

Kenji side-eyes her. "Is British royalty coming to her pop-up opening?"

"Love, don't you know? Everyone is coming," Fable says, still queen-like.

"Also, doesn't *pop-up opening* sound kind of naughty?" Juliet asks with a quirk in her lips.

"Along with *everyone is coming*," Rachel stage whispers.

Kenji clears his throat, shooting daggers at each and every one of the troublemakers. "Ahem, ladies, focus. Chocolate. Now."

"Hello! You're the one who said I sounded British. You began the distraction," Fable says to Kenji with a defiant flick of her copper hair and a return to her voice.

"And I am ending it," he says, firmly, clapping his hands once. "Now eat."

I gesture to the tray. "We're starting with a flirty theme for the first night," I explain. "So this chocolate is raspberries with a little champagne flavor."

"Real champagne?" Rachel asks, intrigued.

I shake my head. "It's not actually liquor. This

chocolate has popping candy in it that makes it feel like champagne bubbles in your mouth."

"Oh, chocolate is magic," Juliet says, her big green eyes widening.

Rachel smiles warmly at her sister. "Never change, my hopeless romantic," she says, then pops the square into her mouth and moans.

Fable follows suit and groans carnally.

Juliet's next and she gasps for a good, long time.

I beam.

"And we have a winner," Kenji declares, then turns to me, his brown eyes glittering. "I told you those would be perfect with the cocktails. Mister Cocktail will make champagne-themed drinks that night," he explains since he's been helping with planning.

"Mister Cocktail," Fable snickers.

I roll my eyes. "Just eat the next one," I urge, pointing to the tray with the chocolate-covered cherries. "They're made with dark chocolate and a cherry filling I canned this summer from fresh farmers market cherries."

Fable flaps a hand in front of her face. "My mouth is watering."

She grabs one, and Rachel and Juliet do the same. Rachel finishes first, with glossy eyes, saying, "I really hope Carter gets home early from practice because this chocolate is turning me on."

"Yes!" My grin spreads to my whole body as I high-five Kenji.

"That's what we want," he says. "Also, I hope your man gets home early too."

"Thanks. Oh!" Rachel bounces in her chair with obvious excitement, fiddling with her heart necklace. "Did you know Carter is friends with Hot Daddy?"

I tilt my head toward Rachel, curious. "Who's Hot Daddy?"

Juliet rolls her eyes. "Elodie, hot daddy is obviously one of your fiancé's many nicknames."

Kenji goes thoughtful. "I do love a daddy. But can he be Inked Daddy?"

"Excellent nickname," Fable says approvingly to the man next to me. "We're keeping you in our crew."

He clasps his hands together in appreciation. "Thank you." Then to Rachel, he says, "Now, dish."

I try not to be too curious. But I am on the edge of my seat as my bestie dives into the gossip pool. "Apparently they're friends. Inked Daddy and Carter. And Monroe too," Rachel adds, nodding to Juliet.

Juliet narrows her brow. "*Monroe*," she grumbles since her podcast co-host on *Heartbreakers and Matchmakers* drives her crazy. The two of them are at each other's throats a lot on the show with their whole frenemies vibe. Which is, admittedly, kind of hot.

"We'll get to that *Monroe* soon enough. Keep going," Kenji says, waving a hand at Rachel, eating up her story.

"And apparently you made quite the impression on Inked Daddy," Rachel says to me, having too much fun doling out these details.

My pulse speeds up. Sure, I knew this because, well, I've experienced it. But hearing about his affection from someone else is next level. "Really?"

"Did you hear that? The way her voice pitched up?" Juliet asks, enjoying my reaction far too much.

"You bet I did," Fable says, then we're all little dogs waiting at Rachel's feet for her to give us more kibble. Rachel looks right at me, a devilish grin on her face. "Evidently he said it was a damn shame that you weren't having another date. He said you were incredible and"— she sketches air quotes—"'she kept me on my toes like no one ever had.'"

It's as if I ate a whole bar of chocolate with popping candy. I'm fizzy inside.

Kenji slaps my shoulder playfully. "You're blushing!"

I lift a hand to my cheek, feeling heat. "No, I'm not."

"Don't deny it," Fable chides.

"Fine, fine. It's not a secret we had an amazing date," I say. *And an amazing sort-of-pretend second date where he nearly got me off with words in a coffee shop.* "But now we're not. And that's fine too." My stomach swoops with a fresh round of nerves. I hope we can pull this off. The pop-up, the plan, everything. "I mean, how hard will it be to resist him?"

It comes out rhetorical, but I mean it. We've sort of been good at resisting so far. Cheek kisses and dirty words surely count as resistance.

Rachel gives a sympathetic hum. "It'll be harder than you think because you'll have to make lovey eyes at him and touch his arm and hold hands and act like you're in love as you work with him."

Can confirm that's hard.

Juliet nods seriously. "I bet all that fake stuff makes you want the real stuff."

I sit up straighter. Steel myself. "I will not let myself be tempted by him, especially since I bet that man has got a major magic dick."

Juliet scoffs. "I don't believe in magic dick."

"I do and I'd like to go to that church every single day," Fable says, sounding a little like she's already in the choir at that house of worship.

Rachel tuts. "There are a lot of people who believe in that but let me tell you, there's no such thing."

Kenji tosses a napkin at her. "Shut up. We all know you're getting magic dick every night. You're not allowed to talk to those of us who aren't getting it."

"Well, if you ever talked to that guy who helps out at Samira's shop you might have a better chance."

He lifts a stop-sign hand. "He's too cute. I just can't."

"You should though. You've had a crush on her employee forever," I add.

"Don't remind me. He came in here the other day with his cute blond hair, and his cute white teeth, and his cute freckles, and I was like...*hiiiii, help has I can you?*"

"So you're definitely not getting magic dick," Fable says dryly.

"I cock-block myself," Kenji says.

Fable points to Rachel. "Then you need to hold your peace if you're getting magic dicked down every night."

Happily—like a woman getting it good—Rachel mimes zipping her lips, but Juliet jumps to her defense. "Look, my sister's right. A man can't just have one. He needs to know what to do with it."

I wave my hand. "Semantics."

"You don't have sex with semantics," Fable warns.

Rachel unzips her lips then points at me. "Well, she's not having sex with semantics or with Gage."

Kenji wraps an arm around me. "And she won't. Because we can't have hot mama getting distracted by daddy's magic dick. Mama needs to make this store soar," he says, finishing the last word like he's singing in a musical, but I hear the desperation we both feel in his voice.

Even if Felix is *sooo patriarchal*, he's not wrong. Romance is more likely to go wrong than right. I certainly don't have a track record of successful relationships. I've had my heart broken more than once. I let men in easily. Too easily. Where are those ex-boyfriends now? Gone from my life. But Gage will decidedly be in my life for the next three months, and I don't want to go to the pop-up every weekend to see the guy who hurt me. Which is what would happen if I let him further into my heart. Or into my panties again. Resolved, I add, "Exactly. Here's to my no-fuck fiancé-ship," I say, ready to charge ahead. "I'm adaptable. I'm flexible. It's only three months. It'll be fine. And you know what? Actually, it'll be fun."

"Fun?" Rachel asks, her tone dubious.

"He's been a single dad pretty much his daughter's entire life. So it'll be educational. I can learn from him. I can grow as a parent. It'll be useful."

My friends all snicker at once. "That's quite a spin job," Rachel says. "You went from him having a major magic dick to you learning how to be a good mom."

I dig my heels in. "A girl's gotta try."

Fable grabs another chocolate then holds it up high. "By the way, these chocolates taste like sex, so good luck not thinking about it with him."

Later that day when I head to meet Gage at the pop-up, I do my best not to think about his magic dick.

How hard can it be? I didn't even get to see it.

18

FAKE FIANCÉ BENEFIT

Elodie

Repeat after me.

I will not flirt.

I will not say naughty things.

I won't even think about sex.

A few dozen mental reminders on the walk over and my mind is completely innocent. Yes, Angel Elodie is in the house, turning on the block of The Escape, walking up the steps, crossing the courtyard and smiling.

That neon sign looks so good.

Gage is here, positioning it just so. His shirt rides up, revealing a sliver of his toned, trim abs. My pulse pounds, and I take a moment to savor the view. Sure, I saw him shirtless the night of our date. But that only made me want more.

Now I'm getting a tease again, and the devil is shoving the angel to the back of the line. With his arms stretched up, his ink is in my crosshairs and I can't look away. I am officially a tattoo girl. I want to touch them. Trace them. Kiss them. "What's all the ink for?" I ask as I reach him.

With a casual glance back at me, he flashes a smile, then glances down at his arm as if he's just noticed the artwork climbing from his wrist up his forearm, a lotus in the center. "All sorts of things," he says, a little playful. He didn't get the *do not flirt* memo, or perhaps he's tossed it in the trash can.

After checking the sign's secure, he lowers his arms, then points to the fine black linework of the lotus on his right forearm. "This one is for—"

"Change!"

The bright, soprano voice comes out of nowhere. I whip my head in the direction of a girl with twin brown braids and bright green eyes heading toward us. "Like when bad things happen and it reminds you that you can be stronger," the girl adds coming from the direction of the lobby and probably the restrooms.

I'm instantly charmed. "I love that. I believe that. Do you...Eliza?" I ask, since she's got to be Gage's daughter.

"Yes. I'm Eliza. And I believe it because the other week, I wanted another chocolate bar, but my dad didn't give me one, so that was a bad thing. But my uncles Zane and Maddox got me an ice cream sundae with that chocolate freeze-y hard shell instead."

I laugh at the lotus of an eleven-year-old's life, and at the analogy that doesn't quite add up. "Confession: I love chocolate freeze-y hard shells."

"Me too," Gage says, then runs a hand down her hair. "Eliza, this is Elodie, my business partner."

"Your fiancée," she corrects, nudging him with an elbow, not surreptitiously at all.

With a grateful smile, he says, "Yes. My fiancée. And Elodie, this is Eliza, my chocolate-loving daughter."

"Nice to meet you," I say, sticking out a hand.

Eliza takes it, giving me a firm handshake. "I looked you up before your date. And I thought you were super fancy, and my dad is not. But that's okay. Not everyone has to be fancy."

"That is very, very true," I say.

"I'm here helping today," she says, then stage whispers, "Don't let him trick you into thinking he hung the sign. I did."

I turn toward the pink words in neon. They're right next to the door, a bright, bold, romantic invitation. "You did a great job."

"It arrived early," Gage explained. "I wasn't expecting it till tomorrow. But Loretta called as I was picking up Eliza, so we came over here together."

"I didn't come over for the sign," Eliza corrects. "I came for the chocolate since I can't be here on opening night."

I nod sadly. "That's true. You'd have to be twenty-one."

She sighs, the aggrieved sound of a child's disappointment. "Yeah. But maybe you can open one for kids?"

"Do it," a familiar voice calls from behind me. I spin around at the sound of Amanda. I didn't know she was coming here. She's with her friend Ally, and they're giving serious twin vibes, with both of them in cropped tops and hoodies sloping off their shoulders, Amanda's revealing pale skin, Ally's showing olive skin.

"What are you doing here?" I ask curiously.

"Way to say hi, Els," Amanda says, her tone dry, as it often is.

"I wasn't expecting you and…hi."

"We were walking home from school and we wanted to check it out. Then get a boba. Is that cool?"

"Of course it's cool," I say, then smile at Ally. "Good to see you."

"How's everything going, Elodie?" she asks.

Before I can answer, Eliza pipes up with, "I love boba! Can I get a boba? Since there's no chocolate at the shop."

"Boba on me," a new voice chimes in—a warm, friendly tone, accompanied by the confident sound of fancy men's shoes clicking on stone.

Hello, whiplash. Gage and I swivel in unison to see Felix striding across the courtyard from the hotel. "This must be the happy family," he says, then beams at the girls.

Oh, hell.

We never trained for this. We never planned a happy family moment. Ally peers around in her glasses. She looks thoroughly confused. But then Amanda drops an arm around Eliza's shoulders and squeezes hard. "We're totally going to be sisters," she says to the younger girl.

Gage's lips curve up in an appreciative grin for Amanda's improv skills.

Not to be outdone, his daughter adds, "I've always wanted a sister."

"Way more than a brother," Amanda says.

Ally looks so lost. "Amanda?"

"You have a sister too," Amanda says to her friend with a big, bright, go-along-with-it smile.

"Yeah, I do. I just didn't reali—"

"And Eliza is basically going to be my stepsister," Amanda butts back in before Ally can say *she didn't realize*. "Since they're getting married." Amanda points to Gage, then me. "Hey, Els, when's the wedding again? Did you say you were doing it on New Year's Eve?"

The little stinker. I grit my teeth then adopt a false grin. "Oh, that was just one of the dates we were talking about," I say, waving a hand airily.

"There was Valentine's Day too, right?" Amanda continues, all deadpan and having way too much fun. "And the first day of spring."

Gage clears his throat. "But we also talked about how very much we like summer. Next summer, right? A fantastic, outdoor, summer wedding in…Wine Country."

Far, far away.

"Or here," Felix says, a matchmaker gleam in his eyes as he gestures to the picturesque courtyard we're standing in with the fountain and its gurgling water, sounding like chimes. And actually…this would be a perfect spot to get hitched.

Not that we will.

"And," he adds, "my daughter Camilla is a wedding photographer. Well, she's transitioning from corporate headshots to weddings. She's looking for a few weddings to do for free. To get the experience."

Oh, god. My stomach drops as it's clear where he's going.

Felix shifts his attention briefly to Gage. "I know your grandmother took those engagement photos, but if you're looking for some more formal couple shots— perhaps for the store, or some of the articles we have planned—she could take those. I'm sure she'd be happy to do your wedding as well. Oh, and I have a florist right here on-site you can use for the big day. Happy to gift those to you too."

Kill me now. Who thought it was a good idea to come here today? Not me.

"Oh, yes, that'd be amazing," Eliza says in a sober voice, answering for us. "Can you give us the name? Amanda and I would love to check them out."

They're in cahoots already? I stifle a groan.

"We truly would," Amanda adds.

"And I've been studying flower arranging, so I'll help them," Ally adds, her tone deadly serious now that she's figured out the ruse.

It's like Harriet the Spy and the Spy and the Spy. I could whistle in admiration if I didn't also want to whisper to these troublemakers *whose side are you on*?

But my fake fiancé has other issues on his mind. "Articles as in media coverage?" Gage asks Felix.

"Yes. I have Silver Zanetti coming to the opening, among others."

"The Dessert Devotee?" I ask, my voice pitching up at the mention of the wildly popular dessert influencer.

She can *make* a shop. Double, triple, quadruple its business.

Gage shoots me a curious look. "Who's that?"

"She reviews chocolates," I rattle off at Mach speed. "She does these videos where she takes bites of chocolate and rates them, and they're so popular."

"For eating chocolate?"

Well, she does it really sensually, like she's having a foodgasm, but I don't say that in front of the kids. I just nod to Gage. "Yes."

"That's great," he says to Felix.

"And many others are coming too. Lots of food press and lifestyle media. And the merch team will have their branded items on sale during the day in about a week, so be on the lookout for that, but sharing the shop should be easy. They don't need more than shelf space during the day."

"Piece of cake," I say, like I'd deny him a thing.

Then Felix turns to the girls. "Kiss My Tulips is the name of the flower shop if you do decide to check it out."

"We most definitely will," Amanda says.

"Right after we get our boba," Ally adds.

"And we should head over there now," Eliza finishes.

Yes, leave, right away!

They wave, then spin around.

"If you go to Farm To Straw, tell them to put it on my tab. Felix Aguilar," Felix calls out as they trot down the steps.

"Thanks, Felix," Amanda says, and the girls disappear.

Felix is enchanted by the troublemaking trio, shaking his head in delight as they go. "They're the best of friends," he says to us.

Gage laughs. "No, they just—"

"They just are," I correct, ready to stomp on his foot. "Isn't it precious?"

Realizing his mistake, he quickly adds, "So precious. Just love it. Love it big time. One hundred percent."

"You have a lovely family," Felix says warmly. The dude is such a grandpa. His warm eyes travel to my hand. "Oh! What a beautiful ring. Is that—"

I've got this. "Yes! It's vintage. Gage's grandmother's ring. We were having it sized, so I was wearing a silly little cocktail ring because I didn't want to go without."

"It's a lovely family heirloom," he adds, and whew— I'm glad I had that lie ready, though I still feel oily. Maybe oily is just my new normal. "And I personally think a New Year's Eve wedding would be great. Stop by the flower shop anytime. We can handle everything."

On that note, he leaves, returning to the interior of the hotel. Once he's out of earshot, I slump against my fake fiancé. "That was…"

"A close call?" Gage finishes, wrapping his strong, capable arms around me.

"Yes, and are our kids actresses or what? They'll be thanking the Academy before we know it," I say, then rest my cheek against his shoulder. "I feel oily again."

He sighs, full of understanding, but then his voice is strong, firm as he says, "Don't, baby. Just don't."

It's said with warmth and reassurance. Protective-ness too, and I try to let those guilty feelings ebb, especially since he called me *baby* instead of cupcake. He called me that, too, the first night we were together. It feels different than cupcake, and I'm not sure why.

All I know right now is that I don't want to leave his arms.

He doesn't let me go either. He's quiet for a beat, stroking my hair gently. "Is this a fake fiancé benefit?" he whispers.

"A hug when you need it?"

"Yes."

I smile against his solid frame. "Seems it is."

A warm sigh. A comfortable silence. Then sweet words. "Good. I like this benefit."

Me too.

19

A BAD IDEA

Elodie

A few hours later, the shop is spick-and-span, and Eliza and Amanda are besties. The older girls took Eliza to a pottery-making studio and are making bowls with cats on them or cat bowls. Or bowls shaped like cats. It's not entirely clear, but they're busy for a little longer with all things feline.

The blinds are down, so Gage and I were free to clean without being caged animals on display. As we survey the little space with the minimalist counter, and the simple tables, and the sound system, ready to play our curated playlists, we're almost ready for Friday.

"I have a good feeling," I declare.

"Yeah, me too," Gage replies as we stop behind the counter together.

I turn to meet his gaze, my eyes finally returning to his ink. "The lotus is for change?"

"Yes," he says, and I expect him to say he got it after his wife died, but he adds, "I got it after I went to therapy."

Is it weird that my heart's skittering that he prioritized his mental health? Maybe. If so, I'll take weird, thank you very much. "I've been pretty much in and out of therapy since college. I have a lot of parent issues," I say with a shrug, then nod to the ink again, recentering the conversation on him. "I love the lotus. Does it help?"

"I think so." He studies the ink again. Does it reconnect him with his past? Or his progress? "I got it after the doctor told me I wasn't going to play baseball again."

That surprises me too. I'd been so sure it was for Eliza's mom.

"Well, not immediately. Once I heard my elbow was toast, I drowned my sorrows for a couple months, turned into a shitty dad, then my grandma and mom told me to get my ass to therapy. I did. And worked on how much I was hurting." He taps the flower authoritatively, like he's in charge of his past, not the other way around. "I got this a few months later. It was sort of like taking back myself, you know?"

"I'm glad it worked. The tattoo and the therapy."

"I still go from time to time. As Grams and Eliza tell me, it's the in thing these days."

"And you started before it was in. That was ten years ago, right?"

"It was." He leans against the counter, his back to the door, rubbing a hand over his scruff. For a few seconds, I figure he's said all he wants to say. That he's opened the door a sliver and is ready to close it.

"I wasn't in a good place, Elodie," he says, his tone stripped bare. "I was struggling with depression. It was after Hailey died too."

My chest aches for him. "Was her passing part of it? The depression?"

He doesn't answer right away, then finally gives a resigned, "yes." He looks to the white blinds covering the glass, like the answer to what to say can be found there. Then, he turns back to me. "That was part of it, but we were struggling. Our marriage was...well. It wasn't perfect."

That has to have been so tough for him to reconcile with her death. I wait for him to say more.

"It started out imperfect," he adds, maybe a little embarrassed as he scratches his jaw. "It was a surprise. The pregnancy. But a good surprise, of course."

"Of course," I second.

"And so I married her. In city hall, not the Conservatory of Flowers or Shakespeare Garden, or what have you," he says, almost apologetic.

"Oh." I pause. "Was that hard for you, when I was rattling off all those places?"

"No," he says, at first, then stops himself, reconsiders. "Not hard. Just a reminder, that's all. But I have no regrets. Not a single one."

I can tell he doesn't want me to compliment him for being an upstanding guy and marrying the woman he knocked up so I just give him a warm smile and nod, so he knows I'm listening.

"Anyway, she died unexpectedly. I lost the career of

my dreams and the mother of my child at the same time."

"That's so hard, Gage," I say, reaching out to run a hand down his strong arm, my loaned vintage ring gliding over his permanent art.

"It was. But hey, now I'm tattooed. This right here?" he says, pointing to a bird on his flesh. "It's for new dreams."

I run my finger along the finely drawn wings. The bird's not macho like an eagle. It's not feminine like a dove. It's simple and a statement—a future, a dream, a new horizon. A slight tremble seems to move through him as I trace it. I should stop. But I don't. I travel along the bird up to the crook of his elbow, then down as it flies into the moon and the stars, the lotus, and the sky. The guideposts on his body. "They're beautiful," I say.

His eyes hold mine, and then he lifts a hand, reaching for my face before he drops his palm with regret in his green eyes. For touching me? Or not touching me? I don't know.

Gage clears his throat. Checks his watch. "We should get the girls soon. We probably need to leave in ten minutes."

I try to ignore the disappointment inside me as I hunt around for the broom I was using. He finds the rags and the spray cleaner for the counters. Then we make our way to the little supply closet down a nook at the back of the store.

I open it and set the broom down. He wedges past me and puts down his items. Then I reach for my purse on a shelf, since I left it here earlier, but Gage steps in, moving faster and snagging it for me.

As he hands it over, the bag buzzes. He cocks his head. "Is your purse purring?"

I should be embarrassed. But instead, I roll my eyes —*at me*. "That's just my Plus One."

He jerks his head. His tone is pure intrigue as he asks, "Plus One?"

"It's the name for this tiny little pocket *friend*," I say, dipping my hand into my bag to find the tiny rose-gold vibe and silence it.

But his hand covers mine. In a heartbeat, he's setting the purse back down then cupping my cheek, holding my face and studying me, like he's weighing choices and consequences. Risks and rewards. The great and terrible appeal of a romance that we won't let be.

We're pretending to be in love while fighting to stay apart.

Yes, it's hard.

But this? Tilting my chin. Parting my lips. Saying yes with my eyes. This is easy. Welcoming his kiss.

He takes my invite and raises it, crushing my lips to his. We kiss more, hungry and urgent. A kiss that's a countdown. A kiss that knows it's running on borrowed time. He bites my lower lip, tugs on it, groaning as he seals his mouth to mine.

He kisses me like a man in charge. Like he has zero regrets. Because this is what's been keeping him up at night—the need to touch me again.

Same here. I feel it too. And I feel swept away by the

insistence of his lips on mine as he grips my shoulders, holds me like he won't let go, marks my mouth.

With a carnal groan, he breaks the kiss, his eyes glinting with desire. "This is a bad idea." But his tone says it's the only idea.

"It is."

"We said we'd be hands off."

I glance at his strong hands, gripping me tightly. "That's true."

He hauls in a breath. Blows it out. Stares at me, then says, "But what if I'm not *really* touching you?"

"You were *really* kissing me," I point out since, well, you can't fuck semantics.

He runs a finger over my lower lip possessively. "I was. It's important that our affection seems real," he says, and there's a wink in his voice.

"Are you going to kiss me like that in front of our customers?"

"No. But no one will doubt I do."

I flash back to Sebastian's eyes on me the other day. To the jealousy I saw flame in them. "No one does."

"But there's a loophole in your purse, baby. I think we should use it," he says, then nuzzles my neck, kissing me savagely, inhaling me, traveling to my earlobe. "Let me."

It's utter desperation in his tone.

And between my thighs.

Who am I to argue? I'm a little helpless to this man today. But then, it's not only today. It's been this way the last few weeks. "Do it now," I urge.

In no time, I'm fishing around in my purse, swiping

past makeup and tampons, sunglasses and energy bars, hair clips and hand sanitizer, then finding the little faux lipstick tube.

He's all determination, the man in the movie tasked with breaking into the vault in less than five minutes. With a feral sort of focus, he tugs up my skirt, turns on the vibe to its lowest setting, then rubs it on the outside of my panties.

"I hate that you were so wet, so turned on, so needy," he says, stroking me with the toy.

I suck in a breath. My thighs tighten. "I was."

"Makes me so fucking sad when you're so wet and I'm not fixing that problem for you." His voice is gritty, needy too.

The toy buzzes, a low hum as he coasts it across my soaked panties, teasing me from the outside.

I'm so aroused already that I barely have any flirt left in me. I just lean my head back against the shelves. "Please," I pant out.

His smile is too pleased. His hand is too skilled. "Please what, baby?"

"Please make me come," I whimper.

"I'm working on it," he says, his grin deepening. This man loves to play. He's sliding the toy slowly in a maddening circle over the outline of my aching clit.

I moan in agony. "Work harder," I demand.

A sensual laugh. Another tantalizing circle. A lingering glide.

I grab his shirt. "Gage!"

He glances down at me, tsking. "I thought we said no touching?"

"Fuck that loophole. You kissed me senseless. That was touching," I say.

He dips his face to my neck again. "You're fucking sexy when you're horny, Elodie. You know that? You're so fucking sexy when you need to get off," he says, stroking me a little faster now, then turning up the vibration a level.

I gasp. Then shudder. "Yes. Please. God."

"Mmm. That's what I want to hear," he says. Then he pulls back from my neck, tugs down my panties, and slides his hand inside. His fingers don't touch me. He's really sticking to his rules as he gives me the relief I seek.

He presses the buzzing vibrator to my aching bundle of nerves.

I grip his shirt harder, my legs like jelly, my stomach flipping. I'm moaning, sighing, melting into him.

Soon, it's only the pulse of pleasure, the heat of my skin, the gravel of his words—words like *yes, so fucking sexy, so hot, love it when you lose control.*

Then I'm squeezing my eyes, my whole body shaking as pleasure blooms exquisitely, then shatters. I cry out. Maybe a yes, maybe his name, I don't even know. It's all just so, so good.

I'm floating on this orgasm high for a minute, or two, maybe more. Till finally, I come down.

He's watching me, looking more pleased than any man has ever looked. But he also looks...hungry.

As he turns off the vibrator, I dart out a hand, cup the hard ridge of his cock over his jeans.

"Fuuuuck," he mutters, slamming his free hand over mine, pressing it roughly against his straining erection.

"Let me," I say plaintively, using his words against him.

He groans apologetically. A rumble that seems to come from deep within his dirty soul. Setting his hand over mine, he pushes, grips, strokes. Then, like it pains him, removes my hand and his. "We should go."

I shake my head, frustrated but getting it. "It's Elodie two, Gage zero though."

He presses his forehead to mine. "I'd argue it's Gage two, Elodie zero."

I pull back. "Math isn't that hard."

"I like making you come. That's what gets me off. That's what I think about at night. That's what I picture in the shower. Making you lose control."

And I want to answer that with a kiss so badly—even though we really shouldn't.

Quickly, we straighten up, pop into the restroom, then leave to head to the art studio. As we walk, his phone buzzes. He glances down, then clicks on an email with uncommon speed. His lips twitch while reading it, as if he likes the contents.

When he closes the email, he says, "Celeste will come to our opening night."

"The landlord? For the place you want in the Marina?"

"Yup."

I smile. "Told you so. I had a good feeling."

"Well, nothing has happened yet," he says, hedging against happiness.

"But it will."

"Don't count your chickens and all."

I roll my eyes. "I know. I won't. I'm just saying."

He stops at the corner, eyes intense, maybe even a little hard. "I shouldn't have done that back there."

I blink, unsure what he means at first. Then, I'm far too sure. Already? He's already regretting getting me off? It was his fucking idea.

I straighten my spine. Raise my chin. "It wasn't you. It was the Plus One."

His jaw ticks. He pauses, maybe absorbing the punch. "Right. Yup. That's what I meant."

"Good."

"Yeah. Good," he repeats, hollow.

We stop at the crosswalk, and I turn to him. My tone isn't icy. It's easy-breezy as I say, "It was just a mistake. It won't happen again."

He nods crisply. "I know. It won't."

"So there's nothing to worry about."

"Definitely. It's all fine."

"Everything is totally fine," I say, even though I feel dirty

That night there's no text from him. I don't text him either.

Sex complicates everything.

Gage

The next night at Sticks and Stones I mess up a drink order—switching an olive for a lemon twist in a martini —because I'm elsewhere. I'm in my head, wondering if I'm supposed to apologize to Elodie.

What would I even say? I mull that over as I remake the drink, then set it down for the customer, who then orders a sandwich and an app of warm olives and hummus.

"Coming right up," I say, like my helpful attitude can erase the blunder, then I turn to the kitchen to place it when I bump into Zoe. The salad she's carrying wobbles precariously on the edge of her tray then tumbles onto the floor.

I curse myself privately as I try to catch the bowl but I'm too late—the salad is the collateral damage...of me.

"Oh shoot," Zoe mutters.

"Sorry. My bad," I say.

"No, it's fine. I got it."

"I'll clean it," I say, insisting.

"It's okay. Let me just have the kitchen redo it and I'll clean it."

"I really will get it. I'm just..." I swallow the words *I'm distracted*. Don't need my employees knowing I'm unreliable right now.

As I hustle to the back of the house to grab a rag and straighten up, this is my reminder. This is why I don't want to get close again. Because it leads to messes, to mistakes, to a lack of focus.

I face the same problem the next day, too, when I go to a fall softball practice with Eliza's team and I'm hardly present. I'm the damn coach yet I'm lost in my head. Am I missing something with drills? With this scrimmage? With the batting practice? I feel like my brain is breaking. It's split evenly between how to field a hard grounder and whether I messed up when I went cold the other day.

But I'm still pissed at myself for giving in to desire in the supply room. It's so easy to give in with Elodie. She's temptation in a clever, bright, loyal, feisty, vulnerable, sexy package of blonde hair, red lipstick, and polka dots.

When I'm home that night with Eliza, I try to reset. She's telling me about what she learned in history class as we unmold the soap we made two days ago—the day I confessed so much of my past to Elodie. This loaf is finally cool and dry enough to slice. Eliza sets it on a sheet of wax paper, then wields a butter knife that's sharp enough. "This is my favorite part."

"It's very satisfying," I say.

"Why is it so fun?" she asks, grinning.

"Because it's the reward. For all the hard work."

"Like chocolate is a reward too," she says, then digs the knife in, the tip of her tongue sticking out as she concentrates.

And I try to concentrate too. I try not to think about chocolate, or Elodie, or the way she listens when I talk, and how she seems to want to know me.

Eliza finishes the first bar, then lifts it high. "Reward!"

"It sure is," I say, staying focused, staying present.

She cocks her head, considering it, then her green eyes sparkle. "What if we gave one to Elodie? Wait. No. They won't be ready. Can we give her one of the grapefruit ones I made a couple weeks ago? You can give it to her as a gift on opening night?"

So much for my efforts to stop thinking about her. "How about you hold on to it for the next time you see her? It's really a gift from you."

"That's a good idea."

"She'll like it," I say, and I feel confident about that.

But I sure as shit don't feel confident about whether Elodie still likes me or not. Or if she even should.

* * *

Alone in bed a little later, I'm still replaying our last encounter on the street. Still trying to figure out if I handled it badly when I got Celeste's email, an opportunity and a Post-it saying *get your focus on*.

I chew on all these questions in the dark when my phone pings with a message from my brother.

Zane: WTF?

I furrow my brow. What is he talking about?

Gage: WTF what?

Zane: I go to London and you got your ass engaged? Am I even invited to the wedding?

Shit. I didn't even tell my brother. I suck. Immediately, I reply and give him the details, and the second I'm done, my phone rings. I answer it right away. "What time is it in London?"

"Fuck all late. It's three-thirty in the morning. But we were at a club and now we're heading back to our flat, and I've seen the pictures online so I'm calling you. So you're fake married?"

I shake my head, scoffing. "No way, man. Just fake engaged."

He snorts. "Doesn't sound that different."

"Look, we're only doing it to impress the guy."

"I don't get how that impresses someone?"

I explain the situation with Felix and the last couple he leased to who broke the agreement, then how Celeste had been playing hardball with her marketing requests. "And the guy who's leasing us this shop is obsessed with marketing. He's a wizard, Zane," I say, excited just thinking about the lineup for tomorrow night's opening. Felix knows how to bring it. "I think this could make the difference in me getting the second location."

Zane knows why I've been chasing expansion for a long time. Hell, he knows better than anyone. When Eliza was younger, I had nothing saved up. No security. I lived paycheck to paycheck. When I was a bar manager in Sacramento five years ago, my boss was a ballbuster, reaming me out every night for every little thing. Nothing made me want to work for myself more than working for someone else.

Zane helped me out big time when he set aside money for Eliza's college fund, and I'll forever be grateful for his generosity. But I won't rely on my little brother for handouts. I'm Eliza's dad, and it's my responsibility to take care of her. There are no guarantees with just one bar. A second though? Maybe even a third one down the road? That's when I won't always be sleeping with one eye open. Always looking behind me. Always wondering when the shoe is going to drop.

I tell Zane about the opening night and some of the opportunities that Felix has lined up. And as I talk, I feel a little more settled. It was right to cool things off with Elodie. It would be a mistake to keep bending the rules and looking for loopholes. "So we cooled it, but we're pretending to be together," I finish.

He's quiet for several long seconds.

"Huh."

"What's that huh for?"

"But you do like her?" It's a legit question.

I answer him from the heart. "I do. But it doesn't really matter. I don't have a good track record with romance. When I go all in, everything falls apart. And you know it."

I put my heart on the line with Kylie and got two hearts broken in return. And well, then there's Hailey. Without her I would never have the love of my life in Eliza.

But the dirty little secret of my young marriage to Hailey—we were both twenty-one when I got her pregnant, and then married a week after we found out in a shotgun wedding—was that less than two years after the city hall *I do*, we were in the process of splitting up. When she died of a brain aneurysm, no one knew we were falling apart. Her sister didn't know. Her parents didn't know. My family didn't know. Hell, I didn't even tell Zane. Only my shrink.

Never her family.

They don't know she was struggling as a new mom. They don't know her postpartum blues hit her hard and for months. They don't know she was ready to give me primary custody and that she needed a break. They don't know any of that because none of that matters now that she's dead.

I just don't see how romance—big romance that you throw your heart into—can lead to anything that lasts.

21

A SWEET TOOTH

Gage

On Friday afternoon, there's barely a second to ask if everything's okay when Elodie and Amanda arrive at my place. My grandma offered to make chocolate chip cookies with them, then take them to the movies later since we'll be busy at Special Edition all night.

Eliza's waiting at the door, both for Amanda and to give Elodie the gift. The second Amanda's inside, pressing a contraband bar of chocolate into Eliza's pocket—which I'm pretty sure they're going to use in Grandma's cookies, along with the secret ingredient of coconut—Eliza hands Elodie a gift bag. "Good luck tonight. This is for you."

Elodie peeks inside, then smiles and sniffs. "Grapefruit soap. I love it. And way better than a chocolate soap someone once gave me."

Eliza's nose crinkles. "Eww. Chocolate is for eating, not cleaning."

"Exactly. But grapefruit? That's for eating *and* cleaning," Elodie adds, and she sounds like Mary Poppins, magical and bright, and I shouldn't love that. Really, I shouldn't. She's not a delightful, fictional nanny. She's a very real woman with very real needs—one who I am really in business with now.

And I can't get in the way of her paying her bills and loans and putting Amanda through school.

Before we take off, Elodie tugs my grandma aside at the door. "Amanda's a vegetarian. She doesn't eat any meat at all. But she's obsessed with cheese."

"Well, so am I," Grams says. "We'll get along fine."

We leave my house, heading for her car where she sets the soap bar in the back seat. As she drives, she's peppy along the way, chatting about a slight increase in traffic at Elodie's Chocolates today with some of the social buzz about the pop-up. She mentions that the woman who owns the perfume shop next door said her business has gone up too, and isn't that great?

But Elodie's almost *too* animated. Too Mary Poppins.

When there's a break in her chatter, I say, "Hey."

"Yes?"

"Are we good?"

She laughs, answering rhetorically with, "Why would we not be good? Now, I've got the playlists ready, and I need to do some chocolate prep, and I wrote out a list of—"

"Elodie, are you pissed at me?"

She slows at a light on Van Ness, tossing me a blank

glance. "No. I don't even know why you think I would be."

"Because—"

But I stop myself. I don't want to be presumptuous. I don't want to be that guy who acts like he expects a woman to be out of her mind when he says we can't do this. When we both said we can't do this.

"Because that's great," I backtrack, then talk business the rest of the way.

Several hours later, I'm amped up from the nonstop lines, the chatter, and the vibe of a packed house. A tiny house, sure. But a packed one nonetheless, with crowds spilling into the courtyard, including Loretta who brought a pack of women friends who all left big tips.

It's just after nine, and I'm mixing a Blushing Mimosa—orange juice, pineapple juice, grenadine, and champagne—and Elodie is plating some of the choco-late-covered cherries along with the raspberry chocolates.

"We're almost out of the popping raspberries," she whispers out of the side of her mouth, concern in her tone. "I don't want to have to close early. We said we'd be open till ten."

"Good problem to have," I say as I fill a flute with the juice mixture, then top it with champagne.

"That's not what I'm saying," she whispers, her brow knitting.

"But the lines, Elodie. Look at the lines," I whisper,

nodding toward the crowd snaking outside the shop. "And they're all posting. They are doing the work for us."

"And if we run out, they'll post that we ran out," she counters, and there's real worry in her voice.

I should reassure her. I'm supposed to be her fiancé. "I've got extra champagne in the supply closet. We'll just serve drinks then." There. That ought to do the trick.

"You have extra?"

"Brought it earlier. I'm a softball coach, remember?"

"Well, I hope you don't bring champagne for the girls."

"Gatorade. But point being…I've got this."

I take the mimosas to a table in the corner, thanking them, then returning to the counter. Next up is Celeste. We have enough for her, and that's what matters. "Good evening, Celeste. How are you?"

She's like the cold lawyer on a TV show, that's how she is. She peers around, and I bet her robot eyes are recording everything. Her hair is slicked back in a bun as usual. She's in a pantsuit as usual, this time in navy. And her tone is no nonsense, like it is every damn time as she asks tonelessly, "What do you recommend?"

"An Aperol Spritz or a Blushing Mimosa have been popular all night," I say.

"Everyone serves Aperol Spritzes," she says with a dismissive flick of her fingers, like I've committed the bartender equivalent of offering cupcakes in a cake jar world.

Think fast.

"I could make you a pineapple mimosa," I suggest,

but I'm officially flustered. I don't know how to please this woman. "The other cocktail we're offering is a blackberry mule with winter melon." That usually wins over the fancier guests.

Her nose twitches. What the hell?

I gulp, glancing *help me* at Elodie, but she's busy with other customers, smiling and holding a cute little pink tray with decadent dark chocolate bonbons and raspberry chocolate squares for a cooing pack of girls in matching black corsets, who are snapping her pic.

"Your bandana," one says.

"Your necklace," the next one adds.

"Your lipstick," the final one puts in.

"Better With Pockets. Bling and Baubles. Mia and Lola," she says, and what language is she speaking?

Celeste arches a brow their way, her machine brain recording the interaction and filing it under *Elodie is better than this guy*. "Or would you rather have some chocolate?" I ask her, flailing around some more. Elodie would know what to say. She's so good on her feet. "Some people don't like champagne cocktails and that's okay."

Have I been a bartender for years or am I a schoolboy, unsure what to say to a stern teacher?

Celeste studies the counter, the chocolates, and the cocktail ingredients when the corset crew leaves, and Elodie slides over to my side. "We could also pour you a glass of champagne or some sparkling water."

She's an angel. She must have heard the whole interaction.

Celeste doesn't smile. But her ruler lips move for the

first time. "A glass of sparkling would be fine. No chocolate though. I hate sugar," she says with a shudder.

"I understand completely," Elodie says with warmth in her voice. "I hate tomatoes."

Celeste's lips twitch.

I'd like to add *I hate things* but I don't think it'd garner the same reaction so I keep my mouth shut as Elodie finds the bottle of sparkling water in the tiny fridge.

Why the hell didn't I think of that? We do have it for those who don't drink. Elodie hands it to me, and I pour it in a pretty flute, then give it to Celeste, who thanks me, then lifts her phone to tap the card reader.

I shake my head. "No charge."

"I insist," she says and the subtext is clear—she doesn't want a tab *with me.*

Once she pays, she takes a sip of the water, sets down the flute at the end of the counter, and leaves, departing on her chariot of efficiency.

I breathe again, but I don't feel settled. I have no idea what to think of that interaction. If it means anything at all. But when I look down at the counter, we're nearly out of chocolate.

Shit.

Elodie was right. I was too focused on myself to think about her running out. I brought extra for me, but she went through the chocolates faster than expected. I hold up a finger to the next customer, then turn to Elodie, ready to fix this, stat, and I know just how to do it. "Tell Kenji to meet me outside the shop with extras… bonbons or whatever he has," I say, since her main shop just closed a few minutes ago, and he won't have left yet. "I'll run down there and get some chocolate."

"You don't mind?" She sounds so relieved. She's got flats on, but I bet she doesn't want to run in them.

I nod subtly to the customers. "You're better with people. But can you make a Blushing Mimosa?"

"Of course I can."

I take off my apron and run the few blocks to her shop, these retired athlete legs still working. I meet Kenji outside.

"Here you go, Inked Daddy," he says, but I have no time to wonder what that name's all about as I say thanks then haul ass back to the shop.

I do it in minutes flat with a stash of chocolates.

I slide behind the counter in the nick of time, tying on the apron and helping handle the rest of the customers.

Including a young woman who's got her phone in front of her face the whole time as she orders. Which isn't strange. It's pretty much par for the course. But this woman is all alone, and that stands out to me. She's got to be someone. With tiny black braids twisted up on her head and silver eyeshadow against dark brown skin, she's dressed in black with metal bracelets jangling up and down her wrists.

That's when it hits me. Silver Zanetti. She must be the Dessert Devotee Felix mentioned. She's talking to the phone camera, then she stops, lowers it and smiles at Elodie.

"Hi, bestie," she says.

I blink. Does Elodie know her?

"Hi, Silver. Love your vids."

"Love this shop. And I've been dying for your chocolate. I'm already obsessed with it, and I haven't even tried it."

Okaaaay.

"But no cocktails for me," she says to me, apologetically.

"It's all good," I say.

Elodie moves quickly, then serves the influencer, who takes the tray to a table in the corner, sitting alone and shooting the whole time as she eats.

Elodie fiddles with her ring, and I want to reassure her, but I don't even know what to say to her anymore after the other day, and the car, and tonight.

Except, fuck it. Sometimes, she just needs to know I believe in her. And I do.

I set a hand on her soft arm. "She's going to love it. Your chocolate is amazing. The best in the city," I whisper.

"Thanks," she says softly.

When I look up, I'm staring at the face of Sebastian. His cap is off today, and his hair is thick, dark, and gelled. He gives off a peddling-life-insurance-to-little-old-ladies vibe as he smiles gregariously at the offerings. "Chocolate-covered cherries. You've really outdone yourself, Elodie."

What does that mean? I want to punch him for no reason.

"Thank you. Glad you like it," she says, clearly trying to be friendly, but there's discomfort in her voice.

"Can't say I'm not jelly though," Sebastian adds, like a

jovial uncle trying to appropriate youthful slang but missing the mark.

"There's room for all of us. Everyone has a sweet tooth," she says, trying so damn hard to play nice with her competitor.

I better aim in the same direction. "You've got a fantastic thing going at your shop, man," I say, trying to defuse whatever bomb is ticking in him. "I gave some of your chocolates to the parents on the softball team, and they went crazy for them."

He turns to me, head tilted, hair not moving, smile etched on. "Oh, you're a softball coach as well as being a former pitcher?"

Dude looked *me* up? "Yes. I am," I say, keeping it simple even as my radar beeps loud in warning.

"Gage coaches his daughter's team," Elodie puts in.

Sebastian arches a brow her way now. "Your...step-daughter's team?"

"Soon. She'll be my stepdaughter soon," Elodie adds.

"When's the wedding?"

"Very, very soon," I add, without thinking, because fuck him. "We can't really wait much longer"

It's not at all what I've said to Felix, but I don't care right now.

"I hope I get an invitation," he says.

There's no reason on heaven or earth why we'd invite this guy, but I say, "Of course you will. Now, can I get you a blackberry mule with winter melon? It's our most elite cocktail. For VIP customers."

Guys like him think they deserve the best.

"Perfect," he says.

When he's served, he sits down at a table with a man who looks like him, and they eat, drink, and rub me the wrong way.

But there's no time to linger on him when Felix arrives near the end of the night, clearly pleased as he surveys the shop. "I had a feeling about you two. I see you met Silver," he says, then rattles off the names of other local foodies who were here. "Keep it up for the next few months."

When the doors close a few minutes later, and everyone's gone, I'm spent from the night, the games, the pretend, and all the uncertainty.

I want to clean up and crash.

But I also know I need to thank Elodie for saving my ass with Celeste. When a text lands from my grandma with a photo of two tired girls conked out on a couch, I show it to her, then say, "Let me treat *you* to some rosemary fries."

She looks like she wants to say no. Like maybe she figures no is the safe answer. But instead she says, "Yes. Also, those were the names of the shops where I got my bandana, my necklace, and my lipstick."

It takes a beat for me to realize she noticed earlier that I must have been wondering. It takes only a second more for me to realize she must notice everything.

22

A LITTLE CAVEMAN

Elodie

Sticks and Stones closes at midnight, so the place is still bustling when we grab a booth in the far back, past the pool and Ping-Pong tables. In seconds, a woman with a pixie cut arrives to take our order.

"Rosemary fries and a chicken sandwich with sriracha times two," she says after we place it. "Aren't you two lovebirds the cutest?"

Gage startles for a second. Then he adjusts, adding a mostly genuine smile. *Ohhh.* His employees don't know this is fake, of course, but he's still adjusting to people assuming we're a couple. He drags a hand through his hair, a sign he's a little stressed, but I hope she doesn't know his tells like I do. "Yup. We both just have good taste," he says to her.

"We do," I second, then she heads off. When she's gone, I ask, just to be sure, "She doesn't know?"

"Nope. And I feel bad lying."

"I get that."

"Well, except to Sebastian," he says with a growl.

I still feel like I need to take a shower because of that guy. But I want to deal with the tension between Gage and me first. I can't let it take up so much real estate. I've been noodling on his *we good* comment since this afternoon. I didn't want to get into it then. I do now, especially after the awkward moments between us tonight, the uncertainty in how we spoke to each other.

But before I can even begin, he takes over with, "Elodie, I'm sorry I didn't listen to you earlier."

His tone is laced with regret. But I don't know exactly what he's talking about. "What do you mean?" I ask carefully.

He rakes his hand through his thick hair a second time, messy at this late hour, unkempt and a little wild. A lot sexy. "You were worried you didn't have enough chocolate, and I made it seem like your concerns were nothing. I was only focused on me. And Celeste. And then I didn't even know how to handle her. You saved me with the sparkling water. Thank you. I was in a big hole there. Felt like I was on the mound with the bases loaded."

I can't help it. I smile. "Is this where I'm the catcher again?"

He leans back in the booth, a little chagrined but also owning his sports speak. "You can take the man out of the baseball game, but I guess you can't take the baseball out of the man."

"We helped each other," I say. "I was seriously

grateful for your save with the chocolate race. That was amazing."

"But I should have listened to you sooner," he says, like he's beating himself up over this. "I was obsessed with Celeste and the location. I can get a little single-minded."

He's so self-aware, it's refreshing. "I noticed," I say softly, exonerating him. "And I understand."

The other day when he shut down after he touched me, I was hurt. I felt as if I'd made myself vulnerable because, well, sex is vulnerable. A few days later, with time and reflection, I could see where he was coming from—he's banking on the exposure this shop can bring. Me too. "And look, I foolishly thought opening this pop-up would solve everything."

He looks confused. "You don't think it's helping?"

"I absolutely think it is and it will," I say, assuring him. "Tonight was a great start. But I suppose I thought it being an overnight sensation would mean I could pay off the loan like that." I snap my fingers. I picture my banking app on my phone, the payments I still need to make. I'm getting closer. But I'm not there yet. "It'll take more than one great night though. More than the buzz we got. And Special Edition is not a magic bullet. There will always be more bills, so I understand why you said we can't do this again. We don't want to mess up our partnership."

"I said it at the wrong time though. In the wrong way. I should have…" But when he trails off it's clear he doesn't know how he should have delivered that truth bomb.

I don't either.

He takes a breath, scrubbing a hand over his jaw, then locks those sinful eyes with mine. "Here's the thing. I couldn't get you out of my head when I first met you. It's still that way," he says, reaching for my hand, like he often does. The man is so tactile. Touch is his love language. He's always putting a hand on my arm, or wrapping one around me, or squeezing my palm. "But I'm terrible at making it all work. I don't know how to do this and everything else. That's why I kind of went cold the other day."

Since he's being patently honest, I give him some of the same. "When you said that can't happen again, you were giving the impression like you thought I was *that crazy girl* you had to break up with." I point to my chest. "I'm a grown woman. I do understand why we set lines and rules. Tonight was a classic example of why we need them. There was a lot happening in the store, but if we're all weird and tense with each other we will make mistakes." I pause to drive the point home. "And we can't afford to."

He laughs, but it's devoid of humor. "Are you saying Felix was right? That new couples are trouble?"

I shrug in admission. "Kind of? I mean, look at us. We were sort of…prickly. We almost let it get in the way of business."

"We did. You're right."

Seconds later, Zoe arrives with the food. "Here you go. I should let you know it's last call, but the kitchen said they'll stay open for you, boss."

"They don't need to, but thank you," he says.

When she leaves, he picks up a fry, but before he eats, he meets my gaze once more and asks point blank, "What's up with that guy Sebastian? Why do I get an ex-boyfriend vibe from him?"

My stomach curls. I knew this was coming. It would be hard to avoid the truth. But it's better if Gage knows anyway. "He asked me out once. I turned him down. I said I didn't feel the chemistry. I feel like that bothered him more than he ever let on. And when he was trying to buy my shop, he sent me gifts like chocolate bath bombs."

He puts two and two together. "That was what you meant by your chocolate soap comment earlier."

I tap my nose, a sign he's got it right. "Yes."

"That guy," he mutters, his tone bordering on caveman.

And I can't resist that tone. "I noticed when he's around you get a little possessive. A little *my woman*."

"Yeah, well, that's how I—"

But the conversation ends when our phones buzz in unison.

It's a text from Felix. He wants to know if I'll be available for the Dessert Devotee to shoot a video with me tomorrow and he's letting Gage know about the video too, even though she only needs me. "This is big time," I shriek.

"You earned it, baby," he says, and that word from him threatens to melt me like it has before.

"We earned it," I correct.

He waves a hand dismissively. "She didn't even want

my cocktails. She's after you, and I'm not surprised. You're a star."

His genuine enthusiasm melts me as much as his nickname. I really need to be careful around him.

As we eat, we read the rest of the text from Felix. He's lining up interviews with local food sites, and we schedule times with him as we dine. He also says he wants to add Special Edition merch to the shop—T-shirts and mugs with the cute little logo. It's all so wild and wonderful.

When the meal ends, Gage nods toward the door. "I should take you back to my place, so you and Amanda can go home. But I need to grab something in my office. Come with me?"

I say yes, and once we're there, he closes the door, then locks it with a definitive click. That sound sends a thrill up my spine. Anticipation weaves through me as the mood shifts.

"I didn't want to say this in front of everyone," he says, gesturing to the bar beyond the door.

"What is it?" I ask, my pulse galloping. He's looking at me with fire in his eyes.

"I feel a little *my woman* with you. That's the problem. That guy gets under my skin, and I barely knew why till tonight. Now I get it. He's fucking jealous, and I hate that he looks at you like he wants you. It drives me insane."

I shudder. Why do I like his possession so much? It's raw and dangerous. "The way you look right now drives *me* a little crazy."

Gage breathes out hard through his nostrils. "Everything about you, Elodie, every single thing, makes you so damn hard to resist."

My skin runs hot. My whole body tingles. "This is a challenge," I tease.

In no time, he closes the distance between us, holding my face. "Maybe we should just agree beforehand that it won't happen again. *Not after*. What if we do that?" The man sounds so desperate for a loophole.

"Is this the *one more time* challenge?"

"Yes. Want to take it with me?"

I shake my head. "Actually I have another challenge for you."

I get down on my knees.

23

PAINTING A PICTURE

Gage

I'm a patient man. I'd never take before I gave.

But ever since she sent that first dirty text saying *I was on my knees,* I've pictured her just like this. Looking up at me with those lush red lips parted. With those wide blue eyes gleaming. With my dick on her mind and soon in her mouth.

Her hands tiptoe up my thighs, climbing higher then tapping against the ridge of my erection.

"You gonna tease me? Is that my challenge?" I ask.

"It's the *great blow job* challenge, Gage. You interested?"

My gaze strays purposefully to my hard-on. "I'd say so, but why don't you find out if I'm up for it?"

She smirks, then grabs her purse from the floor. "I think I will. One sec."

Maybe she's going to silence her phone? Or check it?

I'm antsy as she fishes around in the little bag, then grabs something silvery.

Ohhh.

It's a tube of bright red lipstick, and she applies it seductively—of fucking course, since she does everything seductively—then smacks her lips.

After she returns the makeup to its home, her fingers dance up to the button on my jeans. She pops it open and slides down the zipper ever so slowly, watching me the whole time with avid eyes.

I haul in a breath.

I've never seen so much desire in someone's irises. She looks like she's exactly where she wants to be. It's a heady thought and it's scrambling my brain, the idea that she's this excited to suck me off.

She's practically bouncing on her knees as she reaches the end of the metal, spreads open my jeans, then leans forward, pressing her nose against the outline of my dick. Her eyes flutter closed as she inhales. My legs shake.

This woman.

I am not strong enough to withstand this blow job, but dear god, I'm willing to try since Elodie's cuddling my dick. She's rubbing her cheek against my cotton-covered cock. And all I want to do is say *take it out.*

But all I want, too, is to enjoy every single goddamn second of what she's got planned. So I let her lead as she raises her face, her eyes looking glossy already. Then, with the most devilish smile in the history of the world, she peels down my black boxer briefs, inch by inch, and frees my cock.

Her smile doesn't fade. It grows. Then, she meets my eyes. "Oh yes, I am here for this challenge."

"Take it, baby. Take it fucking now," I say, my voice husky, needy.

We move in tandem. As she dips her face toward my aching shaft, I draw another sharp inhale, letting it fuel me. I tangle my fingers through her soft hair, savoring the feel of her strands.

Darting out her tongue, she licks the tip, and I tremble. "Yessss," I groan.

A smile.

Another lick.

Then, a kiss. Her red lips kiss the head of my dick, and I can't stand how aroused I am.

"Elodie," I murmur.

"Yes, Gage," she whispers against me, then licks a long, luxurious stripe down my shaft, then back up, drawing me in past her cherry-red lips.

I don't even know what I want to say. Except… "Don't stop."

"Never," she says, then sucks me a little deeper, and everything in me snaps, crackles, pops. My cells are like a shaken soda bottle. My fingers thread around more strands as I stare wantonly at my woman taking me deep.

More, more, more.

My world narrows to a pinprick. To the warm heaven of her mouth. The bright red of her lips stretched wide around me. The feel of her tongue sliding along my dick.

And the sounds of her. Soft sighs, heated murmurs, hungry moans.

Then my own noises. Groans and grunts as she licks and sucks. As she wraps a hand around the base, her other palm bracing on my thigh. Pressing hard against me for balance as she hoovers my dick, working me over, driving me absolutely fucking wild.

Wave after wave of lust pounds through my body. Mercilessly.

"This what you pictured?" I grit out.

She raises her face but doesn't stop sucking, doesn't stop gripping.

"That night? In your bed? When you texted me?" I ask again, my voice urgent, my nerves fraying.

She nods, then lets go. "Yes…" She tilts her head. "But also no."

My brow knits as she takes me fully in hand, stroking my length hard, rough.

"No?" I ask. What the fuck does she mean?

But wondering is difficult as she's gripping my hungry cock. As she's holding on to my thigh. As I'm roping a hand through her hair.

"I did picture this…" She takes me back between those beautiful lips, and I sigh happily as my dick disappears down her throat once more.

I can't look away. The view is magnificent. I'm amped up from the sight of this goddess in her dress, on her knees, savoring every second. I can barely think about how she hasn't finished her sentence. I'm just staring savagely at her sucking and smiling. My bones shake.

"Fuck, it's so fucking good," I rasp out without thinking. "Let me fuck you, baby," I beg, getting lost in the pleasure. "Let me fuck you on my desk, against the wall, anywhere."

She drops me once more, tilts her head, slides that talented hand quick, quick, quick along my shaft, then says, "I pictured you coming on my face."

And it's a damn good thing she didn't listen to my pleas for her pussy. Because I'm not going to last. I'm seconds away from shooting as she swallows me whole once more.

She's too good to me. Too sexy. Too perfect.

"God, yes, fucking yes," I say on a pump.

Then, remembering that a man should always listen to a woman, I somehow, some way, find the will to pull out, wrapping a fist around my throbbing cock and aiming.

She gasps in excitement. "Yes," she moans, inviting me to come on her face as she parts her lips and sticks out her tongue.

And like that, I paint her mouth white. My vision blurs, my brain going offline as I come on the woman I just can't have.

It lasts for ages and it's not nearly enough.

And I'm keenly aware of the ticking clock, of the responsibilities we both have, of my employees beyond the door, cleaning up.

But after she grabs a tissue from my desk and wipes her face, I lift her up, set her on my desk, and tell her to lean back.

She complies as I get in the chair and return the

favor. It doesn't take her long at all. Soon, she's where I want her. Hands wrapped around my head, thighs gripping my face, whimpering and holding back her cries as she clenches and comes.

A few minutes later, we leave. I'm both sated and completely unsatisfied.

* * *

The next morning, as I fumble around for a coffee mug in the cupboard, the black box of chocolates from The Chocolate Connoisseur catches my eye.

That's right. Last week, I tucked them away in the cupboard. But now I return to Sebastian's invitation to try the autumn-themed bonbons.

Taking them out of the cabinet, I set them on the counter. As I brew the coffee, I open them. Study each one.

The raspberry is a rich red color. The caramel is a bright gold like fall leaves. The dark chocolate enrobed in a royal shade of burgundy. Then, as I take the first sip of coffee, I get on Elodie's website and click on her gift boxes.

I grit my teeth.

His are identical. The same flavors and colors as hers.

24

A CHOCO-GASM

Elodie

"A chocolate truffle ganache would be perf."

That's the verdict from Silver on Saturday afternoon as the dessert influencer with the sparkly matching eyeshadow and gleaming metal bracelets surveys the display case at my shop.

Which is a smidge busier than yesterday.

I could kiss Felix. No, better yet, I could marry Special Edition. Kenji and Amanda are handling the extra foot traffic with aplomb as Silver studies the options with her practiced eye.

"I've got ganache galore," I say, and I'm not surprised she's picked that treat for the video we're doing. I've watched her channel. Her fans love her shtick. So do I. She's a woman who understands the sex appeal of chocolate. Of whipped cream. Of frosting.

She's not one of the most popular dessert influencers for nothing. She knows her audience, and she knows how to sell sweets to them.

I pick a few ganache, set them on one of my robin's egg blue Elodie's trays, and head to the little café section in the back of the shop where we settle into a plush red booth.

Once she sets up her phone on a small tripod, she hits record.

"Hey, besties! It's your girl Silver here, and I've got something that's going to melt in your mouth. And isn't that what we want from our desserts? Something that gives you a choco-gasm?"

She swings the camera to me, and I say cheerily, "I'm all for dessert climaxes."

"That's what I'm talking about," she says, upbeat and bright. "And those champagne chocolates from your pop-up were top tier. But I bet the ganache is better. And I'm gonna find out real soon. But guests first. Tell us about this ganache."

I pick one up and sing its praises. "It's handmade by me. Crafted from the finest dark chocolate. It's decadent and sinful, and will make your day better Chocolate produces endorphins and they say it makes you feel like you're falling in love. Did you know Casanova consumed chocolate before getting intimate?"

She angles the camera toward me. I'm dolled up, like usual. Coiffed hair, bright red lips, long lashes, and a pretty red short-sleeve sweater. I take a slow, sensual bite of the ganache, sighing in a most satisfied way as I eat it, rolling my eyes in pleasure, then darting out my tongue to catch a drop of the gooey chocolate that slides down my chin.

She swings the camera back to herself. "I'm gonna need some now."

Silver does the same, filming herself biting into a rich piece of chocolate, and she's even louder than I am, slapping a hand on the table with a "yes" as she finishes.

She hits stop, shaking her head in approval as she points to the tray of goodies. "Damn, your chocolate is good. I never fake a dessert *O* or a real one."

I hold up a hand in solidarity. "A woman after my own heart."

I expect her to take off, but we chat some more, and she tells me she studied chemistry in college, attending on a STEM scholarship, and she's always loved the science behind baking and chocolate-making.

"Me too," I say. "I'm a science girl."

"And I bet people think you can't be because you're cute."

I shrug. It's not my place to comment on my looks.

"Oh, c'mon. You are. *We* are. And we can be anything we want. We can be scientists or dessert devotees. We can be pilots or presidents. And we can be sexy if we want too."

"I think I love you," I say.

"Of course you do. I'm very lovable," she says, and she makes no move to go. Instead, I give her a hot chocolate and we chat more about being a woman today in business. I feel a little like I made a new friend.

* * *

That night after we finish at the pop-up and I'm home, Amanda receives a reply from the art school that she passed the first round and they want to see a portfolio. I'm thrilled for her and nervous, too, about paying the tuition bills for her dream school.

I'm worried about something Gage told me when we were closing up. He thinks Sebastian is imitating me. He said Sebastian copied my fall colors chocolate box. And Gage is probably right, as much as I wish he were wrong. Sure, there are staples in the business—everyone carries a box of salted caramels, for instance. But the flavored bonbons in the same colors is a little... unsettling.

Especially since he's offering them for half off my price, I learn when I check out his website.

But there's hardly time to worry once Silver posts her video on Monday morning.

It goes viral by Tuesday.

On Wednesday, there are lines all day at Elodie's. They get longer on Thursday. And by Friday I've hired a temp worker to help out when I'm at Special Edition that evening, where Felix tells us hotel business is ticking up. That night, I make another loan payment.

On Saturday morning, Elodie's Chocolates is busier than ever. Samira pops in, clever eyes crinkling at the corners as she comes around and drops something into the pocket of my apron.

"What's this?" I ask.

But I know—it's my favorite perfume.

"Chocolate and perfume sell well together. My business is hopping," she says. "And it's the perfect timing too."

I pluck out the bottle. "I can't take this," I say.

"You can and you will," she says, then scurries off.

"Thank you," I call out, and tend to the line.

And on Saturday afternoon, Gage meets me to take even more extra chocolate over to the pop-up that night. As he's carrying the first batch over, I head to the back of the store to pop into the ladies' room. When I leave, I'm tossing a paper towel in the bin as I push open the door with my elbow and a familiar newscaster voice says my name from the hall beyond.

"Elodie." There's a pause that slices the air like a knife. "Just admit it. You were always playing hard to get with me."

The hair on the back of my neck stands on end.

25

LITTLE CHOCOLATE DARLING

Elodie

That's hardly the tone Sebastian used when he wooed me. Neither for the date nor to buy my store. I turn around carefully, wishing I had a tray in my hand, a fork, a phone. Anything.

He just came out of the men's room and I'm standing in the small back hall, away from customers.

"I don't know what you mean," I say, but I have some guesses.

None of them are good.

"Why don't we try again? I'm happy to increase the offer." His words are friendly, but the tone is chilly. He gives a new number. A ten percent increase. I hate that it's tempting. But I hate, too, that it's still a low-ball offer.

"I appreciate your interest. Truly, I do, but I'm committed to doing this on my own."

He advances closer, holds his arms out wide, a gesture that says *you have nothing to be afraid of.*

Why does fear slide down my spine then? Why do I want a weapon?

"I'm just down the street," he presses. "You can't fight my shop forever. You're one store here in San Francisco. I'm forty nationwide. It would just be easier if we joined forces. You wouldn't need to rely on a"—he pauses, as if he's looking for the right word—"a titillating video to drive sales."

That *word.* It's said derisively. And with his eyes straying to my chest.

I want to wrap my arms around myself, but I stand my ground. "I don't rely on videos. I rely on ability."

"Right, of course. Sure. But you've clearly seen the benefit of partnership with a man. As evidenced by your partnership with your"—he takes a beat, like the word tastes sour on his tongue—"*fiancé.* Wouldn't it be wise to partner with me as well?"

Why am I not surprised he's sexist too? "Because I can't do this on my own as a woman?"

He rolls his eyes. "No, don't be silly. But you can do it better with me."

Silly? Screw that. "I disagree."

"Fine, I'll admit you've seen a nice increase in business from the video. But it won't last."

"So that's what this is about? You're mad I've gained business over you because of a video?"

"Of course not."

But that's a lie. Of course he's jealous. He's been

telling me as much ever since I turned down his buyout offer.

"You need somebody like me who has deep pockets to keep this going past the viral video." His smile is so patronizing. "That's just a stunt. You need something that lasts."

I cross my arms. "I make really good chocolate. Everyone that's coming in here likes it. That's what lasts."

"Elodie," he says, relentless. "You're a smart business-woman. You wouldn't have built this if you weren't smart."

His gray eyes take a salacious tour of my body, over the bodice of my pink dress with black polka dots, over the swing in my skirt, over my waist. My skin crawls as I say, "Again, the answer is no."

With a shake of his head, he gives a *you'll regret it* sigh. "That just makes me want to compete even harder with you." He smiles, plastic and predatory.

Alarm bells ring in my head, but I try not to let on. "Why is that your first response though? There's room for both of us."

"Ah, but see? That's where we disagree. It would just be so much easier if we could go into business together. I want the shop. I want this location. I want you as the face of the brand." He sounds like a child stomping his foot. *I want the red fire truck.* "Especially after that video. That's why I'm offering you the increase. How about fifteen percent? That lasts. You could use that to take care of Amanda. Surely that's the responsible thing to do."

Fear slides down my neck. He knows her name? I can't believe he's using her in this clearly hostile attempt at a takeover. "The answer is no," I bite out.

But he doesn't seem to care what I say. He steps closer, crowding me toward a wall. "You won't have to worry about whether a provocative video will bring people here to...well...to see if you'll put on a show for them."

"I'm not going to apologize for making a fun video," I say, trying to stay tough as panic rises in my blood, in my brain.

"*Fun video?*" he asks with a scoff. "More like strategic. Talk about using your best assets," he says, his awful eyes lingering on my mouth, then my chest. My skin crawls.

"You don't see me making videos like that. You don't see the men who own shops making videos like that. You want to be treated like a businesswoman, then you go make a salacious video like that?"

I'm shaking all over. Wishing I knew martial arts. Reaching for my mace, but I don't have it right now because why would I have it right now? "Leave," I hiss.

"You need someone like me because you can't run a business to save your life. But you sure know how to steal the spotlight."

A million responses start to form in my head but I don't know how to get them to my mouth. I'm stuck in a nightmare, trying to shout and scream but no sound is coming out. I can barely even hear anything but the rushing of blood in my head.

Then, there's the sound of boots.

A growl.

And I feel an arm wrap around my shoulders. Strong, possessive, and, most of all, *wanted*.

"Don't talk to my wife like that."

I'm frozen. I can barely even process that my fake fiancé just upgraded me on the fly to protect me.

For a few seconds, Sebastian sputters out a *what*, clearly knocked off his game. But then, Sebastian's eyes narrow at Gage and he lashes out once more, the little boy wanting the truck at all costs. "She's not even your wife."

Gage isn't one to debate dates, titles, or legalities with this asshole. "All you have to worry about is that she's *mine*."

Sebastian arches a doubtful brow. "Is she though? She never even mentioned you when I asked her out. That engagement ring she wears? That's not the ring she had in her social feed a few weeks ago."

A chill seeps into my bones. Sebastian's right. Of course he's right. I hate that he's right. I hate, too, that he's so obsessed with me he's studied my social feed for details.

Gage doesn't dwell on that though. He keeps me close and says, low and calm, "You think *when* I gave her my grandmother's ring has *anything* to do with what you saw in pictures on the fucking Internet? Get out. *Now*."

Sebastian isn't moving though. He wags a finger at me. "This engagement is a PR stunt. The two of you are trying to look like the cute, fun couple. Trying to impress somebody. And I can guess who that might be."

His eyes are gray pools of jealousy as he looks my way. "I made you a good offer. Your store should be mine." Then, he turns his focus back to Gage. "And I don't believe you're getting married. As I said, she never even mentioned you when I asked her out two months ago. I bet you don't even know her."

Gage breathes fire, moving me behind him as he advances toward the man. Sebastian backs into the corner of the hallway as Gage stares him down. "You think I don't know the woman I'm marrying? Think again. I know her favorite food is a chicken sandwich with sriracha. Her favorite artist is Roy Lichtenstein. Her favorite sport is football. I know, too, her favorite color isn't red. It's yellow because she wore a yellow dress the day I asked her to marry me, and I know she made me so damn happy when she said yes. She buys Mia and Lola makeup, and looks spectacular putting it on, and looks even more beautiful without it. I know she listens to her friend's podcast, and shops at her other friend's jewelry store, and can make friends with anyone. I know she's fearless and brave. I know she's the best listener and has the biggest heart. I know exactly why she loves to make chocolate, and it's about so much more than money, and you will never know these things about her. I know, too, that she loves cherry scents and soap that smells like fruit, *not* chocolate bath bombs." Gage takes a deep, fueling breath, then cocks his head and says, "And I know the sounds she makes when she calls out my name." His voice is filled with the fury of a thousand suns and the protection of an unbeatable army. "Now get the fuck out of her business, and if I ever see you here again, I won't be so nice."

My stomach flips. In the midst of all this heat and rage, all these arrows thrown, it actually flips from the way Gage speaks—so possessively, so passionately.

Sebastian lifts his chin, then holds up a hand as if to say *you've made your point*. He wedges past us toward the store, but turns back once again.

"You can give speeches all you want. But I know this is a game." He points to Gage, then me. "And I'm not going away easily. First, I'll tell your happy little land-lord that you're faking it, and then I'll let the world know." His gaze slithers to me then. *Only me.* "And see if you can be everyone's chocolate darling when you're just a liar."

For the next five hours, Sebastian's parting words echo in my head.

You're just a liar.

It's savory night at Special Edition. We spend the whole evening serving chocolate squares with potato chips, chocolate truffles with everything bagel season-ing, and chocolate truffles with—of all things—olives.

As Gage makes dirty gin martinis, and everything bagel seasoned ones too, I spend savory night watching, waiting, fearing.

Every time the door opens, I tense.

Check for Sebastian.

Wait for him to blow our cover.

He never shows. Neither does Felix.

I feel oily the entire time. I feel exposed. I feel... afraid.

And I fake it, smiling and serving. The lines are certifiably to die for, and yet, I want to curl up in a ball.

Mercifully, at ten p.m. we close. Gage and I haven't had a chance to talk since Sebastian left. It's been go, go, go.

Once everyone leaves, it's just us at last, and I want to collapse in his arms. Just like a real fiancée would do.

26

A PROPOSAL

Gage

Talk about a Freudian slip.

At the end of the evening, my own words are still playing on a loop in my mind.

My wife.

That asshole was right. Of course she's not my wife. But the words slipped off my tongue so easily. Without a second thought.

But with zero regrets.

Even when he called me on it, I felt no remorse for having said it.

His accusations only fueled me. Made me want to protect Elodie even more from him.

I still do.

Now that the lines are gone at Special Edition, I lock the door, lower the blinds, and pull her to me. Instantly, she buries her face in the crook of my shoulder, like she's wrung out. "I'm so sorry you had to deal with him," I say, apologetically. "I wish I'd been there sooner. I wish I hadn't gone to the other shop. I hate that you had to deal with him alone."

"Don't be sorry. I'm glad you were there at all."

"I heard the tail end when I came back. I could barely believe what he was saying," I say, and my tone is gentle for her, but inside I'm seething still, hearing his smarmy voice, picturing him standing too close to my woman.

"Me too," she says quietly, in a small voice that hardly feels like my Elodie. I pull back, meet her gaze. Her eyes are shining with tears. "He mentioned Amanda."

I breathe fire. No. Just fucking no. There's nothing gentle in my voice as I ask, "Are you serious?"

A tear rolls down her cheek, then another as she nods. "He didn't threaten her. But he wanted me to know he knew her name."

But that's a threat in its own terrible way. Fact is, that asshole threatened me too when he showed up here the first night. "Like he did last week when he wanted me to know he'd looked me up," I grit out, my jaw ticking. My entire body is a high tension wire.

"He's onto us, Gage. Everything we've been building in a few short weeks and he's just going to upend it?" Her voice is quavering. "We're not famous. Not even close. But he *could* do something. He knows we're faking it. He knows we're not really engaged."

"I know," I mutter, so damn frustrated that the guy

has something on us. I've got to find a way out of this mess. I've got to help her.

"We've got all this attention on the shop," she continues, sounding desperate. "We're being written up and talked about. We're being featured. Felix has said there's more business to the hotel thanks to us. What if that all goes down the drain? All Sebastian has to do is plant the seed of doubt and he could ruin what we've built."

Not if I can help it. I shake my head. Grip her shoulders fiercely. "I won't let him."

"How can we stop him?" she asks, like she doesn't think I can fix this.

But I can. I know exactly what pitch to throw to strike him out.

A crooked smile tips my lips. "Marry me."

27

FASTEN YOUR SEATBELTS FOR TAKEOFF

Elodie

Don't get me wrong—TSA pre-screen is one of life's greatest inventions. But why does it have to be more crowded than regular security on a Sunday morning at five-thirty? We've been trudging through this line for forty-five minutes already, and my nerves are frayed as thin as my cuticles.

I check my phone for the departure time. Again.

Gage peers around the coil of bleary, annoyed travelers ahead of us, trying to get a view of the checkpoint. "We should be fine. We still have forty minutes," he says reassuringly, but all I can think is *forty minutes to back out, forty minutes to walk away.*

I haul in a big breath. "So, this will just be for—"

But before I can even recap the rules of this marriage of convenience one more time, the line starts flowing. Suddenly, we're moving along, then we're showing IDs to a sturdy TSA agent. With eagle eyes, she stares down at Gage's driver's license, then back up. Down, up.

My pulse gallops.

What is it? Does his face not match the ID? I try to check his license to figure out the issue. I catch a glimpse of his middle name, but I don't even have a second to ask him about it because the agent's suddenly satisfied, dismissing him and nodding to me. "Next," she barks.

I stick mine out at her. She gives a serious perusal. My stomach churns. Has my license expired?

No, of course not. But I feel like it has.

A nod my way, then a gravelly, "Next."

All business, Gage urges me over to the security checkpoint he's picked, reaching for my purse. I hand it to him and he sets it on the conveyor belt with a chill that I simply don't possess. I don't get how he can be so…calm when I'm so frazzled.

My purse slouches onto his neatly folded leather jacket. Even his jacket looks cool, while my bag is chaos as they trundle away.

I hustle through the scanner, then out the other side, but right when I'm grabbing my phone and purse from the belt, he's pulled aside for a random screening.

"Are you kidding me?" I mutter.

But there's no joking at security.

Five minutes later, his hands have been wiped down, his jacket scanned, and his tablet confirmed unthreatening. He tips his forehead to the row of departure screens as announcements ring out overhead.

"The international terminal is this way. The flight to JFK is now boarding. Please don't leave your luggage unattended."

I check for our flight, my shoulders dropping. "They changed gates."

"It's at the end of the concourse," he says. "And it's boarding." His eyes travel quickly to my shoes. Converse sneakers today. "Can you run?"

No. God no. Running is awful. "Of course," I say, then he grabs my hand and we're trotting through crowds, weaving through parents tugging toddlers and couples in sweats wearing neck pillows.

As we race toward the last gate at the end of the concourse, I'm certain this is how I'll die. My lungs are staging a mutiny. My thighs are screaming obscenities at me.

And yet, I choose this moment to try again. "We're just doing this for the length of the lease, right?" I say as we jog past a shop selling *I left my heart in San Francisco* sweatshirts. Or maybe *my mind*, in my case.

He's not even startled by my abrupt return to the rules of the road. He nods, cool and controlled. "Yep. We'll get that guy to back off and then we'll just…" But he trails off, maybe uncertain for the first time since he offered his hand last night.

My worry skyrockets. Is it us he's freaking out about? Something else?

"Get a divorce," he finally adds, as if the word tastes like sour candy on his tongue. "I don't know if we can get an annulment after two months. I'll have to look that up."

"Or I can," I offer as we race past gates like partners in...romantic crime? "I guess people have gotten married for less," I say, trying to normalize the insanity of this choice.

"People get married on a dare from their friends. People get married because they're drunk. People get married and then they just get divorced as soon as they can." He lists off reasons steadily, a man in charge once more. "At least we have a reason."

I picture the insidious look on Sebastian's face less than twenty-four hours ago. His parting words. The power he possesses to ruin me by revealing our lie. Somehow, he's so threatened by my modicum of success, and by my *no*, that he's declared me his enemy. With his fat bank account and his suspicions, he *could* take me down.

A real marriage neutralizes the threat of a fake engagement. I swallow past a knot of fear.

"Flight Thirty-two to Las Vegas. All groups must board now," a tinny voice rattles as we reach the busy gate, packed with people.

"I can't believe there are this many people going to Vegas on a Sunday morning," I say, though what I'm really thinking is *I can't believe I'm going to Vegas less than twelve hours after you proposed to me for a second time*.

I lean closer, trying to lighten the mood, to slow my still surging pulse. "Are they all plotting their fake marriages?"

He tugs on my hand, his eyes darkening, his mouth serious. "This one is real."

I'm speechless for several seconds. "I know," I say, my stomach flipping with nerves.

"Real for two months," he adds, like a reminder, but it hardly seems like a reminder for me.

It's more like he's reminding himself.

We reach the jetway, where a man in a starched blue suit gestures to the scanner. "Boarding pass, please."

Gage scans his mobile phone. "How you doing?"

"Good. And you?"

"Great," Gage says, but does he mean it?

The man smiles. "Good luck."

After I scan my pass, we walk down the jetway in silence. My worries crawl back up my throat.

"Hey, you okay?" I ask. "You can back out." Maybe he needs a parachute. Maybe he regrets his throwdown. "I'm the one who needs this. Sebastian's after me. Not you."

Gage's head tilts my way. His eyes study me. "He's after us. We're in this together."

My heart pounds mercilessly. "We are?"

"We are," he says, strong, certain. "One hundred percent."

"But you really don't have to do this," I say. I've never seen anyone step up like he has. I didn't know that was a thing men did. Or people.

"You're looking at me like you think I regret this."

Busted. I purse my lips as we near the mouth of the plane. "I just thought maybe a few minutes ago…you were regretting it. When you sort of trailed off."

He squeezes my hand again. "I was thinking. That was all. Just about…"

"The last time you got married?" I supply.

His smile is soft, a little wistful. "You're a great listener. And yes, I was."

"I had a feeling," I say.

"But I'm sure of this," he adds, curling his arm possessively around me like he did yesterday. "We have a plan and it's a good one. A Special Edition Marriage."

With our plan and our chutzpah, we step onto the plane on a Sunday morning. We're not even going to stay overnight in the city of sin. We'll be back in the early afternoon. Amanda spent the night at Ally's house. Eliza is with her grandmother. There were no appointments today in San Francisco to get a marriage license, so this was our best option for a quick marriage.

We find our seats quickly in the twenty-third row, my engagement ring glinting from the sun rising outside the little window, my phone buzzes with a text.

This confirms your wedding at 10:00 AM at The Extravagant Chapel. Congratulations, and we will see you soon.

I breathe out, talking back to my buzzing brain that's telling me I'm still so impulsive. *It's no big deal. It's for less than two months. It's just to save my business and, you know, my life.*

I steal a glance at Gage, at the steadiness in his eyes, the sturdiness in his broad shoulders, the calm in his handsome features.

No, it's *our* business. We're in this together.

"Thank you," I say, my throat tightening with emotion. Then I add, "Gage Reginald Archer."

He dips his head, laughing. "You were checking out my ID?"

I shrug playfully. "Maybe I was. Is that a family name?"

"My grandpa's. Margo's late husband. He taught me how to throw a fastball. What's your middle name?"

I wish mine had such a good story. "Calliope."

He waits for me to say more.

"My parents claimed it was for the muse," I explain, and I don't hide my skepticism.

"And…?"

"But I found a photo where they met. A bar named Calliope."

He nods, seeming to take that in, then adding thoughtfully, "We met at a bar."

"Your bar. You weren't drinking. Neither was I," I point out.

"And I'm stone-cold sober now," he says.

And marrying me anyway.

"Please fasten your seatbelts," the cheery voice of a flight attendant says overhead. "We're about to take off."

Yes, we are.

28

IT HAD TO BE YOU

Gage

Fake engagement. Real marriage. Both have an expiration date, so what's the difference? This next legal step is just more of the same.

That's what I tell myself to keep my focus narrowed on the mission today in Las Vegas—getting hitched. That's the one goal I have. I'm not going to linger on what's next. I'm not going to think about how much I like spending time with this woman. How often I think about her. How deeply I want to protect her from anything and anyone. Most importantly, how hard it will be for me to pretend my feelings for her aren't fast becoming real.

I'm going to stay lasered in on the goal like I've done all morning so far. First at the airport in San Francisco, and now as our Lyft arrives at The Extravagant Hotel on the Strip. I thank the driver, then step out of the sedan, marriage license in hand.

Our flight landed right on time so we cruised over to the Clark County Marriage Bureau, striding in the second the doors opened at eight. Now, it's eight-thirty, and our *I do* appointment is in one and a half hours.

With no luggage and no room to check into, I figure we'll grab a bite to eat, maybe brainstorm the Special Edition menu for next weekend over eggs and coffee. We head through the revolving door into the opulent hotel, its lobby glittering with a huge chandelier that's dripping with faux gemstones. I picked this hotel for one reason only—its chapel had the earliest opening in the city for a no-frills wedding. But as I walk past a fountain that's sparkling with imitation sapphires and rubies, I wonder if I made a mistake with the all business strategy. I glance skeptically at my clothes—boots, jeans, a long-sleeve shirt, cuffs rolled up.

"I should go get a sports jacket or something," I say, plucking at my white button-down.

Elodie stops in front of a roulette game, the wheel spinning, as she gestures to her shoes. "Don't you dare. I'm wearing jeans and sneakers. You said casual last night," she says sternly. "So I followed orders."

"Right, right," I repeat. "Just a no-big-deal wedding. Like we agreed to."

Hell, this quickie wedding is more shotgun than my actual shotgun wedding more than a decade ago. I suppose there's no point in dressing up. We've got a two o'clock return flight, which should give me just enough time to make it to Eliza's karate class this afternoon.

Still…

Something nags at me. I should look good for Elodie. That's what she deserves. A man who shows up. "We could shop for something fancier since we have an hour and a half free." I remember the website for the chapel and the list of extras. "Come to think of it, we can rent tuxes, dresses, and flowers at the chapel."

Do I sound as jittery as I feel? I hope she can't tell.

With a curious tilt of her head, she asks, "Is that what you want?"

I want to make you happy.

She has to want more than a no-big-deal wedding, even for a fake real wedding. Back in Felix's office the other week, she provided a road map, didn't she? Elodie detailed all those romantic venues. Even though this is a temporary tying of the knot, I need to try harder. "Do you want me to take you shopping? For a dress or something? And I can rent a suit."

Before she can answer, her phone buzzes. She lifts a finger. "Hold on."

She checks her texts, then meets my gaze with something like delight in her irises. "It's the chapel. The nine a.m. wedding ceremony was canceled so they're offering us the slot. Want to get married early and see if we can catch an earlier flight?"

She sounds…ecstatic.

It was ridiculous of me to think she'd want all the trappings. This is an arrangement, and she's always been a smart businesswoman. I'm not even upset. Not one bit.

"Let's get hitched, baby." I take her hand, and I'm strangely eager to get to the chapel.

Just to get a move on, I'm sure.

That has to be it.

* * *

But the velour burgundy jacket is irresistible to Elodie.

The second the officiant, a bald white guy with a pro wrestler's physique and name, Hitch Malone, shows it to us in the foyer of the chapel, she turns to me, eyes glittering, mouth wide with excitement.

"Gage, you would look so good in this on social. So handsome," she says, advancing toward me. "We could rub Sebastian's face in it."

And that's irresistible too. "How are you even hotter when you go for revenge?"

She smiles coyly. "It's one of my many charms."

"There's a dress for the lovely bride too," Hitch adds, then swaggers to a mirrored door, swings it open, and gestures to a wardrobe full of gowns. "The missus and I stocked it with all the sizes."

Elodie rubs her palms and marches straight over, flicking through choices, then picking. The matching dress for the bride is stunning—it's cut short and it has all sorts of cleavage.

"Sold," she says, then waggles her credit card and presses it into his beefy palm. "The clothing rental is on me."

I smile privately. She did want the trappings. I was

right. I pat myself virtually on the back for knowing my woman.

Not gonna lie—I'm pleased, too, that she wants some frills.

Because I do.

Ten minutes later, I'm tugging on the cuffs of my wine-colored jacket that makes me look like a lounge singer. I wait at the head of the chapel while Hitch Malone sets the rings I bought from him on a white satin pillow on the altar.

A woman with the attitude and dress of a burlesque singer fiddles with the music. She's his wife, and her name is Matrimony Maven.

"You want 'It Had to Be You,' right, hun?" she calls out to me.

I picked that one, figuring it was one of Elodie's favorites since she named a line of chocolates after the tune.

But a coil of doubt winds tighter in me. Is this tune sending the wrong message? Will she think I'm making more of this match than I should?

I wish relationships came with recipes, like cocktails. Or rules, like baseball.

But…in for a penny, in for a pound. "Yes," I answer.

I tug on my bow tie as Matrimony Maven cues up the music and Hitch Malone pats me on the shoulder. "It's all right, kid. I was nervous before I married Maven," he says, nodding toward his wife. "Nerves are good. They mean this matters to you."

"That's not why—"

But I swallow my denial when the music begins and

the door opens. Elodie strides in, and my nerves simply vanish, like smoke in the fog.

I can't take my eyes off her. Her hair is twisted up in a clip, blonde tendrils framing her face, her cheeks rosy, her lips the color of cherries, her blue eyes bright and playful, but also…hopeful.

I think.

Or maybe I want to think it's hope I see in the tilt of her lips, the softness of her smile, the tenderness in her eyes. The burgundy velour dress hits at her knees, accentuates her waist and full hips, and hugs the curves of her breasts. Her engagement ring from Grams shines on her right hand today. She switched it so she could put the band on her left hand. She's still wearing her Converse, and somehow the incongruity of my dressed up woman in sneakers makes my breath catch.

And my heart beats faster.

Clutching a bouquet of yellow roses, she's walking toward me, dipping her face, then meeting my gaze, then looking away, and holy shit, is she truly nervous? Or is that excitement?

I don't even know. I just *feel* right now. I feel… tingles as she walks past empty chairs and the romantic song swells, the crooner's lyrics filling the corners of my mind.

It must have been that something lovers call fate.

I'm not a fate guy. Don't believe in it one bit. Not after the way my life has gone. But in this moment, I believe in something bigger than me. I believe Elodie came into my life for a reason.

The reason is the partnership, surely. That's what I

tell myself. But I can't seem to hold that idea in my head. It falls away like sand as Elodie closes the distance between us while Maven clicks, clicks, clicks on her phone, snapping photos.

For a brief, dangerous moment, my imagination runs wild. Maybe that's inevitable, even when you're playing pretend. But when I'm with Elodie, I don't feel like I'm faking a thing. With her I don't feel like I'm constantly racing toward the future. I feel like I'm living in the moment, and each moment with her is the only place I want to be.

It had to be you.

When she reaches me, Maven fades the song into the background, and I lock eyes with my bride. "Hi." It comes out rough, like sandpaper.

"Hi," she says and it's bright, bursting with sunshine.

"You look…" I stop, like I can find the best word for her. But in the end, I return to the simplest. "Beautiful."

"You look so handsome," she says, her tone surprisingly vulnerable.

It's like we're saying more even as we compliment the surfaces. Or maybe I just want to believe that.

Out of the corner of my eye, Hitch Malone seems to be fighting off a smile. "Dearly beloved, we are gathered here today," he begins, and he wastes no time moving through the script he must know by heart, then saying, "And do you, Gage Reginald Archer, take this woman to be your wife?"

Electricity crackles through my bones. "I do," I say, holding tight to her gaze.

"And do you, Elodie Calliope Starling, take this man to be your husband?"

There's no hesitation as she says, "I do."

"The rings please."

Maven hands Hitch the $129 wedding bands we picked out online last night. I slide hers onto her ring finger, staring at the sight of the metal hugging her skin.

She slides mine onto my finger, and I savor her touch.

"I now pronounce you husband and wife. You may kiss the bride," he says.

I cup her cheeks and drink in our first kiss as a married couple like it's my favorite wine. The softness of her breath, the silk of her hair, the sweet cherry scent of her skin. I kiss her deeper as the scent goes to my head. But really, it's her.

The way she is. The hold she has on me. How she makes my heart hammer.

I'm going to have to be seriously careful because I could fall for my wife. When we break the kiss, she looks up at me with heat in her eyes, and something more.

Something like gratitude.

Like safety.

Like…calm in the midst of chaos.

Then she whispers, "Thank you," and I can hear how much this means to her. But there was never any question for me.

After we sign the marriage license and return our clothes, Maven says she sent the pictures over via email. We thank her, then leave the chapel. Elodie nods toward the casino, promising hours of entertainment. "Our flight doesn't leave till two. Want to play the slots?"

I shake my head then haul her against me in the middle of the hallway outside the Vegas wedding chapel. "I have another idea."

She shudders, her voice trembling as she asks, "What is it?"

I press a possessive kiss to her lips. Passionate, and a promise too. This is not a fake engagement anymore. This is a marriage, and I want something badly.

Deeply.

So much I can feel it in my marrow.

I pull back. "I want to fuck my wife."

29

TAKE ME

Gage

Thank fuck the hotel isn't sold out today. But if it were, I'd have marched to every hotel on the Strip to find some privacy for even fifteen minutes with this woman.

When we reach the door to our room, she smiles coyly. "You and me and hotels. This is becoming a habit."

"Hotel sex should be a regular one." I stop for a second. "No—sex should be a habit," I quickly revise... *because seriously*. There's no point playing the virtue card any longer. Hell, we've barely been playing it so far. I move behind her, sweep her hair off her neck, and dust a kiss there as I swipe the key over the pad. "Can this be one of the perks of our temporary marriage?"

She murmurs as I kiss her. "Let's see how good you are at convincing me of the marital benefits."

I growl against her skin as I turn the handle. "I'm

very persuasive…Mrs. Archer," I tease, even though she didn't take my name.

A laugh comes from her as she steps inside. "Or maybe it's Mr. Starling."

The second the door shuts, I haul her against me, her chest flush to mine. "Call me whatever you want…when you're coming undone."

"Deal," she says, and then I start making good on my part of the bargain. I back her up to the wall, hold her face, and crush my mouth to hers.

Like I wanted to do in the chapel. At the front desk. In the hallway.

Finally.

It's such a relief to kiss her behind closed doors. To kiss her without worrying about who's out there in the store, or in the restaurant, or in the bar.

I kiss her deeply, thoroughly, like I plan to take her apart, orgasm by orgasm, here in this hotel room high up above the city of sin.

I devour those sweet lips, kissing off her lipstick as she ropes her arms around my neck, warm and pliant, tipping her head back.

A sign.

Letting me know how she wants to be kissed.

Like she's *not* in charge.

I wrench apart from her, tilting my head, stroking her cheek. "You like orders?"

She gives a tease of a smile. "Try me."

A rumble works its way up my chest as I reach for her wrists, then pin them over her head in a blur.

"You're fast," she says, her blue eyes sparkling.

I dip my face to the hollow of her throat, kissing her there before I let go and meet her gaze again. "Turn around. Hands against the wall."

She spins, and I press her breasts to the wall, then brush her hair to the side. "Your neck," I murmur, coasting my lips across her skin, inhaling her cherry scent, then running my nose into her soft hair. Her shampoo's different. Something subtler, something clean and sweet I can't identify. I roam my hands down her arms.

"Do you have any idea how many times I've wanted to touch you?" I drop a kiss on her collarbone as I slide her sweater down her shoulder.

"How many?" She's breathless as I travel across her soft skin.

"Can't count that high," I murmur then give a flick of my tongue over the shell of her ear.

She shudders beautifully. "Me neither."

Her desire rushes through me, mingles with my own, grows stronger, digs deeper. I gather her hair in my hand, tug on it.

She gasps.

Setting a hand on her chin, I angle her toward me, exposing her neck. I coast my lips along the column of her throat, her pulse hammering against my touch as I go.

When I stop, I turn her around once more so she's facing me. Then I grab her ass and hike her up. "Wrap those legs around your husband," I command.

And my obedient, horny wife complies, squeezing

those lush thighs around my hips as I carry her to the bed.

"I'm such a typical bride," she jokes, then glances down at her very non-bridal attire. The sweater, jeans, and sneakers.

"It's perfect for you. All of this. Everything," I say as I promptly remove her clothes, then hiss out a breath between my teeth when she's naked and glorious, full breasts, soft stomach, creamy skin. "My wife is so fucking sexy," I say, and I'm about to push her down, then climb over her when she shakes her head.

She twirls a finger at me. "Your turn, husband."

I'm standing at the foot of the bed and she's sitting, watching, pleased.

I give her a lopsided grin as I undo the buttons on my shirt, but when I'm halfway done, she's crawling to the end of the mattress, kneeling, taking over.

Elodie Starling is an interesting mix of bold and submissive, and I am going to have a fantastic time exploring the cocktail of her. After she tugs the shirt from my jeans, she slides it down my arms, and I let it fall to the floor.

She takes several seconds to stare at my chest, my arms, my abs, and I do not mind the admiration. I like her eyes on me. *So much.*

"Feels like forever since our failed one-night stand," she says, unbuttoning my jeans.

"Failed? I seem to recall you riding my face. I call that a win."

She shakes her head as she unzips my jeans. "It'll be a

win when you push me down onto my stomach and fuck me like that."

I...blink.

Then groan.

Next, I drag a hand through my hair as I take a fucking minute to absorb the beautiful, filthy specificity of that image. "That something you picture at night? When you're all alone with your toy collection and your fantasies of me?"

"I do. A lot," she says, pushing my jeans down, then my boxer briefs, freeing my cock. Which is very, very happy to see the Mrs.

She wraps a hand around my aching dick, staring at my length like she's never been this hungry before in her life. My legs shake.

As she strokes languidly, she nibbles on the corner of her lips. I tremble.

I could savor this. Standing in front of her, letting her play with my cock, cataloging her excitement.

But that's not what the woman ordered.

I bat her hand off, then shed the rest of my clothes. "I'm gonna give you everything you want, but before you get my cock, I need to make sure you're good and ready. How does that sound to you?" I ask, tugging on her ankle and pulling her down the bed, manhandling her since I'm pretty sure she likes that.

The shiver that runs over her body says I'm right. Then she does, too, as she says, "Sounds so good."

I climb onto the bed, nudging her thighs apart and kneeling between them. I run a hand up her soft stomach, then to her beautiful, majestic tits. And finally, at long fucking last, I play with them.

These gorgeous beauties.

I bury my face in them, and I never want to leave. She grabs my hair, curls her fingers through it, jams my face against her tits with a loud moan. Heat roars through me. Her reaction revs my engine. But I'm pretty sure nuzzling her tits isn't going to be enough.

As I fondle them, I move over, lying next to her. My eager fingers coast along her belly, down between her thighs, finding her slick center. My breath hitches. Hers stutters. "You're soaked," I say, marveling. She's hot and silky and so turned on.

"Do something about it," she says, at the same time as she parts her thighs for me.

"So greedy. So bossy," I mutter against her tits.

"Do something about it *now*," she demands, arching into my hand, and then using my hand as a toy.

Thrusting against it, rocking into it, seeking contact.

I follow her lead, playing with her pussy the way she wants. With teasing circles on her clit, then deep thrusts inside the warm, wet paradise, I draw a nipple into my mouth as I slide my fingers inside, then along her clit, enjoying the welcoming warmth of her.

The needy moans that fall from her parted lips.

The thrust of her hips. The journey of her hands—up to her hair, like she can barely handle how good she feels.

I stop licking since she's breathtaking to watch.

But I can't watch for long because she likes it too much when I play with her tits. I kiss and lick her breasts while I stroke her sweet pussy, listening to her noises, responding to her plaintive cries.

More, please, now.

Till she's shaking, trembling then arching into my hand.

"Yes, yes, yes," she chants, crying out, then shuddering as she comes undone.

When her eyes open, I bring my fingers to my mouth and lick her off each one. "You taste so fucking good. And now I get to feel you at last. Been wanting this for so long. Let me get a—"

But before I can say condom, she sits up and kisses me, cutting me off with her greedy mouth. She's sucking on my lower lip, sending sparks through my whole damn body, making my fucking toes curl, and that has never happened to me before.

"Gage," she says, breaking the needy kiss, her voice more vulnerable than I've ever heard. "I don't want to use a condom."

I pause. Process. Picture.

My dick turns to granite. My blood is on fire. And my mind is vibrating.

Before I can even rasp out a *yes*, she adds, "I'm negative. And on birth control."

Her words are like a filthy poem.

"Negative here," I say with a smile.

She roams a hand down my chest. "Take me."

Two words.

They're all I want.

All I need too.

Then, because a man should listen to a woman, I flip

her to her stomach, raise her luscious ass, and kneel behind her.

"You picture this, baby?"

She gasps at that last word. "Yes."

"You like when I call you baby?"

"I do," she says, and she sounds drunk on this. On us.

Same here.

It's barely been a month since I met her and yet...I feel like I've been waiting forever to get close to her like this.

To feel our bodies connect.

To rub the crown of my cock against her pussy.

To hear the hitch in her breath, the gasp in her voice as she asks for me.

"Please, Gage. Fuck me," she says, begging beautifully.

"You want your husband's cock?" I say, teasing my throbbing dick against her wetness.

"So badly," she says on a whimper, her fists curling around the sheets.

I sink into her, savoring every single second. It's so good, it's unholy.

It's electric.

Pleasure grips me hard, and I'm buzzing everywhere, a circuit breaker reaching maximum. I set a hand on her sexy back and push her down. Like that, I pin her, my chest to her back, an arm roped around her tits, my other hand gripping her hip.

I fuck her good and slow.

Deep and passionate.

Letting her feel every inch of me with every goddamn thrust.

Reaching that sweet spot inside her.

She grips the sheets, parts her lips, begs for me. "Yes, more, so good."

My nerves fray. My brain goes haywire. And lust consumes every single thought.

Except...maybe not all of them. As I fuck her harder, I'm keenly aware that today is not a one-time thing. That she is already so much more than a habit. That I'm already a little wild for my wife.

"Oh god. Yes. So good," she says, my noisy, horny, greedy, wildly aroused wife, who seems to love it when I fuck her.

When I slide a hand up higher, past her breasts, she's lost. Moaning, writhing, murmuring.

"The sounds you make," I mutter then thrust deep, reaching the end of her.

"The way you fuck," she murmurs, arching back against me.

"How we fit," I say, holding her tight, swiveling my hips, and taking her. Just fucking taking her.

Pleasure blasts through me, a torrent of impending bliss, and I've got to get her there soon. But she's already helping herself along, maneuvering her hand between her legs.

"Fucking love that you're playing with your clit," I praise as I ease out then drive into her.

"Feels so good with you inside me," she murmurs then cries, "Oh god, deeper."

I obey, fucking and filling her, and losing my mind,

and I'm sure my soul, to this exquisite bliss as she shouts and screams then shudders under me, coming hard and beautifully, and I'm right there with her.

Pleasure jolts through me, hard and recklessly.

And even if this ends, I won't regret a second of it.

I mean, *when* it ends.

* * *

Fifteen minutes later, we're freshened up and curled together in bed, smiling dopily as we contemplate room service. "Do we even have time?" she asks.

The clock ticks close to eleven. "We do," I say.

But before we can order, we're kissing again, then fucking again, then room service is the last thing I'm thinking about as I bend my wife over the couch and fuck her for all of Vegas to see.

It's a damn good wedding day. Especially when she says, "You convinced me of the benefits of marriage."

"And I won't stop convincing you."

Yes, she's the best kind of habit already.

* * *

We land around three-thirty and snag a Lyft, returning to our all-business mode, making plans for the week ahead, all the things we need to do for the shop, and all the things we need to do for our temporary marriage.

Like, where to live. We can't just stay in separate homes. That nosy fucker would sniff around, figure it out, lash out again.

I drag a hand through my hair, offering up suggestions. My home in Russian Hill has two small bedrooms. She says hers in Hayes Valley is about the same. And while we're both fairly confident the girls will approve of our decision to tie the knot, we don't think they'll be up for sharing a bedroom.

"It's a little overwhelming. All these details," she says, apologetically.

I cup her cheek, catching her face in my hand. "Worth it. And don't worry. We will figure it out," I say, then look out the window. We're on Webster Street now. "And this will be worth it too," I tell her as the car slows to a stop outside The Chocolate Connoisseur.

"Be right back," I say, then I grab a souvenir from Vegas, march to the door, and yank it open. The store's full of customers and I don't give a fuck about making a scene. I head straight to the counter and ask a young man with glasses for Sebastian. "You can tell him Gage Archer is here, and I've got the receipts he requested."

The employee blinks, then says, "Umm." Maybe the boss isn't in today. That's entirely possible. I'm taking a chance, after all.

But Elodie's ruthless competitor must hear me since a few seconds later, the man with the smarmy face and the asshole interior strides from the back. He sports a sharp, expensive tailored shirt and ire in his eyes.

Curiosity, too though. I knew the fucker couldn't resist seeing me.

A wary cat, he tilts his head. "What can I do for you?"

The second he reaches the counter, I slap down the paper in my hand, then stab it with my finger. "See this?

It's our marriage license." I point to the names. "See that? Elodie Starling. Also known as…" I raise my chin, take a long, satisfied beat as I meet his beady gaze, then I let the words roll off my tongue like chocolate. "My wife."

He blanches, his expression nothing but pure shock. Yup. He played chicken with the wrong guy. "What? You got married?"

I lift my left hand, rub my forefinger along my gleaming gold wedding band. The gesture isn't lost on him. "Do not underestimate me. Do not underestimate the things I will do for my woman. And, like I said yesterday, don't come around to the store and threaten my family." I take the marriage license and sigh deeply, full of satisfaction. Worth it. So damn worth it. "Oh, and feel free to jump in a chocolate fountain."

30

A GIANT PRANK

Elodie

The second the soles of my sneakers hit the top step on Juliet's floor, my friend swings open the door to her apartment. With eager eyes, she declares, "Everything. I need to know everything."

"You know everything," I tease, but my stomach flips with butterflies, making a liar of me.

Undeterred, Juliet shuts the door behind her.

Stares me up and down.

It takes her three seconds to diagnose. "I knew it! You got banged in Vegas."

"Shh," I say since Amanda's just beyond the door in her apartment. Juliet—my friend, my savior—picked her up from Ally's house this morning, and they hung out together for the day.

I love my friends so much. They're like Amanda's aunts.

Juliet scoffs, flapping a hand behind her. "Sawyer's here. They're playing Mind the Gap and Amanda's got music blasting at a ridiculous decibel. Tell me everything."

Sawyer is Juliet's big brother and he's as obsessed with board games and video games as Amanda is. Two decades older, he's like the fun uncle she never had. He's a ruthless competitor, too, so I'm sure they're neck and neck in pop music trivia from the new game Amanda picked up a few weeks ago.

Juliet makes a rolling gesture with her hands. "So you got married, and then…"

A tingle runs down my spine as I picture this morning in the hotel room. A smile takes me hostage. "And then my temporary husband gave me the best sex of my life."

She squeals.

"Well…we *had* an extra hour. What else were we to do?" I ask, ever so innocently.

"I'm finally getting a pancake-breakfast-worthy update," she says, gathering my hands in hers. "Details."

I tell her about the wedding, then how we upgraded our clothes, then the music, then the room.

Juliet holds up a stop-sign hand. "I do want to hear about all the in-room services, but first…you rented a dress? And he got a suit?"

It's like she's caught me in the act of…something. "We did. Why are you asking like that?"

She hums as if it's obvious. "Because it meant something to you."

"Well, I *did* marry him. It didn't mean nothing."

"I know. But it sounds like it meant more than you expected. More than a marriage of convenience."

I want to deny it, but instead I give a one-shouldered shrug. "Look, you know I like him. I always have. It just doesn't mean *everything*."

She hums again, doubtful this time. "Doesn't sound like it means *nothing* either."

I remember the way Gage looked at me as I walked down the aisle—like I was a mystery he wanted to uncover—then relent. "You're right. It meant something. But it can't mean what your big, squishy heart wants it to mean."

She rolls her eyes. "Fine, fine. Tell me about the magic D then."

I give her a few more details, finishing with, "He's just...he's great, Juliet. He's truly great. I've never met anyone like Gage. But it's just an arrangement, and I can't get caught up in it."

Words to live by. Words I'd better not ever forget.

"It's a wonderful arrangement though."

"I suppose it is. But it's also surreal. And a little terrifying. Because now I have to deal with *what's next*."

"And what's that?"

I gulp. "Gage and I talked about it in the car. But I should probably tell Amanda first," I say, and all at once, my sex high wears off. Reality slams into me. "I just got married to ward off a threat to my livelihood, and I'm also trying to raise my sister to be a good person who doesn't lie. What does this say to her about how I solve problems?"

Juliet grabs my arm, squeezing it like she's trying to

impart all her boldness into me. "That you're a mama bear."

I frown. "Juliet. You can't believe that."

She squares her shoulders. "I can and I do. You're busting your cute little butt for your sister every day. You're finding new ways to take care of your family. You're fighting and working it. Do not dismiss that."

My throat catches. "Really?" I need this so badly— someone's reassurance that I'm doing this right. Or at least, not wrong.

"Yes, you may be unconventional in your methods, but your heart, friend?" she says, then points importantly to the door. "It's beating for that girl in there."

As if on cue, my chest swells with emotions. "I have no choice. I must hug you right now."

She widens her arms. "Incoming hug."

We embrace, and buoyed by her strength, I go inside. Girl pop is blasting from Amanda's phone in greeting as I prepare to tackle the start of what's next.

But first, Amanda and Sawyer are facing off on Juliet's couch while a black-and-white cat paces, watching them like an official in a tennis game. Amanda slaps a palm down on the couch cushion. "Zendaya doesn't have a last name, bro!"

"So I was right then," Sawyer insists, "when I gave her first name."

"She's not Zendaya Smith," Amanda argues.

"But she *is* Zendaya. I got that part right. The rest is details," he says, ever the businessman, trying to talk his way out of a situation and looking the part, too, in a crisp tailored shirt, even on a Sunday.

"How do you not know who Zendaya is?" Amanda continues.

"How does she not have a last name?"

"That woman from your generation doesn't. You guys have all those celebrities with no last names. Madonna and...you know."

Juliet clears her throat. "Hello, Madonna is our mama's generation."

"Yes, kiddo," I add, backing up my friend and my generation.

"It's all the same. It's old," Amanda insists.

"Fine, fine. Don't give me credit for Zendaya Smith. I will still destroy you," Sawyer warns, but ten minutes later, he's schooled by my sister. She lifts her arms in victory. "I am the trivia queen," she says, then glances at me, then my shiny gold ring. "So the outfit of the day is married, I see?"

I gulp, hoping Juliet is right. "It is."

* * *

Before dinner that night, Gage calls, and I can hear the pride in his voice, a man who's solved a problem. "I have a proposal for you," he says, as I turn the heat down on a pan of sauteed broccoli and carrots.

"But you already proposed. Kind of twice."

"Woman, there was no kind of."

I smile. "For real twice."

"A man should do all good things in multiples. Orgasms, proposals, and purchases of chocolate."

"I don't disagree," I say, plating the veggies on top of the fluffy rice I cooked earlier.

"So, what do you think about this…" He details the idea, and it feels a little like a fairy tale.

After dinner that night, I tell Amanda the plan for the next two months, the time left on the lease, and she just shrugs a yes. "I guess it sounds cool. Like a vacation for the rest of the year or something."

She sets a plate in the dishwasher. How can she be so level-headed about it? My stomach churns with another set of *am I doing this right* worries as I rinse off a bowl to hand to her. "You really are good with it?"

"Sure. I mean, it's weird, but whatever."

Is that a *good* whatever or an *I can't be bothered* whatever? I don't know. I turn off the faucet and dry my hands. Rather than guess, I flash back to advice my shrink has given me over the years. *Be kind and be honest.* "Amanda, sometimes I feel…" Then I just rip off the Band-Aid. "Like I'm doing a terrible job with this whole thing. With you. Raising you."

"With me?" she asks, incredulous.

"Yes." That's honest.

She shakes her head, shutting the dishwasher. "I don't think so." She's certain where I'm not.

"You don't?"

She's quiet at first, then swallows and says, "You're around more." Her voice starts to crack.

Mine does too. "Than Mom or Dad?"

She nods, her blue eyes glistening.

"They weren't around that much?" I ask to be sure

since this is news to me. "I thought…" *I thought they raised you differently than me.*

"Els, they were kind of obsessed with recovery. That was their thing. Sobriety coaching. Being sponsors. Being there for their sponsees," she says, her tone so vulnerable that it breaks my heart a little.

"I thought they were super parents," I say, taking a beat to process this new intel.

"I mean, I loved them. I miss them. But I don't think you're like…a bad guardian."

I laugh at the half compliment. "Thanks."

"I mean it," she says, genuinely. She dips her face, and when she raises it and meets my gaze I can tell she has something important to say. Maybe something that's been weighing on her. "Sometimes I feel bad though. You had this whole life at age twenty-eight. You probably wanted to get married and settle down. And then I landed in your lap."

My heart breaks even more. I reach for her, curl my hands over her shoulders. "Don't ever doubt that this is where I want to be. With you."

"Are you sure?" Tears slip from her eyes. I wipe them away.

"I never hesitated to take care of you. And I never will," I say, my tone brooking no argument. "You're mine. Do you understand?"

She places her head on my shoulder, pressing her face to me, nodding against me. "I like that you're around. I like that you come to the studio. And play trivia games. I like that I get to work in the shop. I like that you tell me your crazy things. Like getting married. I never knew what was going on with them."

I stroke her hair, marveling at this seismic shift in my view of my parents and maybe myself. Here I thought I was the wild, impulsive, irresponsible one. Maybe I am. But maybe there's another side to the impulsive coin. Being honest with the people you love. "I never thought about keeping any of my crazy life from you, including this married part."

She pulls away gently, offers me a small smile. "It's kind of fun to be in on it. It's like a giant prank. Or a game. And that dude is the worst," she says, her nose curling as she brings up Sebastian.

"He is."

I haven't told her much about him. She doesn't need to know all the things he's said to me. But she knows I don't like him. She knows he's a bad guy. And she knows, too, that if he ever comes into my regular shop when she's at the counter, she needs to find someone else—Kenji or me—to deal with him.

"But thanks to him, I get a pinball room, and a movie theater, and a pool for almost two months," Amanda says.

My sister might be the most adaptable person I've ever known. It comes from the harshest kind of necessity, but she is, after all, forged from the fire.

But perhaps I am too, and maybe I'm not so bad at setting an example of how to step up for your family. "Then later this week let's move into my temporary husband's rich brother's mansion."

31

UNDER ONE CONDITION

Gage

"And in this room, my uncle Zane has a popcorn machine," Eliza says, going full tour guide as she tugs Amanda by the hand down the hallway on the garden level that leads to the home movie theater.

"Dude! No!" Amanda says, her gaze briefly meeting Elodie's as if to say *is this for real?*

"Dude! Yes," Eliza confirms. The kid is practically strutting her way to the room where she's spent many a night convincing Uncle Zane and Maddox to let her watch *just one more*. "And the seats go all the way back. It's pretty much the best."

"We should watch something tonight," Amanda declares. Not *can we* but *we should*. It's a school night— Wednesday now—and we've all brought our suitcases to the palatial three-story in Pacific Heights. Zane bought this place a few years ago when he renewed his contract with the San Francisco Dragons.

Elodie and I hang back in the hall as my daughter shows Amanda into the state-of-the-art home theater, complete with four chairs you can swim in, surround sound, and the aforementioned popcorn maker.

The hallway is adorned with artsy, moody black-and-white photos of London, Tokyo, Prague, and other cosmopolitan cities around the world. Elodie gestures to the framed prints. "No baseball photos? Awards? Trophies?"

I squint, picturing Zane's home gym, which we haven't checked out yet since the girls aren't that interested in bench presses. "Pretty sure those are in the gym. But Eliza would know. She spends a lot of time here," I say.

"I can tell."

"Dad! Can I make popcorn?" Eliza pokes her head out the door, fastening on her *please, pretty please* grin that I know so well. "Amanda says she knows how to make cinnamon popcorn, and I think I might die if I don't have some right now."

"That sounds dramatic," I say dryly.

"It's a need," Eliza insists.

Amanda presses her palms together, batting her big blue eyes. "It's so good. You can have some too, Mr. Archer."

I laugh at the name, but then I stop laughing. What the hell is she supposed to call me? Stepdad? I cringe at the last one. Before I can spiral down that rabbit hole, I say, "Sounds great."

The girls rush past us in a blur of ripped jeans, friendship bracelets, and long hair, racing up the stairs to the gleaming new kitchen, leaving Elodie and me alone.

I turn to the photos again, answering her in more depth. "They like to travel a lot. My brother and Maddox. They take pics of all the places they go. They're in London right now, which is kind of like their second home. They have some friends who spend time there too."

Elodie gazes at the images one by one, softness in her eyes as she slowly checks them all out. The River Thames at night. A tea garden in the afternoon. A castle in Prague, enrobed in fog. "It's like a wall of memories. All their favorite places," she says, and why the hell is my heart beating faster from that?

She's talking about my brother and his dude, and *their* lives.

But really, it's the simple and real understanding of what matters to someone. It's the easy way she sees people and knows their minds. She's a woman who can get along with anyone, even people she's never even met —like my brother.

"I want you to meet him," I say immediately.

"You do?"

"Of course I do," I say, and the idea takes hold of me. I can picture a dinner, a night out, a mini golf game with the four of us. This has to happen. "You already met my grandma. Many times. You need to meet my brother."

"Well, I am playing house in his house," she says,

then furrows her brow. "He really didn't mind us converging on his place?"

I've already reassured her a few times, but I'll do it again. I tuck a strand of blonde hair behind her ear. "It was his idea," I say, reminding her. When I called him Sunday evening to tell him about the wedding and to ask if we could hang out in his empty home while he was traveling, he beat me to it. "He offered it up before I could ask."

"That's family for you," she says.

"He's great," I say, looking around at his gorgeous home. There are five bedrooms, a couple living rooms, a private gym, and a pool. Sure, sometimes I've been jealous of him, especially because we started our adult lives the same way—on the baseball field. But the funny thing is I haven't felt that way lately. Haven't experienced those pangs of envy over the last few years. "Maybe when he returns we can all go out? Have dinner?"

"Isn't that in the new year?"

Translation: we won't be together then. Like we discussed on the way to Vegas a few days ago, our marriage will end when the lease ends. When the year ends. That's in less than two months. For now, we've neutralized the threat to her business and our business.

"Yes," I say darkly, but then I try to shake off that cloud. I drop a kiss to her nose. I don't want to linger on the end. Some topics are best avoided. "Let me show you the rest of the house."

The herd of elephants known as teenage girls race back downstairs on their way to the popcorn machine, with a bowl of, presumably, cinnamon and sugar in hand, and Amanda shouting, "Want some, Mr. Archer?"

Before I answer, I lift a brow Elodie's way. "What should she call me?"

With a *you're so cute* smile, she pats me on the arm. "Your name, Gage. Your name."

Well, duh.

"Call me Gage," I call out. "And maybe later."

"Okay, Gage," she says, and we head upstairs where I show Elodie the pinball room, the rooftop pool, then the bedrooms on the third floor.

Except...

Shit.

As we're standing in front of two guest rooms, I'm kicking myself. This basic detail slipped by me.

Elodie shoots me a curious look. "Are we...sharing a room?"

"That's the question, isn't it?"

We're not lying to the girls about our relationship ruse...but they don't need to know we're *actually* sleeping together.

I drag a hand through my hair, thinking, messing it up. "We should have separate rooms," I say, turning to her. "Since they don't need to know I'm a little addicted to my wife."

She slides into my arms and kisses me. And later that night, when the kids are asleep, I slip into her bed.

We're both quiet as I cover her soft body, kissing her till she's writhing and moaning, arching and gasping, then pushing my head down. "Please," she whispers.

"Please what?"

"Please…go down on me," she says, desperate and needy.

I palm her breasts, teasing at the peaks of her nipples. "I will under one condition."

"Anything," she whimpers.

"Be quiet," I say, even though the house is big and we're not on the same floor as the girls.

"I will."

I settle between her thighs, my hands on her soft flesh, and I lick a long, lingering line up her sweet, hot pussy.

She shudders. Then lets out the neediest little moan as I flick my tongue on her clit, then suck on it.

"Shh, baby."

She nods, then obeys.

Her desperate little noises guide me on, and under the covers, I worship her pussy, kissing her like I'll go crazy if I don't, then stopping right when she's getting close.

"Gage," she urges, tugging my head back.

But I'm a tease tonight, here in the dark as we play house in San Francisco, and I drive my wife a little wild under the covers over and over as I bring her to the brink, then stop. Then do it again.

No, make that *a lot* wild judging from the way she grips my head with her thighs when I finally let her come quietly on my mouth.

In seconds, I flop to my back. She climbs over me, sitting on my dick, and riding me like I'm her bucking bronco.

I think I'm going to enjoy the next several weeks very much.

* * *

The next night, a couple of friends amble up to the bar at Sticks and Stones. Before I can even say a proper hello to the pair of hockey players, the guy with the beard blinks at my wedding band.

"Wait. Let me see *that*." Hayes Armstrong is a long-time friend of mine and a star winger on one of the city's two hockey teams. He's at the bar with the team captain, Stefan Christiansen. They're both married to the same woman—the team mascot. That makes the three of them one of the city's handful of hockey throuples. Something is definitely in the water there in the arenas. Or the ice.

"Oh. This?" I deadpan, showing off my ring, raising my hand for the whole world to see.

"When the fuck did you get married?" Hayes asks.

Stefan rolls his eyes and pats his teammate on the shoulder. "Do you seriously never look at social media?"

Hayes jerks his head to his buddy. "Do I look like I enjoy pointless arguments with strangers along with photos of lunch?"

"Kind of," I joke.

"Also, what does social media have to do with it?" Hayes asks, grabbing a stool and parking his burly frame on it.

Stefan, who is known as The Viking, thanks to his Scandinavian looks, takes the seat next to him then tips his forehead to me. "Gage and Elodie posted their wedding pics on social. Our friend and his bride said *I do* in Vegas last week. And the groom wore...velvet," he adds, in a gossipy TV announcer voice.

"Correction: it was velour," I say, having too much fun with the tale. Well, it was a damn good day in Vegas. Best day I've had with a woman in a good, long time.

"Nothing but top-shelf for our friend," Stefan says.

Hayes is a dog with a bone though. "Can we back it up to you being married? What's up with that?"

Since they were out of town for a long stretch of away games, they haven't been around for more than a week. I glance around the bar, checking for, well, Sebastian and his spies, but seeing only familiar faces. Still, I lean in and lower my voice. "It's an arrangement. We needed to do it for this business thing," I say, explaining a few more details.

"A marriage of convenience," Hayes confirms when I'm done.

"Yes. It is." I run my finger absently over my wedding band.

Hayes chuckles, shaking his head in amusement. "And you gave me a hard time when I accidentally married Ivy in Vegas once upon a time, then told the team owner we were happy newlyweds."

Stefan clears his throat. "Now, now, Hayes. That was you putting your foot in your mouth with the owner when you and Ivy were on the way to get an annulment." Stefan will probably never stop teasing Hayes about how the fake real marriage transpired.

Hayes arches an eyebrow at Stefan. "And we all

enjoyed the benefits of my wife. Now, *our wife.*" He spins his focus back to me. "But also, you gave me a hard time."

I nod, owning it. "I did."

"I guess it's payback time."

"Sure, give me hell about how a smarmy, oily, man threatened her business because she wouldn't sell it to him, and I stepped up and married her to protect our families," I say, *bring it on* style.

Hayes lifts a finger, parts his lips, then says, "Well played, sir. And on that note, I'll take a pale ale."

I turn to Stefan. "Stout for you, Viking?"

"That'd be great."

After I pour their beers and set them down, Hayes shoots me a quizzical look. "But is this really just a business deal? You're into this woman, aren't you?"

More than I ever expected to be. But I'm curious how he figured that out so quickly. "How can you tell?"

Hayes swallows some beer, then sets the glass down. "The way you're showing off your ring. You're proud of it. Proud of her."

Stefan whistles. "Damn, that's some serious emotional intelligence," he says to Hayes.

I'm a little floored myself. I peer down at the gold on my finger, then rub my thumb over it once more. I do like it. I am proud of it. He's not wrong. I meet his gaze. "Yes, but a deal's a deal."

I have to say it for myself more than them. To remind myself that we made a business deal. To grow Sticks and Stones. To help Elodie's Chocolates. To gain financial security for our kids. We're just two single parents trying to stay ahead.

The other reminders come all night in a packed bar. Business has been slowly but steadily picking up since Elodie and I opened Special Edition a couple weeks ago. I can't complain about the increase in revenue.

And I can't complain about the email that arrives from Celeste the next time I check my phone. It's short and to the point.

I am impressed with Special Edition. Keep it up.

I can't wait to tell Elodie. When I head home a little later, eager to sneak into bed and let her know, I pass The Chocolate Connoisseur on the way.

A new sign in the window reads *Half Off Everything*.

I groan. That guy can't leave well enough alone.

32

POP-UP HUSBAND

Elodie

It's a spicy kind of evening at Special Edition, since that's our theme for this weekend.

Gage serves a jalapeño margarita along with a firecracker strawberry daiquiri.

"Oh! What's bringing the heat?" a woman in rose-gold glasses asks as she takes a drink of the pretty red cocktail with the kick.

"Cayenne pepper," he says proudly from behind the counter.

"Bring it on," the woman says, then heads to a table with her friends. As they drink, they snap pictures of their reactions—a lot of hands flapping in front of faces and *oh-oh-ohs* moaned loudly.

"It's the universal code for I drank something fiery or I'm feeling really, really good," I say to Gage, feeling saucy tonight.

I guess good sex every day will do that to you. Every night too. Living with this man just has its perks. But there's no time to linger in sex memories when I've got a line of customers eager for my contributions to our fiery Friday night menu.

I plate some of my cinnamon and cayenne pepper truffles for a pair of couples on a double date, I suspect, telling them, "Enjoy the heat."

"We will," one of the women says.

When there's a brief break in the line, I turn to my… *husband*. I'm still getting used to that term. *Temporary husband*, I remind myself.

Like this shop is temporary. A pop-up shop and a pop-up husband. I grin.

Gage swipes a thumb across my bottom lip. "What's that smile for?" He dips his voice. "You thinking of how I woke you up this morning?"

Electricity sparks down my spine. This man and his appetite. Well, it matches mine.

"Maybe," I tease, remembering the sun peeking through the window, his arm roped around me, his fingers trailing along my belly. Then, in my still sleepy state, I pushed his hand between my thighs. It was a very good morning, even though we had to hustle out of bed before the kids woke up. "Or maybe I was actually thinking, you're just like this shop."

His brow knits in confusion for a few seconds, then understanding. "Thank you. I am spicy," he says proudly.

I shake my head. "You're a pop-up husband, I mean."

I expect him to laugh, but his expression is blank for

a moment. Unreadable. Then he offers a smile that feels like a cover-up. "That's me," he says, then turns to help an older man at the counter. "What can I help you with, sir?"

I paste on my shop owner smile too, but the vibe between us feels weird now as we wait on a new rush of customers.

Why did I blurt that out? Did I say the wrong thing? I was only trying to make a joke. To keep things light.

My mind clatters with worry for the next twenty minutes as I serve trays of spicy treats and Gage mixes drinks.

But an approving whistle pulls me from my dark thoughts, and I turn to see the face of…a rock star.

In. Our. Store.

Ethan Adair is here, and my mouth is a fish's. I'm all agape at the sight of the front man for Outrageous Record two feet across from me.

With inked arms and soulful eyes, Ethan's become a heartthrob, and he has the talent to back it up. His band has skyrocketed to stardom in the last few years. The woman by his side is the drummer for the band, and I'm pretty sure they're a couple.

"Everything looks good," he says to her. Tess, I think.

"Because you like it hot," she teases, nudging his shoulder with hers.

"You know I do," he says, then flashes warm eyes at me. "Hey there. Couldn't resist checking out this shop when we heard about it on social."

"Hi," I say, a little breathy, eager to profess my adoration. "I love…welcome to Special Edition."

And fangirling almost got the better of me. But he probably wants to just grab a drink like a normal guy.

Gage shoots me a curious look, maybe wondering what's up. But now's not the time for me to whisper *there's a rock star here. Two, actually.*

Ethan surveys the menu with the chocolate offerings. "Apricot and chili pepper, enrobed in Aztec chocolate—sounds like my dreams."

"Chef's recommendation. You should try it," I say.

"I'll have that and the whole flight of chocolate," he says, then turns to his girlfriend. "And you?"

"Make it a double. And let's get one of each drink and we can do a taste test," she says, and quickly, we serve them.

As the cool and beautiful couple take their trays and drinks to a corner table, every single phone in the house lifts and snaps.

Gage tilts his head, whispers out of the side of his mouth, "Who's that?"

God, he's cute, not knowing. "The front man for Outrageous Record, and the drummer," I whisper surreptitiously.

His eyes widen then swing to the couple in leather and ink, then back to me. "Damn. Their songs are good."

I set a hand on his strong chest, smiling. "I'm relieved you know their music at least."

"Know them. Love them," he says, and he's a little starstruck. And that's cute too.

I let go of my worries about my pop-up husband comment.

For now.

* * *

After we close, I check my phone and it's lit up. As I
wipe down tables, I read my texts, going to the group
chat with the girls first.

> Juliet: Why did you not get him to sing
> "Blown Away" in your shop?

> Fable: Or better yet, write you a song! I
> can hear it now. "You Melt In My
> Mouth!" "You Make Me Moan!" "You Are
> My Truffle!"

> Rachel: Ladies and gentlemen, Fable
> has a new career as a songwriter. Watch
> it, Taylor.

> Fable: Please. We're gonna duet "You
> Are My Truffle."

> Juliet: And you can debut it tomorrow
> night at the Outrageous Record concert
> in town.

> Hazel: Wait, wait. What if we all go and
> beg him to write a song called "Pop-Up
> Love?"

I'm laughing as Gage cleans the glasses, asking,
"What's going on?"

"Apparently everyone posted that Ethan Adair was
here with his girlfriend," I say, bringing him my phone,
showing him some of the pics of the rockers on social,
then the texts from the girls.

He reads them quietly, and when he's done, he says,
"That's cute. Your messages with your friends."

Huh. I didn't expect that warm reaction. I thought he

was still irked about the pop-up husband comment for some reason. And you know what? If he is, I want to know. I set a hand on his forearm, covering his lotus ink with my palm. "Hey, are you annoyed about the pop-up joke?"

He takes a breath, and for a second I think he's going to lie. But instead, he says, "I was. But I don't even know why." He gives a *no idea* shrug.

My heart races with worry. This is why relationships are scary. When you start to care, you can start to hurt each other. If he sees the real me, the less than flirty, less than fun, less than bright and bubbly me, will he still like me? But it's too late for that question. I'm already barreling down the real path. "I'm sorry. I sort of blurted it out without thinking."

"Don't be," he says, exonerating me. "It was short-lived."

I grab the front of his shirt, tugging him closer. "I don't want to hurt you."

He drops a kiss to my nose. "We're all good. I promise."

I feel calmer. "Was that like a mini fight?"

His green eyes flicker with dirty thoughts. "No, but we can have make-up sex anyway if you want."

"You know I do," I say, and I'm glad we're good, though I don't understand why it bothered him.

But this time, I have to let it go for real. I'm his temporary wife, not his real wife. I don't need to push him.

* * *

The next morning, as I'm sliding my fork through the delicious pancakes Gage made, Eliza clears her throat. "Attention! Today is the monthly beach cleanup with the Oceans Are Cool crew. Are you in or are you in?"

Over a cup of black coffee, Gage gives a decisive nod, then lifts a hand. "In."

Amanda yawns as she shuffles past me, sniffing the pancakes. "What's that?"

"Pancakes," Eliza says matter-of-factly.

"No, I mean the beach thing."

"It's a volunteer thing I do. Because plastic sucks, and it's everywhere, and it hurts the ocean and animals," Eliza says.

Amanda perks up. "Ooh, I hate plastic too. I'm there."

That leaves me and it's a no-brainer. "Count me in."

Thirty minutes later, we pile into my little car and head to the ocean, passing one of Sebastian's shops along the way. I spot the *half off* sign that Gage told me about the other night. "That guy," I mutter.

"He's my mortal enemy," Amanda seethes from the back seat.

I peer into the rearview mirror. "Is that so?"

"His chocolate isn't even that good. I've tried it," she says.

"It's not as good as Elodie's that's for sure," Gage seconds and I love their support, from their mouths and their stomachs.

"Nothing is, except for cookies," Eliza says, and we shift to cookie talk and that's far better than Sebastian chatter.

* * *

Early that afternoon, the Pacific is crashing gently against the shore and we've collected eighty-eight bottles, twenty-two cans, a couple dozen plastic forks, an empty can of chickpeas, an unopened can of chickpeas, a set of rusty fur-lined handcuffs, and a metric ton of takeout containers.

And a used condom.

I found that one next to a rock, gingerly plucking it with my gloves and trying not to gag as I tossed it in the trash bag. When we're done, Eliza dusts one covered hand over the other then tugs off her racoon gloves. "Good job, team."

She's such a cute kind of bossy. Like father, like daughter, I suppose.

"We're basically a turtle's best friend now," Amanda says, then her stomach growls loudly.

I crack up. So does Gage.

Amanda clutches her belly as a sea breeze whips through her blonde hair, making wisps flutter near her face. "I guess beach cleanups make me hungry."

Gage hums thoughtfully, staring away from the shoreline toward the businesses lining the beach. "There's a great vegetarian sandwich shop here in the Outer Sunset. We could get a late lunch before Elodie and I have to leave for work."

My. Heart.

It's thumping so hard. We've had a couple meals together as a foursome and they were accidentally vegetarian—pasta primavera and mushroom risotto. But I've only mentioned Amanda's food preferences once—to his grandmother the first night of the pop-up shop.

And he remembered.

"Say less," Amanda says, and we're off for a family lunch.

I mean, a temporary family lunch.

Over sandwiches, Amanda asks about the menu tonight, and we tell her what we'll be serving. "I wish we could go with you. I like serving chocolate," she says wistfully, and I flash back to her comments from last week about how she enjoys helping in the store.

"I wish you could too, bug."

When we're done, we take them back to Zane's house, where Gage's grandma is waiting with cookie supplies and time.

Lucky Grandma.

* * *

That night, Amanda's comments play on a loop as we work.

I wish we could go with you.

The hotel staff set up tables in the courtyard and we've hired some temp workers to help us serve, thanks to the influx of crowds from the chocolate viral video and the rockers' pics.

It's another busy night. When we close, we've exhausted our supply of extra jalapeños and chocolate, but I haven't exhausted my brainpower. I'm still thinking about possibilities when Felix raps on the glass door.

Smiling, naturally.

It's the first time we've seen him since the wedding. He's been out of town for business this past week, though he congratulated us online.

Gage unlocks the door and lets him in.

"The Mr. and Mrs." Felix beams, and the man couldn't be happier we're hitched. You'd think he was a matchmaker or something and we were his prize clients. "You must have really wanted to get married."

"We sure did," Gage says, upbeat and telling the truth, though leaving out a crucial detail. *We have an enemy who wanted to tell you that we've been lying to you.*

My stomach twists. The fact that Gage and I legit like each other is irrelevant. We lied, bold and bald-faced, to snag this coveted property.

And we're raking in the business thanks to trendsetters coming here.

"We did," I echo but I feel hollow. Guilty. Gage squeezes my waist, maybe a sign for me to perk up.

Felix strokes his beard, his eyes twinkling. "I wouldn't mind if you wanted to add another day. Maybe Sunday?"

I grimace privately, but before we can answer, his phone rings.

"Be right back," he says.

As Felix steps into the courtyard, I turn to Gage with some hesitation over adding a day.

I'm relieved his expression matches mine.

Uncertainty.

It's written all over his face.

"I don't want to take time away from…the girls," I confess.

"Same here," he says and I'm so grateful to be on the same page.

"But I have another idea." It starts as a kernel but quickly, a few minutes later, it's fully formed.

* * *

The next Sunday, we're in the shop with the girls in their aprons for the Sunday Special Edition: Hot Cocoa and Grandma's Chocolate Chip Cookies.

And it's open to families.

33

SOMETHING, SOMEONE

Gage

Over the next few weeks, we fall into a surprisingly easy routine. School, the occasional fall softball practice, taking Amanda to ceramics class and Eliza to karate. The four of us spend Thanksgiving together, eating at Grams' house and having too much food and too much fun. Amanda is right—the sides are the best part.

So are dinners at our so-called vacation home when I'm not at the bar.

And I'm not always at the bar.

Sticks and Stones is busier than it was before—a lot busier thanks to the word of mouth from Special Edition—but I'm able to hire a couple new servers and an extra bartender, while Zoe and Grams handle managing the place when I'm not around.

Like, when I'm having dinner with the women in my life. *My temporary life.*

I try not to think about the looming end date too much because *this*—life as I know it—is too good.

One morning in December, I wake up next to Elodie in the early dawn, the sky still inky dark, the stars still winking. After slipping out of bed early, I head to my room to pull on running shorts and a long-sleeve shirt. Late fall in San Francisco is never too cold. I'm about to pad out of here quietly but something pulls me back to Elodie's room.

Something.

Please.

More like someone. Someone I'm addicted to. Someone I can't resist.

Elodie's curled up under the white duvet looking devilishly angelic with her blonde hair spilled across the pillow, all mussed up from sex last night. I head to her, dropping a kiss to her cheek, murmuring devotions against her skin. "Thanks for taking Eliza to school," I say.

"I haven't seen you run since that first night at the shop," she muses. "When you took off for chocolate."

"I work out, *woman*."

She turns toward me, smiles sleepily, eyes roaming up and down. "I'm aware of that. It's just usually at the gym."

There's a gym right next to the bar, and I try to get in quick workouts before work though sometimes I work out in my brother's gym. But today I'm taking off for a rare morning run with a friend. I need to meet Monroe in twenty minutes.

"I appreciate you letting me get this time now," I say

sincerely since she's taking them to school, and that's how I have time to run with a friend. It's a gift to have a little help with parenting.

I come in for one more kiss before I go. As I brush my lips to hers, I catch the taste of her breath—minty fresh. "Did you brush your teeth?"

I know what this means. She loves morning sex but hates morning breath.

She just smiles wickedly my way.

"Fuck," I groan, then glance at the time. Monroe's house is ten minutes away.

"It's okay. I have toys," she says, a teasing note in her voice, and a delicious image lodged in my brain now. Elodie fucking herself with a dildo.

My nostrils flare. "I'm your fucking toy."

She casts her gaze down to my shorts. "Then use that toy on me."

In a nanosecond, I shed my clothes, climb into bed, and slide a hand between her thighs. Silky paradise. "Baby, were you playing with yourself when I was getting dressed?"

She rocks up into my fingers, so eager, so ready, "I was. I want you."

My chest rumbles. "My wife is so fucking horny."

She gasps, parting her lips, her head falling back onto the pillow.

"You love it when I call you that," I observe, stroking her as she turns wetter and hotter. I dip my face to her neck, murmuring up to her ear, whispering hotly, "*My wife.*"

"I do like it," she says, arching her hips, seeking more of my fingers. "Do you like calling me that?"

This is just a game. A word game. A sex game. And still, I play it, taking her hand and curling it around my cock. I'm steel right now. "That's how much I like it."

"Gage," she moans. "Fuck me."

I can't deny her. I love teasing her hot, wet pussy with my fingers. Driving her wild with my touch. But I relent, giving in to her gorgeous demand.

I let go of her then smack the side of her ass. "Get on all fours like a good wife."

With a naughty grin, she gazes at me from under her blonde hair, then shifts to her hands and knees. Taking her time. Getting in position.

"Is this how you want me?" she asks, so innocent, and yet not at all as she offers me her beautiful body.

Back arched. Ass up. Hungry eyes on me.

Dear god. She's fucking incredible. All soft and warm, aroused and eager. As I kneel behind her, I run a hand down her body. My fingers are electric from touching her. "Just. Like. This."

I rub the head of my dick against her slick heat, then sink inside.

"Oh god," she gasps, then thrusts a hand between her thighs.

Holy fuck. She's so damn ready.

Before I can even fill her to the hilt, she's stroking herself feverishly, using me to get off, and I can barely stand how good this feels.

The heat of her pussy.

The smell of her desire.

The strength of her want.

I drive into her, gripping her hips mercilessly as she plays with herself, getting closer and closer then arching her back.

Soon, she's groaning, almost too loud. "Quiet, baby," I warn.

But she can't seem to help herself. She can't stop moaning. I slide one hand up her chest, coasting over those bouncing tits, up her throat, then I cover her mouth.

Her breath stutters against my palm before she mutters a strangled "coming."

Seconds later, I am too, the morning blurring into pleasure, then I collapse onto her, holding her close, wrapping her in my arms.

Her heart beats against my hands. It's addictive. Just like her. I don't want to leave.

"You need to go," she whispers.

"I know," I say reluctantly.

But first, I head into the en suite bathroom, grab a washcloth, and return to clean her up. When I'm done, I kiss her goodbye. "Thanks again," I say.

She knows I don't mean the sex. She knows I mean the early morning run with a friend. Something I haven't done since I was in the majors. "Anytime," she says, and I feel a pang of missing.

For the *anytime* with us that won't happen, even though I almost, *almost* believe that it could.

I go, sliding into sneakers then leaving my brother's house and this perfect morning behind. Once outside, I pick up the pace and sprint a couple blocks to Monroe's home. I make up the minutes lost. He's exiting right as I'm arriving, and he hits the ground running with a crisp nod.

Together, we run toward the Golden Gate Bridge. "We haven't done a morning run in a long time," he says.

"I know. Elodie is taking the girls to school," I explain.

He shoots me a curious look. "Aren't you domestic?"

I flash back over the last few weeks. We've been busy, yes. But we've made time for dinners together. For mac and cheese, for couscous and cauliflower, for salads and pasta dishes, for rice and beans and Thai noodles. "Eliza has started eating just like Amanda," I tell him. "Vegetarian too."

"So the girls' habits are rubbing off on each other."

"They're scarily alike," I say, picturing the way the girls interact. "Amanda's into pottery. She's so talented she made me a vase for the bar and I filled it with some fall lilies, and now people are asking where to get it. She applied to art school and should find out soon. But I know she'll get in. She's that good."

Monroe arches a brow as we near the bridge. "That's impressive."

"Art school. I know," I say, pride rushing through my bones.

"I meant you knowing all the details about Elodie's little sister," he corrects with the thoughtful cadence of a shrink since, well, he is one.

"It is?"

"You care about her," he observes.

"No shit. She's a good kid. She likes Eliza, and she's

got this fierce attitude about the world and women. She loves board games and art and rolling her eyes and hanging out with her friends, and she has strong opinions but a tender heart."

"That last one sounds like your wife."

I slow my pace as we near the bridge, absorbing that observation for a moment. "That's true. They have a lot in common," I say, maybe smiling, maybe sounding a little hooked. Or a lot. "This run with you this morning —it was Elodie's idea," I say, giving him more insight into *why* I'm able to run with him.

"And you're letting this woman get away at the end of the year?" he says.

It's like a punch in the gut—the reminder of the end of the year.

"I can't keep her just because she helps out with the kids...I mean, my kid."

"But it sounds like you meant kids plural." That's the problem with having a therapist as a friend. They can read between the lines far too well.

"Look, it's nice, all right? There. Are you happy?"

"Aww, was it hard for you to admit your feelings?"

"Nope. It's more than nice. It's great," I say easily, just to prove I can talk about my emotions, even if they're going nowhere. But I don't want to spend too much time on things I can't have so I take a detour. "Business is going great."

I barely want to breathe this out loud, but I'm finally feeling like the security I've been seeking is in my grasp. "I've got a meeting with Celeste later in the month about the second location. I still need to make sure my ideas for her are amazing."

The truth is I haven't really added any marketing ideas beyond the fairy lights. Beyond the games. I probably should. I *definitely* should. But I've been having too much fun with the girls and with the woman in my brother's house to think about more than them.

"I'm sure you'll impress her," Monroe says as we reach the mouth of the bridge, weaving past other morning warriors as we run through the fog. "And all I can say is this domestic life is treating you well."

It is. But soon it won't. Soon it'll end. A weight sinks in my gut. I don't want to think about the end of the year. "What about you? What about the crush you've had on your fellow podcaster for years?" I ask, turning the convo back on him.

Monroe's brow knits, like I've tossed him a math problem he can't untangle. "I don't know what you're talking about."

"Juliet. I listen to the two of you. You have that frenemies vibe," I say.

"You listen to me. That's so sweet."

"Don't change the subject," I say.

"Don't *you* change the subject. What are you going to do at the end of this year, Gage?"

There it is again. The inevitable end. The end we've always been moving toward since before we were married. Since we were just fake fiancés.

But it's an end I want less and less each day.

I drag a hand through my hair as my lungs work hard, my breath coming fast.

The end of the year is the expiration date I don't want to face. "I'll figure it out," I say as casually as I can. "There's a lot happening before then. In a week I'll be taking a trip with Eliza when she finishes the semester. I always take her to Darling Springs for the night. She loves it there."

Monroe shudders at the mention of the small town along the coast.

"Come on. Your hometown isn't that bad," I say.

"Maybe," he grumbles.

But as I think about the annual trip, for the first time I feel like something is missing. Or maybe *someone*.

I run harder, faster through the fog on the bridge, and as I peel off the miles I start to wonder—what if we don't end? And what can I do to romance my wife before time runs out?

34

THE MESSY ME

Elodie

I walk Amanda and Eliza to school, and the girls do what girls often do—speak in their own language with acronyms and *did you see this*, and *I have to show you that*. Eliza is telling Amanda she can teach her to make soap, which leads to them bent over phones, watching time-lapse soap-making videos, then Amanda tells Eliza she can take her to the pottery studio again that afternoon, then Eliza asks if she's heard from the art school.

"Just a few more days," Amanda says, and I can tell she's trying to be stoic but she's barely hiding real nerves.

"I can't wait to celebrate," Eliza says, ever the cheerleader.

Amanda's school comes first, so I wave goodbye to her—hugs are verboten—and then I echo, "Just a few more days."

She offers a hopeful smile, then says to Eliza, "Ally and I are getting boba after school. Want to come with us?"

Eliza says yes so fast.

Over the next eight blocks, Eliza's a chatterbox. I barely get a word in edgewise, but I don't need to since she's rolling on, telling me about a new TV show she found to stream, then how someone in her class got a hedgehog and named it Gary, and then there's a new glove she wants for softball, and before we know it, we're at her school.

I offer to take them again the next day so Gage can run with his friend a second time, and it's chillier today. We look up at the swollen clouds in the sky. "Do you think it'll snow?" I ask.

"That would be so cool," Amanda says.

"We could have a snowball fight," Eliza says.

"Or make snow angels," Amanda suggests.

"Or more hot cocoa and warm up by the fire," I offer.

"Yes! I swear I am not tired of hot cocoa even after Sundays," Eliza says.

"Facts," Amanda agrees.

Once we drop off Amanda, Eliza rappels right into another conversation, screw the preamble. "I want to learn to make chocolate too. Like Amanda. Does she make chocolate or is that just you? And where do you make the chocolate? Do you have a chocolate factory in your store?"

I laugh, shaking my head. "My store's small batch. We make everything in house in the back of the shop.

I'm not big enough to have a factory. That's for bigger shops, like—"

Eliza growls, curling her little fingers into claws. "Like our mortal enemy's."

"Yes," I say, but I'm really trying not to linger on that guy. Besides the bargain basement sales and the clear copycatting, Sebastian's been relatively quiet in recent weeks. He hasn't come by my store or the pop-up shop. It's been peaceful to have him out of my life. When he slithered into my shop that day, I tried so hard to be calm as he spewed trashy words. Like when I had to be the steady, stable one when my parents came home drunk. Often, it was a relief when they ignored me as a kid. I feel like that with Sebastian now, grateful to be ignored at last.

"But enough about him," I say to Eliza. "Why don't you tell me why you started doing the beach cleanups? I'm more interested in you."

With wide eyes and the confidence of a fearless eleven-year-old, she shares the things she's learning in school about the oceans and marine life and plastic, and how she just wants to make the world better by doing her part.

"You have a good heart. You're a lot like your dad and your grandma."

Her green eyes look up at me, like she's wrestling with something, then she pins it. "I really liked Kylie, but I like you better. She never asked me all these questions. She was fun and everything, but it's more fun talking to you. Does that make sense?"

That last question is such a thing people say these

days when they're uncertain. Eliza's hardly ever unsure. Gage has spoken broadly to me about his past relationships before. Rather than lingering on the differences between Kylie and me—since, really, they aren't *that* important—I focus on giving her what she needs.

Reassurance.

"I like listening to you," I say genuinely, even as my heart aches for the future. Come January will I even have the opportunity to listen to her stories? To wonder about the bright and curious mind of this young person? My heart climbs into my throat as I curl a hand over her shoulder and squeeze it. "Now, have a good day at school and come home and tell me more stories."

"I will."

She heads inside, and since I'm not due at my shop for a couple hours, I walk back to Zane's home, logging into my banking app as I go. A warm, glowy feeling spreads in my chest as I see the loan balance shrink more and more each day.

I made *this* happen. All by myself. With no role model, no guidance, no handbook.

Though I didn't do it alone. I did it with a partner. I wouldn't have seen the uptick in business without Gage.

That fizzy feeling expands as I reach the house and head inside, following the clink of a ceramic mug against the counter, then the glug of coffee being poured.

My heart thumps harder, as I head into the kitchen. There he is at the counter, holding a spoon over a mug. Pouring his coffee probably. His dark hair is wet, slicked back, the ends curling up at the back of his neck. He's freshly showered from his run, wearing jeans and a gray T-shirt. He's so handsome, my chest hurts.

Immediately, I want to know everything about him. All the things I don't know. Like his favorite book, if he still longs to play baseball, what his next tattoo would be, and why he makes soap. Why didn't I ever ask him these things before?

I need to know them. *Now.* I need to discover every detail of Gage before time runs out.

I walk right up to him from behind, wrap my arms around his waist and rest my head against the back of his shoulder, inhaling the clean, soapy scent of his neck.

Setting down the mug and spoon, he spins around, catching my mouth with his.

A soft kiss that makes my knees weak.

Strong hands wrap around my hips.

Bright eyes look into my soul.

My heart stutters.

I want to know, too, if he likes the real me, the messy me, the me that's not the happy-go-lucky, flirty, dirty girl he met at Sticks and Stones. The one who had to pick up the pieces after her parents died, and take out a loan, and raise a kid with no handbook.

"What's your favorite book?" I ask impulsively.

His lips crook up in a lopsided grin. "*The Joy of Sex.*"

I swat his chest. "For real."

"That's a trick question."

"How is it a trick question?"

He lets go of me, then answers. "If I say something literary, I sound like a douche. If I say something by a dead white guy, I sound patriarchal. If I pick something by a celebrity, I sound star-obsessed."

"Are those your favorites?"

"No," he says with that familiar twinkle in his eyes.

"Then why don't you just tell me your favorite book?" This is important. I need to know him.

"The truth? The one I'm currently reading," he says, and honestly that's a pretty good answer. He reaches for his mug and I expect him to take a sip, but instead he hands it to me.

"I don't like—" I swallow the word coffee because it's a vanilla latte.

"I know," he says with a smile. "I made you a vanilla latte. Just the way you like it. With two shots of vanilla and extra foam."

Oh. My chest warms, a little tingly now. He was making a drink for me. Like we're having a coffee date. He picks up a cup of coffee. He must have poured that before I came in.

I take a drink and my taste buds dance. "Stop making such great lattes," I tease.

"Not likely to happen," he says, then takes a swallow of his coffee. "And you? What's your favorite book?"

"The next one my friend Hazel writes."

"Good answer," he says with a chin nod.

"Do you miss baseball?"

He pauses, giving that some thought before he nods. "I do. But I think I always will. And I'm okay with that. I loved it madly as a kid, as a teenager, then in college. It was my whole entire heart growing up and it's gone." He gives a wistful shrug. "But at least I got to play. And I played at the highest level—one year in the majors is nothing to sneeze at."

"One year is amazing. And it was an incredible season," I say, since I researched his stats. "I even saw some of your videos on YouTube."

His grin is nothing short of magical. "You did?"

"I looked you up. Watched some clips of you on the mound. You were ice."

Impossibly, his grin grows even wider. "Best compliment ever."

"You looked good. You looked great," I say.

"It was a good year. I try to remember that. I achieved my dream."

"You did." I hesitate but ask the next question anyway. "Is it hard watching your brother play?"

Without a second thought, he shakes his head. "It's one of my favorite things. I love rooting him on. You really need to see him play. We should go to a game."

He doesn't say *next season*. But I flash back to when we first moved into this house a few weeks ago. He said he wanted me to meet his brother, and right now it's all I want. This time I answer him a little differently. "We should."

It's not quite a promise. More like a hope.

"What about you?" he asks. "Do you miss...your parents?" It's said so gently, without any judgment in case the answer might be no.

"I wish I missed them more," I say, sadly.

He runs a hand down my arm. "I understand. I do." He lifts his cup again and swallows, then meeting my eyes, like he's trying to figure me out, he says, "You're awfully curious today."

"I had a nice chat with Eliza this morning," I admit, then take another drink of the latte.

He lifts one brow, inviting me to say more. "What did Miss Chatterbox talk about? She's been telling me how much she wants a snow day. She's never had one."

"She mentioned that to me too. Amanda hasn't either. But she also…" Should I mention Kylie? Gage and I haven't really talked about exes in detail. But I *am* intrigued by her comment. Kids see things we don't. "Eliza said that she liked the way I listened and *maybe* she compared me to somebody else who she didn't think listened as well," I say, but once the words land, I wish I could take them back. Comparison is the thief of joy. I wave a dismissive hand. "Ignore me. I sound like I'm fishing for compliments."

I take another drink of the latte, not only because it's good but maybe to hide my face.

When I set down the cup, Gage links our fingers together. "You don't sound that way. But you deserve compliments. And the truth." He pauses, then continues, "Kylie was my last real relationship. We were together for a year and she was fun and outgoing, but Eliza's right. Kylie was a little caught up in herself. She was in love with her career. She got a job in New York and she left. That was that." With a thoughtful sigh, he scrubs a hand across his jaw. "But maybe I was caught up in myself too—at least caught up in my own obsessions about the future."

The Gage picture is becoming even clearer. "That's

why you think things don't work out. From baseball, to marriage, to romance."

"Way to see inside my soul," he says dryly.

"I just want to know you," I say feeling desperate, feeling ravenous. I look at the clock on the wall. I need to go to work soon. Time is running out. This temporary marriage is like a rich, decadent chocolate bar that makes me feel *all the things*, and I'm not going to leave a single piece of it in the wrapper. "When we went to Vegas you were thinking about the first time you got married," I begin, returning to something that's stayed with me.

"I was," he admits, studying me, waiting for me to say more.

"And you said you were sure of *this*." I drop our hands, gesture from him to me. "What we were doing." I pause before I ask the hard thing. "Were you not sure of things with Hailey?"

His sigh is heavy, full of the weight of sadness. He leaves his coffee on the counter. With a hand on my back, he guides me to the table, sits me down, gathers my hands in his. "We got married because of the pregnancy. Did I love her? Probably. But we weren't a great fit. That became clearer as we went on...and when it ended," he says, then stops.

I'm on the edge of my seat.

He lifts his chin, like he's girding himself. "She'd asked for a divorce."

My jaw falls open. I'm frozen. A statue. Finally, I whisper, "I had no idea."

"I've never told this to anyone except my therapist.

She was really struggling, Elodie. She was never diagnosed but I suspect she suffered from postpartum depression. She was giving me primary custody of Eliza. She said she needed some time alone to sort out her thoughts. And when she went away on a trip—just for herself, something she needed—that's when she died all of a sudden. And I never told her parents what had been going on. The custody, the separation. I never told anyone."

My throat tightens, like a hand is gripping it. My eyes sting with tears. "Oh, Gage. You've carried all that for a decade?"

"I had to. What choice did I have?" He leans back, eyes flickering with the shame of secrets. "But people treated me like I was this noble widower and that was awful in its own way too. Truth is, I didn't want her family to know or to think differently of her. She had an aneurysm. It was unpredictable. It was unexpected. She was so young, and I felt confident that even after we divorced, she'd have realized that she still wanted to be a mom. That she'd have become involved again with Eliza. She just didn't live long enough to make that choice," he says, and his voice is rough, full of hurt for the mother his daughter will never know.

Tears trickle down my face. His protective streak is so much deeper than I could ever have imagined. "You were protecting Hailey after her death. You were preserving a memory for her family."

"And for my daughter," he says quietly, that guilt resurfacing. "So I lied."

No. No. No!

I shake my head, firm, adamant. Holding his hands tighter. "It wasn't a lie. It was a gift," I say, fiercely. "Her family didn't need to know she was trying to find herself. It's okay that you kept her secret. It's an act of love. An act of protection. It doesn't mean she wasn't a good person or a good mom. It just means she was in a really hard place," I say, this close to breaking apart. But this isn't my story to wallow in. It's his hurt, his pain, and all I want is to help him see he doesn't have to carry it. "And you helped her after death. And your little girl."

He lifts a hand, swipes the tears from my cheek. "I hate to see you cry, baby…but I kind of love it too," he says, almost sheepish as his eyes well with tears.

"Why do you love it?" I ask, laughing lightly.

He presses a palm to my chest, covering my heart. "Because I like your heart. You have the biggest heart I've ever known."

And I let go of a fear I've been carrying. "I was worried for a long time that you wouldn't like the real me," I say, and it's my turn to be relieved.

"What? Seriously?"

"The messy me," I add with a shrug.

"I like all of you, messy and wild and even with morning breath," he says.

"Do not ever speak of such horrid things."

"But I will. I like you when you wake up, and when you fall asleep, and when you're frustrated, and when you're worried, and when you need a hug. I like you when you're upbeat and flirty and outgoing. And I like you when you're honest and open."

My feet aren't touching the floor. I'm sure I must be

floating. He clears his throat, his gaze vulnerable, like it costs him something to say the next thing. "Have you been in love before?"

Right now I think I am.

"Not *before*," I say carefully, then since he likes the real me, I don't hide my romantic heart this time. I open up to him, flinging open the windows on a sunny day. "But I like romance. That's why I liked your proposal so much by Cupid's Span. That's sort of what I always imagined someday. Someone who was wildly romantic and who wanted only me. And I was always drawn to men who seemed romantic. Who made big gestures of flowers and wine and weekends away." I lock eyes with Gage, my heart beating like a hummingbird. "But never anything like marrying me to protect me."

He lifts his chin, a proud and deservedly so smile on his face. "Maybe that makes me the almost romantic." He kisses my cheek, kissing away the remnants of my tears.

"Or more than romantic," I posit as he pulls back.

"Perhaps I am." Another kiss. Another embrace. Another stroke of his hand along my hair.

I'm shimmering under my skin. I'm about to ask if he wants to do this again the next day. But he beats me to it. "Want to meet again tomorrow like this? A secret date in the morning? Just you and me?"

And now I'm glowing. "Yes. I can take the girls to school. You can run. We can meet back here before work."

"Yes. We can." He runs his knuckles down my cheek. "My more than romantic wife."

Yes, I'm definitely floating. Or perhaps, falling.

Trouble is, the landing is going to hurt so much. Especially when he sends a bouquet of yellow roses to my chocolate shop that afternoon.

And a note with the words, *Like the ones you carried down the aisle.*

35

THE MAESTRO

Elodie

The next morning, the girls make plans to have boba after school again, this time with Margo, before they come to my shop. I say yes, then after I drop off Eliza, I'm doing math in my head. Calculating when Gage will return from his run. How much time I have.

Just enough.

I'm compelled. Utterly compelled. I'm not even sure why specifically, but there's something I want badly for our secret date.

And I want it now.

Picking up the pace, I race walk the final blocks to Zane's house, fingers crossed. When I unlock the door, I check the foyer for the sign of running shoes just shed. Nope. He must still be pounding the pavement in his sneakers.

I kick off my shoes.

Rushing upstairs, I head to my room, strip out of my exercise pants, then shimmy into a black bustier and matching lace panties.

I hustle over to the nightstand, grab a friend, then lie back on the covers. I click on my favorite site, finding a video I bookmarked a while ago. One that just gets the job done.

I get myself in the mood.

A few minutes later, the door snicks open.

I smile mischievously.

I shift to my side, my back to the door, the phone propped against a pillow. The woman in the video does the same, her hand playing the role of the vibrator, coasting down her curves and over her breasts, then settling between her thighs.

With her first throaty moan, I tremble too, picturing what's to come as I rub the toy against my panties.

On the screen a man arrives in the doorway, leans his forearm against it, watches her.

My breath catches.

I turn the toy up a level, brushing it against the dampening lace, over my clit. The man stares at her for a few hungry seconds, unbeknownst to her. She startles, but not for long. She turns to him, a come-hither look in her eyes.

My pulse surges as the man on the screen stalks into the room. Then it speeds even faster when Gage calls out, "Hey, baby."

My eyes flutter closed from the nickname.

"Upstairs," I call out, a little raspy already.

His footfalls echo on the steps as adrenaline spins higher in me, as my fantasy meets my reality.

Gage has no idea what's in store for him. Just like I had no idea what was in store for me that morning at Cupid's Span. I'm returning the favor. A thrill rushes through me knowing how much he'll like his surprise.

Opening my eyes, I rub the head of the toy cock right where I want it, arousal spiking in me.

His footsteps grow louder. He's almost here. I rub a little faster, more urgently. Then he stops and a low, appreciative groan rumbles across the bedroom. "Best day ever."

I smile wide and pleased, but I don't turn to him yet. I keep playing with myself as he stalks over to the side of the bed behind me.

"Fuck, baby. You're so fucking sexy. Is this what you were doing when you would text me at night?"

Shuddering from the heat of his words, I nod, keeping up the rhythm. "Yes," I say, and then I shift to my back, and meet his gaze. He looks rabid. Then he looks to the screen, his lips parting as he watches for several seconds the scenario unfolding on the phone. The man on the screen is now lying naked behind the woman on the bed, working the toy on her.

My breath comes faster. Gage's comes in a carnal groan, then a demand, "Let me do it."

It's said full of need, full of savage want. He barely waits for me to answer. Just reaches for the waistband of his shirt with one hand and tugs it off in the swiftest, sexiest move.

"Are you sure you can handle it? It is The Command

Performance after all," I say, grazing the toy over the now soaked panel of my panties.

He moves across the bed like a cat. "I'm fucking sure, *wife*."

I shiver from that name too. "But this toy works really fast. That's why I didn't take my panties off yet. I didn't want to come too quickly."

He drags a hand down his face, like he's trying to get a grip on the situation. "Thanks for that warning."

In a flash, he's at my feet, grabbing the toy from me, tearing down my panties.

"Look at you, baby. Just fucking look at you. So turned on for your man," he praises as he hands me the toy again. "Show me."

I obey, running The Command Performance through my slick folds.

He doesn't look away from my center. He's mesmerized, and it makes me feel powerful and beautiful all at once. He roams his hands up my calves to my knees, then spreads me apart. Staring wantonly. "Show me how you fuck yourself with it. I want to see exactly how you work it so I can do it the way you like."

My nipples harden. I love that he doesn't think he can do it better than the toy or better than me. I love that he just wants to know exactly how I want it so he can give it to me that way. I show him, teaching him, pleasure pulsing through my bones as I rub the toy against my swollen clit, arching into its vibration, gasping out shuddery breaths.

Tingles race through my body, everywhere.

He holds out his palm. "Mine. Now," he barks out.

Excited by his order, I hand it over. He slides the toy against my clit and I howl in pleasure.

It's more than good. It's fantastic. His eyes stray again to the phone where the man on the screen has tossed the toy aside and has entered her.

Gage's eyes return to me. "You watch porn," he says and he sounds amazed, delighted too. "And you like when your man finds you playing with yourself."

I nod quickly. Urgently. Clawing at the sheets. "I do." The pleasure is so intense I can barely think. I can barely speak. He pushes the toy into me, going deeper, filling me with it. "God, yes," I shout.

In seconds, he's owning me with the dildo I bought the night I met him, fucking me deep, artfully.

"I've never done this before," I say, a vulnerable confession, but one that answers my *why*. This is why I raced home. This is why I wanted to surprise him. To give him this first of mine. To experience a first with him.

"Me neither," he says quickly.

Colors dance before my eyes. Pleasure multiplies in me.

I wasn't expecting a first for both of us. But I wasn't expecting any of these feelings for Gage Archer. The way I want him. The way I need him. The way our intimacy keeps surprising both of us in the best of ways.

As he fucks me with the toy, he praises me. "Fucking beautiful. So fucking sexy. So fucking *mine.*"

That last word thrums through me, lighting me up everywhere. Pleasure coils in me, tighter, then I burst, grabbing the sheets as I shatter.

When I come down, he eases out the toy, turns it off, and tosses it on the covers.

I push up on my elbows, greedy for him to return the favor. "Show me how you got off to me."

"I fucking will, baby." Like he's never wanted anything more in his life, he shoves down his shorts. He slides a hand between my thighs and slicks up his fingers with my orgasm. Gripping his hard shaft, he coats his length with my arousal.

His fist is shuttling his cock, his jaw tensing, and he's so incredibly sexy like this. "Fuck, baby, I need to feel you. I need to feel you gripping me. Let me fuck you," he says.

"Please fuck me," I answer. His shorts vanish and he's climbing over me, guiding his eager dick inside me. Then hooking my legs over his shoulders. I can't move like this, and I don't even want to as he sinks into me.

"Oh god, it's better," I say.

His grin is savage. "Yesss."

He can barely speak. He just fucks me hard and deep. His grunts are long and feral. He takes me urgently, a man needing his woman. But he has other needs too.

Mine.

Even though I came already, he's got that determined look in his eyes. The one that says his woman comes first and second.

He maneuvers a hand between us, stroking my swollen clit and driving me wild till I'm begging for him harder and deeper. And he gives me everything I need till I shatter again. He's right there with me, breaking apart on a loud, passionate grunt.

Then collapsing onto me.

Kissing my collarbone. My jawline. My cheek. Sighing against me, a man content. "Gonna call me Maestro now?"

I laugh. "Maybe I will…Maestro."

He smiles against my neck. "Mmm. That was the best surprise."

"I'm glad you liked it," I say.

"I like everything with you, Elodie," he says, his voice rough with sex, but then soft, too, when he repeats one word: "Everything."

I don't think he's just talking about the sex. I'm not either when I say, "Me too."

* * *

Fifteen minutes later, we're good boys and girls, dressed and ready to head to work. On the way out, his phone buzzes. "Grams," he says, then clicks open a text. After a few seconds, he rolls his eyes. "It's Sebastian."

I tense, fear gripping me. "What is it now? Did he tell Felix? Did he smear us on social? Did he say we lied about being fake engaged—"

"I'm sorry. I didn't mean to freak you out. No, he just started this new campaign. He hired a bunch of pretty women to eat chocolate seductively."

I grimace. "He is the worst." But then, he hardly matters. "He can do whatever he wants. My chocolate is five million times better, and he'll never get my recipes."

"Damn straight your chocolate is better. Also his views suck," Gage says.

"Karma," I say, and karma is this too. "And I'm paying off the loan on Friday."

"Congratulations." He picks me up and spins me around. "I always believed in you."

And the thing is, he did.

When he sets me down, his green eyes sparkle with mischief. "Enjoy work today," he says, and there's a secret in his voice.

"What's that for?"

He shrugs innocently. "What's what for?"

"That!" I point at his crooked grin.

"You'll see."

"Gage!"

He drops a kiss to my forehead on the front step. "You'll find out at the shop."

"Are you sending me something again?"

"Maybe," he says, then heads down the steps, waving goodbye.

But I race down after him. "You sent me flowers yesterday."

"I know."

"And you just told me you always believed in me."

"I know that too."

He's doing so many things for me. Words and deeds. They're both terrifying and thrilling.

"I love them all. And I love these secret dates."

"Me too."

But I still don't know what to do with all these new emotions jostling around inside me. I rise up on my tiptoes and kiss him once more. Then I look up. Sigh. Shake my head. "No snow today."

"Maybe tomorrow."

He leaves and when I get to work, a delivery woman heads into the shop a few minutes later. "Are you Elodie?" she barks.

"Yes."

She hands me a white envelope the size of a card. I rip it open. Then laugh. It's a print of one of the graffiti roosters from our first date. I open it and read.

Remember our first date? That time we went on a ferry ride and had our first kiss. Meet me at the ferry terminal tomorrow morning for our secret date.

I clasp it to my chest, my heart fluttering.

36

OUR SECRET DATES

Gage

"Let me get this straight. You're recreating the dates you never went on? The ones you used when you made up the backstory of your fictional romance?" Grams asks as she makes an early morning run to the restaurant supply shop with me.

"Creating them," I explain as I put bags of chocolate chips into a shopping basket.

She shakes her head, but doesn't try to hide her amusement.

"What's so funny?"

"Gage Reginald Archer," she says, like the grand cat who ate the canary.

"Why are you Gage Reginald Archer-ing me?" I ask as I locate some organic coconut in bulk and scoop some into a bag.

"Because you're falling in love with your wife," she declares. And before I can even respond, she cackles, then pumps a fist. "And I knew it. I knew it the night you two were flirting at the bar. I knew it when you went to the back of the bar and she was waiting for you, looking for you, hoping you were going to come back out."

My lips twitch in a smile I try to fight off. "She was?" This detail makes me unreasonably happy.

"Yes. And I told her to keep coming back...so I'm going to take credit for this union."

"Because you told her to return to Sticks and Stones? You tell everyone to return," I say, dumping the final scoop of shredded coconut into the bag. "That's just good business practice."

"And good meddling grandma practice, so yes, I'm officially responsible for the glow on your face."

"I'm not glowing," I grumble.

"You are," she says matter-of-factly.

"I do not glow."

"Yes, you do." She doesn't stop gloating till we're out of the store and loading the cookie ingredients into her car.

But before she starts the engine, she fixes me with a serious look. "You don't dispute you're falling in love with her?"

Lying to myself has come somewhat easily from time to time. But I've never been good at fibbing to Grams. Especially when my heart feels ten times lighter just thinking of Elodie. But also heavier, since there's a part of me—the dark, heavy part of me—that keeps wondering…what if this romance ends the way the others have?

"I am falling," I admit, and this feels like stepping off the ledge of a tall building. "And it's really fucking scary, Grams."

She pats my shoulder sympathetically. "All good things are. Love, roller coasters, and eating shishito peppers."

* * *

An hour later, I'm buying round-trip tickets for the ferry, setting my hand on Elodie's back, and walking with her onto the big boat.

My palms are slightly sweaty. My heart is jittery. Grams was right. This is scary. It's one thing to want to romance my temporary wife. It's another to realize I've already fallen in love with her.

Pretty sure I know exactly when it happened too. Gradually, as I got to know her, then all of a sudden. The other morning when we talked in the kitchen and she helped me to see my past differently—that was when I knew I'd broken my own rule.

The one I set in Vegas when she was walking down the aisle.

When I warned myself to be careful or else I might fall.

Lot of good that rule did.

I've broken it, and I need Elodie to know what the other morning meant to me.

A December breeze whips by, blowing strands of her

blonde hair as we board. Once we're on the boat, I snag a seat by the window since it's too cold on the deck. "Remember the other morning? When you asked about Hailey?" I ask immediately.

"Of course."

Travelers shuffle past us, slumping down into seats, toggling onto laptops, tapping away on phones.

"I don't think I realized I'd been carrying that for so long," I admit. "How heavy it was too. You helped me to see that."

Her smile is bright and hopeful. "I'm glad you could start to let that go."

"I feel lighter in my own shoes," I say, and holy shit. Nerves roar through me. It's like I'm stepping into the future, leaving my old ways behind. It's nerve-wracking, but exhilarating too. "For years, a decade, I held on to that. Kept it to myself."

The horn blows and the ferry pulls away. "It's a relief to let things go."

"It sure is. So thank you for helping me."

She nods, then she's quiet for a beat before she says, "For a long time, too, I thought my parents became super parents with Amanda. I thought I wasn't good enough. But a few weeks ago, she told me she liked that I shared my life with her, that she got to work with me, that we could walk to school together. And it meant the world to me that the things I'd been doing were the things she needed."

"You're a great mom, Elodie," I say, wrapping an arm around her. "And sister."

"Thanks," she says. "I believe that now. She helped

me to see that. But you did too. You helped me see that I'm not just impulsive. Even though, yeah, we are pretty impulsive," she says, shooting me a playful grin. "You'll probably never let me live down the *we're marrying the hell out of each other* comment."

"I might," I say. *If you stay with me.*

"But your faith in me—like with the loan, and the shop, and what we could do, and my potential as a businesswoman—helped me see other parts of myself. Like how maybe I'm not as chaotic as I was raised. Perhaps I'm actually—gasp—responsible. Empathetic too."

"I don't know anyone who's more like that."

"I'm not sure I would have seen those sides of me without you," she says, her blue eyes filled with emotion, and maybe possibility too.

And…hell.

I'm so fucking in love with my wife, it's ridiculous. I'm going to need to do everything to keep her— starting with not scaring her off with a love confession too early. She's spent a long, long time worried she's impulsive. But she's not. She's thoughtful. I can't risk losing her by moving too soon, by playing into those things she's trying to leave behind.

We've got a few more weeks of working together. Then I'll tell her. That gives me a few more weeks to win her big, beautiful heart.

It. Is. On.

* * *

The next morning, I take her to the de Young Museum for our secret date. She shows me her favorite Lichtenstein titled *View from the Window*. I'm not sure I have the tools to say anything intelligent about art, so I just ask, "Why do you like it?"

"Because it's colorful, and it reminds me to see things in new ways," she says, then turns to me with curious eyes. "Are you going to take me to the tea gardens soon too?"

That was on the list of our fictional dates. "Yes."

In the new year, I add silently.

And I'll be counting down.

Until then, I've got my work cut out for me. Elodie's a package deal, and I want my wife to know I'm all in when it comes to her and the fantastic young woman she's raising.

Today's a big day for Amanda, and I'm ready, if all goes well.

37

SNOW DAY

Elodie

After our secret date, I pay off the loan. It feels great to see the balance dwindle to zero.

What a beautiful number.

But Friday afternoon, something even better happens when I hear a shout from the back room where we make the chocolate shortly after Amanda arrives.

"I got in!"

I swivel around, excitement whipping through me. "Bug!"

With her bandana on, Amanda rushes from the back room, squealing as I wrap her in a big congratulatory hug.

Kenji's here, and he gets in on the act, embracing her too.

"I knew it! You're going to be the world's greatest potter," he declares.

When she breaks the hug, she says, "Ceramicist."

He wipes a hand across his brow. "Oh thank god you said that. I hate the word potter."

"Me too," she says, then I hug her again.

"I'm so proud of you," I sniffle into her hair.

"Thanks. Me too," she says, and I can hear all the emotion in her voice. It's so well-deserved.

There's no time to linger in it, though, since the bell chimes and a customer walks in.

We're busy for the next few minutes, and when there's a break, she asks earnestly, "Can I go to the art school though?"

My heart climbs into my throat, tightening with all the emotions, and pride, too, that I can make her dreams come true thanks to this little shop that fed Special Edition.

"Yes."

* * *

That afternoon when we leave, I do a double take. Scents & Sensibility next door has a sign in the window that says *For Rent*.

"Huh. I wonder if that's what Samira meant by perfect timing," I muse, thinking back to when she popped into the store a few weeks ago. Good for her. She seems to be nearing retirement age. She probably just wants to be a real estate magnate now.

"Probably," Amanda says. "Maybe it'll be a cool pottery place."

"A girl can dream," I say.

We head to Zane's home so I can change and freshen up before Gage and I go back to work at Special Edition, and when we arrive, Eliza is peering out the window that looks onto the front entrance.

Her eyes widen, then she swings open the door. "It's a snow day!"

I blink then smile, amused by her use of metaphor. "Yes, it's a snow day," I repeat. "With Amanda's good news and all."

"Shoes off. Let's go," Eliza says.

Amanda toes off her Converse in no time, asking, "Where are we going?"

Eliza zips her lips, then grabs Amanda's hand, and tugs her through the home. Amanda eagerly follows the younger girl, laughing. I kick off my shoes and go too, curious where Gage is. Margo is watching the girls tonight, so maybe he's already at Special Edition. But he said we'd go over together.

When I reach Amanda's room, Gage and Margo are waiting outside the closed door.

"Since it doesn't ever seem to snow in San Francisco, we brought the snow to you," he says, then gestures to the door.

"What is this?" Amanda asks.

"Congratulations," Eliza says, and when Amanda opens the door, I'm stunned. Her floor is covered with white packing peanuts easily a foot high. It looks just like snow.

"We can make snow angels and have snowball fights," Eliza says.

"Oh my god," Amanda says, then walks into the indoor winter wonderland.

I turn to Gage, jaw agape. "You did this?"

"I helped him," Margo says proudly.

"It's incredible," I say, awed.

"They're made of cornstarch, so they're biodegradable. Eliza's idea. When they're done, I can take the *snow* out to the yard and hose them down and boom. They disappear," he says.

I can barely handle how my heart is melting for this man. This is such a gift. *He* is such a gift. They are a gift.

I can't help it. As the girls make snow angels, I smack a kiss to Gage's cheek. Then it hits me. That's the first time I've kissed him—a chaste kiss—in front of them.

I'm not sure they've noticed, but Margo does since she clears her throat and says to her grandson, "Roller coasters. Like I said."

I give him a questioning look.

But he just shrugs like he has no idea.

The theme that night is the holidays, and we serve up truffles on Friday and then Saturday night with the richest chocolate filling and candy cane flakes, along with gingerbread martinis and hot buttered rum.

The crowds are vibrant, decked out in their holiday gear, with reindeer antlers and elf hats.

When a woman in a sexy Mrs. Claus costume orders a martini, I compliment her outfit, then I briefly picture wearing an outfit like that and surprising Gage. I bet he'd love to see me in it. But I bet he'd love me in baggy jammies and thick socks too.

It's a strange thought. A wonderful one as well. And it has me thinking about other holidays. Other celebrations and average, ordinary days too.

For several seconds, as Gage heads to the courtyard to bring some martinis around, I'm a little lost in a haze, but then I snap out of it when a familiar and unwelcome voice says, "Happy holidays."

I blink up at the face of Sebastian at the counter, and my blood goes cold.

"Your business isn't welcome here," I say firmly.

He waves a hand. "Don't worry. I'm not getting anything. Just wanted to let you know we'll be next door neighbors. I've made an offer to lease the shop right next to yours."

Then he leaves, shooting Gage a smug smile as he goes.

My shoulders sink.

Everything was starting to feel too good to be true.

38

HARRIET THE SPIES

Elodie

Fuck him.

Seriously. Just fuck him.

Last night, I was shocked. A little depressed. But in the morning, as Margo takes the girls out for breakfast, I'm mad as hell.

I'm pacing in the state-of-the-art kitchen with Gage. "I'm not going to take this. That man has been nothing but a thorn in my side since the day I met him. And his chocolates suck," I tell Gage. "The gloves are coming off."

Gage smiles as he thrusts a latte at me. "You're hot when you're mad."

I take it and down a swallow of the drink that's almost too hot. But the burn fuels me. "I'm not going to let him get away with this."

"So, what are we going to do? I've got some ideas."

But I can't keep turning to Gage to save me. I need to save Elodie's myself. "I'm going to make an offer on the location," I say.

He blinks over his cup of coffee. "You. Are?"

I've shocked him. Well, I've shocked me too. "It's a little crazy, isn't it?"

"You just paid off the loan," he says, then pauses before he says, "Let me help—"

I cut him off. "I have to fight this battle on my own. I can take out a line of credit and use it to lease the perfume shop. It's a tiny space, but I can use it for the website orders maybe? My web business is way up thanks to Special Edition."

"It'll probably pay for itself pretty quickly then. You won't need to go into debt after just getting out of it," he says, and he sounds enthused for me. Like he's always been.

"I think you're right. I can manage things. I can do this," I say, resolutely. I've spent the morning checking my books. Special Edition has made a lot of things possible. But it also gave me the confidence I needed. "I'm a damn good businesswoman and chocolatier, and I want a chance to lease that property." I check the time. "Samira's usually in on Sundays. I can catch her when she opens and before we do the cookies and cocoa."

He sets down his coffee. "Let's go."

I pause my pacing. "You're going with me?"

"Of course I am."

We leave together, determined. When we arrive at the corner where my chocolate shop is—Elodie's opens in an hour—Gage gives me a kiss on the cheek. "Go get 'em."

I hand him the keys so he can wait inside.

I cover the twenty feet to Scents & Sensibility alone, brightening when I spot Samira inside. But she's taking down the *For Rent* sign.

All my adrenaline burns off. Turns to ash.

I'm too late.

My heart sinks like an anvil dropped from a cartoon skyscraper. But I knock anyway.

She glances at the sound then smiles warmly. She's practically floating as she heads to the door, then swings it open. "Elodie! Want a trade?"

"I want to make an offer," I blurt out.

Her brow knits. "On your regular perfume? I told you trades are the only thing I'll accept. Though I should give you a lifetime supply of La Cerise since I'm retiring now. I got such a great deal."

But maybe she hasn't signed the paperwork yet. Maybe I can make a better offer. "I didn't know it was an option, though, to rent this space. I'd love to have the chance to—"

"It's not an option," she says, and she's smiling. So bright. So broad.

I should be happy for her. She deserves to retire. To live the good life. Still, so should I. "I have a plan for—"

I'm cut off by the ringing of her phone. She glances at it, smiling again. "Oh! I need to take this. Don't want to leave the new tenant waiting. But come back."

Hopes dashed, I leave, trudging to Elodie's. I'll just have to deal with Sebastian.

I make better chocolate.

I have a classier shop.

I'm nicer.

If he drives me out of this neighborhood, I'll start over again with a new location. That man won't put me out of business. I won't give him the power.

When I pull on the door to Elodie's, the comforting scent of chocolate greets me.

But so do Amanda, Eliza, Ally, Kenji, Margo, and Gage. They're all bursting with smiles.

"We have some good news," Kenji chirps.

Amanda grabs my wrist and tugs me to the café section.

"What's going on?" I ask, every single molecule confused.

Once I'm sitting, Amanda clears her throat. "Confession: Eliza, Ally, and I haven't been going to get boba after school."

Worry prickles along my spine. "What have you been up to?" I ask carefully.

"It seems…they're detectives," Gage puts in, clearly amused.

Okay, not drugs.

"And so am I," Margo says, then shifts her head back and forth, hedging. "Okay, more like the getaway driver."

"Ooh, can I be the hacker then in our heist crew?" Kenji asks, enthused.

"You didn't really hack," Ally points out.

My head spins. "Can someone please tell me what's going on?"

Amanda picks up her phone to check the screen, and I'm about to lose my mind. I'm not typically an impatient person, but right now that's all I am.

"It's Silver. She'll be here in a few minutes," Amanda explains.

"That's me," Kenji says, tapping his chest. "I'm the Silver connection."

"Exactly, not the hacker," Ally adds emphatically.

"Guys!" I shout.

"Tell her," Gage instructs.

Amanda meets my gaze with some nerves, but mostly…glee. "Okay, you know how we kept saying The Chocolate Connoisseur's chocolate sucks?"

"I remember that fondly," I say.

"We decided to have a taste test to see if we could figure out why," Eliza jumps in, clearly eager to take a turn in the tale. "Because my dad brought some of it home that day."

Amanda grins. "And the funny thing is it tasted really, really familiar."

"Like a certain store-bought chocolate," Ally adds, then names a very popular brand.

Like household-name levels.

I sit up straighter. "It does?"

Eliza nods, big and long. "Yes. So much."

Amanda sets a hand on my arm, a subtle sign I might not like what she's about to say. "And we really wanted to find out if it was this store-bought brand he was using, so we went to his little factory. It's in a warehouse over in the Mission District. So we were going there instead of going to boba," Amanda says, adding a *please forgive me* grin.

"How did you get to the Mission District?" My voice is on helium.

"We took a bus," Amanda says.

A bus? Alone? Oh god. I'm freaking out and I don't even know why. Except, she's mine and have we gone over the rules for buses? I hope so. I really hope so. The Mission District isn't too far away. But it's not their stomping grounds.

"My sister takes them a lot," Ally explains. "She helped us figure out the routes."

It's fine. A bus is fine. I'm fine. "Okaaaay."

"And we really wanted to go because when I was looking up salad recipes last month I read an article about a restaurant in Los Angeles that claimed to be vegan," Amanda says, sounding just like a detective indeed. "But it turned out they were lying and using real butter and a food writer busted them by looking through their garbage."

"You looked through his garbage?" Helium times ten.

"We used gloves," Eliza explains matter-of-factly. "It was just like the beach cleanup."

I blow out a breath. She has a point. "So, you took it upon yourselves to be investigative chocolate reporters," I say, making sure I've got ahold of the facts.

A warm, reassuring hand slides up my back. "Just let them tell the story."

Amanda bounces. "Anyway, so when we were there, we found out that…"

In unison, all three girls say, "We were right."

That's the real too-good-to-be-true. "You were right?" I repeat slowly because I can't quite believe it. Except I want to believe it so badly.

Kenji hoots. "He doesn't make his own chocolate like he claims. He's not only *not* bean to bar, he's not even chocolate to confection."

The day I met him at the chocolate show, he went on and on about his bean-to-bar creations, with his subtle implication that his small-batch style made him better than my approach as a chocolatier, who sources chocolate to use for her confections.

When he's neither.

He's not a chocolate-maker, nor a chocolatier. He's simply a copycat.

Margo grins sagely. "Apparently, he's the grocery-store-to-Chocolate Connoisseur."

"For real?" I whisper, tingles spreading across my skin. This is too delicious. Too wonderful. I'm holding my breath.

Amanda swipes her thumb across the screen, showing me damning photo after damning photo. Wrappers from bulk-size store-bought brands fill the dumpsters at the factory where The Chocolate Connoisseur produces its cheap chocolate knockoffs that it claims it makes from Ecuadorian cocoa.

More like candy-aisle cocoa.

But…what's next? "So, now what?"

Kenji preens, blowing on his nails. "This is where the hacker comes in. I maybe, possibly hooked them up with Silver. I thought she might want to know about how Mister I Make My Own Chocolate From The

Very Best Beans is actually not making his own chocolate."

"And I brought them to meet with Silver this morning," Margo puts in. "Hence, the getaway driver."

"And what's Silver doing?" I ask.

"Making another video," Eliza says with utter glee in her voice.

As if on cue, there's a knock on the door, and it's Silver, dressed in black with her signature silver eye shadow bright on her glowy skin. She waltzes into the store. "Hey, besties. I posted it," she says, waving her phone as she comes over to join us at the table. She sits down with a certain charismatic panache. "If you're gonna imitate me, I'm gonna call you out."

Take that.

"Already, the video's at more than five thousand views and I posted it a few minutes ago. Pretty soon, word will get out that he's using the cheap chocolate we all use at home."

Kenji parks his hands behind his head. "And that, my friends, is what you call karma."

I sit back, still amazed at this turn of events. But not entirely surprised. A man who'd threaten me the way he did is exactly the type of person who'd lie to all his customers in forty shops across the country.

Then, a dark cloud passes over me. I can't revel in his hoodwinkery.

We lied too.

But lying to customers and the world about the product you sell them is entirely different than lying about who you go home with at night.

I glance at Gage. He looks relaxed, content, and happy. He's running a hand along my back, and enjoying the company of all of us—this ragtag crew. I think about our secret dates. The roses, the lattes, the ferry ride, the art museum. The beautiful care this *not* almost romantic man—this *most* romantic man—took in recreating our fictional dates and turning them so very real. I think, too, about Friday's snow day for my sister. *Our girls.* The joy they found in it. The joy he put into making it happen for them.

My heart stutters then speeds up. It's racing inside me, beating in overtime as it rushes headlong toward this man.

Nothing between us is a lie. And I suppose our romance has never truly been a lie either.

There's just one little issue. "But Sebastian might still be working next door to me," I say.

"He won't last," Gage reassures me, then snaps his gaze to the door. Samira is rapping on it while checking her watch, then glancing back down the street, urging me to come closer.

"Give me a second," I say, then hurry over and step outside.

"I'm sorry to go cliffhanger on you," she begins. "Like I was saying, that was my new tenant, and I didn't want to leave her hanging."

"About that. I'd really like the chance to match…" My brain replays the last pronoun. "Wait, did you say *her*?"

"I did."

"It's not Sebastian Roberts and The Chocolate Connoisseur who's leasing the space?"

She pffts. "Of course not."

"Why of course not?"

"You run a chocolate shop and the store to the right of me is a lingerie boutique. I'm a smart business-woman. I'm not going to lease the space to another chocolate shop. I want all of you to drive business to each other, not take away."

Oh. Well. That does make perfect sense. "Who's leasing it then?"

"Risqué Business is opening another shop," she says, her eyebrows wiggling. "I'm a devotee."

A smile takes me hostage and I don't ever want to be freed. "Me too."

"Doesn't that sound simpatico? Chocolate, lingerie, and sex toys," she says.

It sure does.

It sounds a lot like karma too.

An hour later, Kenji and some part-timers are handling Elodie's while the rest of us take cocoa ingredients and cookies over to the Sunday pop-up.

As I set up a display tray of mouth-watering choco-late chip cookies at Special Edition, a throat clears.

It's Amanda. Eliza's next to her. For a few seconds, I worry it's bad news. Maybe I always will. But Amanda just crosses her arms. Then rolls her eyes. "So, listen. We know you two tried to trick us."

I steal a glance at Gage, asking *what now* with my eyes.

He just shrugs.

"Yeah, but we're pretty smart. We know you two like each other," Eliza says.

"We knew it was real all along. And we think you should go on a real date. So we booked Grams to hang out with us on Tuesday night so you can go to dinner."

"Before my dad and I go to Darling Springs."

I feel like we just got parent-trapped, and I don't mind it one bit. I look to both of these young women. So strong already. So passionate. So damn determined. "You two are pretty smart. And you're right." I turn to Gage. Meet his eyes. Answer them as I look at him. "It's all real."

39

THIS WHOLE REAL THING

Gage

I'm counting down the days, the hours, almost the minutes till my date with Elodie.

If she thought the recreation of our fictional dates was romantic, wait till she sees what I have planned for tomorrow night.

I'm at Sticks and Stones on Monday evening, "handling the bar" as Zoe would say, when I steal a glance at my watch. It's seven, so twenty-four hours to go.

I finish prepping an old-fashioned for table fourteen, handing it to the server to take there when there's a break in the action. "So, when do you find out?" Zoe asks as she reaches for an olive for a martini.

My brow knits. "About…?"

She rolls her eyes. "Hello! The second location."

Yes. That. Of course she means that. "Tomorrow. I

have a meeting with Celeste at five." Right before my date.

"You ready for it?" she asks.

"Absolutely," I say, since that seems like the right answer, even though I feel a little disconnected. Probably because I've been chasing this so long. I've given Celeste all I can. I marketed the hell out of Special Edition. I've proven I can run a successful bar here. I'm not sure what else I can do.

"Let me know. Because maybe you'll promote me from assistant manager to manager if it all works out," she says, bold and straightforward.

Huh. That's not a bad idea. I hadn't given it much thought, but she's onto something. "Maybe I will," I say when Russ arrives. The regular customer parks himself on a stool, saying hello and diving right into hockey talk.

As I pour him his regular brew, we shoot the breeze about how the Golden State Foxes are shaping up two months into the season. Carter and Monroe amble in and grab seats at the bar too.

I excuse myself from Russ, and head over to say hi to my friends. "Always looking for a free drink," I deadpan.

"Free?" Monroe asks, perking up. "Now we get drinks for free?"

"This is news to me," Carter seconds. "But I'll take two then."

I roll my eyes as I set down a pair of coasters. "What'll it be?"

They order their usual, so I pour a scotch for Monroe, and a pale ale for Carter. When I hand them their drinks, Monroe lifts his glass, then says, "To tomorrow night."

I tilt my head. "What do you mean?"

"You mentioned this morning on our run that it's your *real date* with your wife. Does that mean you've figured out what to do at the end of the year?"

Now that's an excellent question. One I've put a lot of thought into.

Carter leans forward. "We're all ears."

I draw a deep, fueling breath. "I think so. When we finish Special Edition, I'm going to let her know I want to keep up this whole...*real thing.*"

Monroe clinks with Carter, then toasts to me. "Good for you for making a decision. Now stick to it."

"I intend to," I say, resolute and so damn ready.

The next day, I'm dressed for my date early, since I want to give Elodie time at the house to get ready and do the whole girl thing with, well, the girls. Plus, Celeste moved our meeting back to six.

I head down Chestnut Street in the Marina, making my way to her office, using the time to reconnect with the location I want. Reminding myself of what I want to do at the potential upscale Sticks and Stones with its brick facade, bright green door, and large windows.

As I stare into the glass, I picture my plans. My vision. What I've been pitching Celeste. And sure, I can see it all clearly.

With that in mind, I head inside. Just like she was the

first time, Celeste's waiting for me, wearing a black pantsuit again, with her tight bun.

"Hello, Mr. Archer. Good to see you," she says, then nods to her office.

"Good to see you," I say, antsy to get this meeting over with.

She gestures to a chair. I sit. She moves behind the desk.

"Thank you again for the ideas you shared. The decor, and the bocce ball, and the added games are smart. So is the upscale menu. It's a very good plan." She sounds exactly like she did that night at Special Edition —removed, robotic. Then she pauses, takes a breath that's not at all robotic. That's far too easy to read. It doesn't take a genius to know what her answer is. "But it can't hold a candle to Special Edition. I know what you're capable of, Mr. Archer, and I wanted that. If you think you can show me that, I'd love to talk again."

After I manage a thank you I barely feel, I walk out of there, shell-shocked. Detached. Scratching my head.

But when I walk past the location I thought I coveted, the picture I saw clearly disappears.

A new one takes its place.

40

A NEW FIRST DATE

Elodie

"That one."

Amanda wastes no time delivering a clothing verdict. She's pointing authoritatively to an emerald-green dress hanging in my temporary closet at Zane's house.

The dress hits at the knees in a swingy skirt, and has sheer three-quarter length black sleeves with embroidered black hearts on them. It's sexy and sweet and has great access, but I keep all that to myself, instead saying, "The OOTD…is dating my husband."

"You're such a weirdo. And…yes," Amanda says, decisive.

Eliza faux coughs. "I don't even get to look?"

The indignance of an eleven-year-old budding fashionista.

Amanda shrugs in acquiescence, but she's a dictator

when it comes to clothes. "I mean, you can pick the shoes, Liza."

Liza, not Eliza. She already has a nickname for her.

I try to hide my smile but likely fail.

"Cool," Eliza says, taking the opportunity and seizing it, even though I didn't bring too many options to Zane's house. Just some Converse, a pair of flats, and a cute pair of strappy two-inch black heels, but Eliza selects those with obvious care, showing them to Amanda. The older girl gives an approving nod...sort of like an older sister would do.

I blink off that wild thought. It's too much. Too good. I don't want to linger on it too long in case it fractures.

Once I'm dressed, Amanda spins me around and studies my face. "A bit more eye shadow." She turns to Eliza, this time inviting her in. "What do you think?"

Taking her role seriously, Eliza tilts her head. "Maybe a touch more mascara."

"And how about that silver necklace with the star for Starling?" Amanda suggests.

Eliza spins around on her pink fuzzy socks. "I'll get it," she says, then rushes over to the bureau and skids to a stop. "Ooh," she says, picking up something shiny, then turning back to me. "Can you wear this too?"

She returns with the cocktail ring.

I smile, the kind that stretches through my whole body, down to my toes. "Yes."

I don't even know what Gage and I are doing tonight, but it'll be fun to wear the ring that got us into this fake fiancé-ship-turned-marriage-of-convenience in the first place.

"It's a good luck charm," I say as I slide it on my right ring finger. Maybe it'll be a talisman for me. Perhaps it'll give me the courage to tell that man how I feel.

My stomach dips as I think of the things I want to say.

I focus on the task at hand—finishing getting ready. I add some shadow, slick on some more mascara, then touch up my lipstick. I turn around and hold out my arms, waiting for my stylists to sign off.

"You look good," Amanda says.

"So pretty," Eliza says, then pats my shoulder. "Now don't worry about us. We're going to heat up my grandma's mac and cheese. She makes the best mac and cheese."

"And then we're going to watch a movie," Amanda adds as they shoo me out of the room and down the stairs. "Margo's going to come over at nine," she says, reviewing the plan. They'll have a couple hours to themselves because they're old enough but then, in case we stay out late, Margo will be here.

When we reach the door, Amanda clears her throat and adopts an older voice as she wags a finger at me. "And you don't have a curfew tonight."

"Thank you so much," I say. I grab my swingy polka-dot purse and a faux fur bolero jacket, but before I go, I turn around and say to both of them, "But don't stay up too late. Amanda has school tomorrow."

My little sister groans. "One more day before break."

Eliza squares her shoulders. "And I'm already on break," she says, gloating.

"You're so lucky," Amanda says.

I go, heading down the steps and then slipping into the waiting Lyft. Gage ordered one for me so I'm not even sure where we're going, but I am sure I'll like the destination.

With him.

After I say hello to the driver, I open my phone. I send a text to Juliet as the red Prius peels away from the curb and into the evening traffic.

Elodie: I'm off to my date.

> Juliet: Every date is a new chance for love, but especially this one.

She said something similar before my first date with him. At the time I replied, *what would I even do with love?* Now, I know what to do with it.

Keep it.

Elodie: I hope so.

41

THE MOST ROMANTIC

Gage

Powered by fast legs and determination, I walk to our date, doing what I often do along the way—think about the future.

But this time it's different.

I'm not *obsessing* about security. I'm *hoping* for something else entirely. Nearly an hour post-meeting with Celeste, and I'm not at all shell-shocked anymore. Not one bit. Everything is clear.

Sometimes you don't get what you want. Or, really, what you thought you wanted. But I don't want that second location anymore. I don't think I have for a while. I'm not even sure I realized that until Celeste said no.

But when she did, a light flickered on. I hadn't given the location much thought recently. I hadn't invested energy in it. I'd lost interest in it because I want other things now.

As I pass the courtyard at The Escape, I glance at the fountain in the cobblestone courtyard, then beyond to where Elodie and I had our first kiss, a kiss that changed who I thought I was—a guy who believed things didn't work out. That's not me anymore. Thanks to her.

I turn the corner. The Lyft app tells me that she's now in the car. She'll be here in ten minutes. I'm almost at the restaurant where we had our first date nearly two months ago. Where I hope we can recreate it tonight.

I reach the Mediterranean-fusion café, then pace in front of the restaurant till the Lyft arrives and the woman of my dreams steps out.

My heart stutters. My breath catches. I've won the lottery for all time.

This is what I want.

Her. Us. Our future together as a family.

I head over to her, take her hand, and then drink her in. With her hair curled at the ends, her shoes clicking, and a little faux fur jacket over her shoulders, she is a vision in retro pin-up.

She's always been beautiful. Her face captivated me the night I met her. But as I've come to know her, I've learned her heart is her most beautiful feature.

I'm about to tell her I can't breathe without her but she speaks first.

"Tell me everything," she says eagerly with avid eyes, squeezing my hand. "How did it go? Did Celeste love your suggestions? Did she say yes?"

"Nope."

Elodie blinks, irked for me. "What? How could she say no?"

I wave a dismissive hand, not for Elodie, but for the location I no longer want. "She said Special Edition was worlds better," I explain quickly. "And it's all good."

There is no more waiting. There is only now.

Letting go of her hand, I cup her cheek. Hold her face. "I promised myself I'd wait until the new year. Until we'd finished working together. But I just can't wait any longer. I can't hold this in. I am out of my mind in love with you. I love you so much," I say, and her eyes sparkle, more blue, more bright than I've ever seen. Now that I've started, I can't stop. "I love you madly. I'm so in love with you, all these feelings drive me wild every single day. I couldn't wait a second longer to tell you that you are the love of my life."

A shudder seems to slide down her body.

Her lush red lips part slowly, full of wonder, like she can't believe what I've said. She's the one shell-shocked now, and I wish I had a camera to capture this moment, but I also know I will never forget it for my whole life.

"You don't have to say anything," I continue since I didn't tell her to hear it in return. "You don't have to say it back. I just couldn't take another breath on this earth without telling you how I feel. I don't want you to feel like you have to be impulsive. I just—"

She covers my mouth with hers and shuts me up with a kiss that makes my heart soar. That melts me. I feel this kiss deep in the center of my soul. It's a kiss that says, *I love you too.* I can feel it in the way her lips coast over mine, in the way her fingers play with the back of my hair. When she breaks the kiss, her gaze is vulnerable, full of the same raw hope I feel. "I'm so in love with you."

I breathe the biggest sigh of relief in the world. And joy too. Unmitigated joy. "Thank god," I say with a little bit of a laugh.

"I love you. I love you so much," she repeats, then laughs too. "It's so good to say it. To feel it."

"Yeah?" I can't quite believe it. It's almost too good.

"Yes, I love you so much. You're the most romantic person I've ever known, and it's all real. You're romantic because you listen to me and you care and you love and you give and you protect and you make me feel incredible." She grabs the collar of the shirt I'm wearing, as she fiercely says, "I'm not letting you go."

I press my forehead to hers, feeling calm, feeling peace. And seeing the true future. Not the one that I'd thought was lined with financial security. But the one that offers the possibility of soul-deep love.

I breathe in her perfume.

Slowly, she pulls back, meets my gaze. "How do we do this?" She sounds hopeful but nervous too.

There's so much to figure out. Our marriage. Special Edition. The girls. The house. The details are a little overwhelming. But if there's one thing I know about my woman, it's that every now and then, she likes it when I take control.

"We'll figure it out after my trip with Eliza. Just know that we're in this together, and we'll work it out like we've worked out everything. Let's just have fun tonight. Let's enjoy our date," I say, then nod to the restaurant entrance.

She smiles. "You're recreating our first date."

"I am."

We go inside and after we order, she asks with some concern, "You really didn't get the place? And you're not upset?"

I shake my head, take her hands in mine, and say, "I have everything I want right here."

A smile. A pause. A moment I want to cherish.

Then her words: "Me too."

* * *

When dinner ends, we head to the hotel where I booked the same room we had the night our first date was cut short. Once I open the door, Elodie acts coy and playful, tapping her chin. "Where did we ever leave off? If memory serves, I was unzipping your jeans," she says, then her hands play with the ridge of my erection.

I shake my head. "If memory serves, you were sitting on my face."

"No, you finished me."

"I'll finish you again." I toss her over my shoulder and take her to the bed.

This time I undress my wife all the way.

This time when I lay her down on the white duvet, naked and resplendent, I place my hand on her neck, curling it over the creamy skin of her delicate throat, feeling her pulse beat beneath my palm.

For me. With me.

Her eyes are wide, flickering with excitement, passion.

Her gaze follows my hand. Then me as I stare at the metal of my ring, glinting against her skin. This is where the gold band belongs.

I run my hand down her flushed chest.

Every breath she takes is shaky, excited. "Are you staring at your ring as you touch me?" She sounds enchanted.

I nod, enthralled by her, owning every second of this new kink of mine. "I am...*wife*."

A tremble runs through her entire body as she watches my palm coasting over her breasts, then down her belly. She shivers under me, her smile burning off. "Keep going...*husband*."

I move lower, settle between her thighs, spread those beautiful legs apart, and gaze once more at the ring on my hand as I touch her soft flesh. "This ring means you're mine," I say.

"All yours." Then her head falls back against the pillow, her hips arch up against my face, and I kiss her. It's a recreation of our first date, but really, it's a whole new first date as I savor the taste of my wife on my tongue, my lips, my face. She gives herself over to me, gasping, clawing at the sheets then coming apart on my mouth with a needy cry, my name a filthy prayer.

I'm undressing as she shakes off the fog of her orgasm, sitting up, reaching for my pants to undo them. "My turn," she says like she did that night.

I shake my head.

She pouts. "Why not?"

"Baby, I need to be inside you. I need to feel you."

I step away from the bed, shed my pants and boxer briefs. My cock springs free, eager, hungry for her.

I climb over her and she pulls me close. For several mind-numbing seconds we kiss like that, naked, skin hot, mouths finding each other. Saying nothing out loud but saying everything with our bodies and our lips. Until I can't take another minute. I break the kiss. "Need you," I say.

"Have me."

It's a wonder I've waited this long to tell her how I feel. And as I sink inside, I know. I just know. She is the rest of my life and it starts tonight.

42

ALL OUR ANYTIMES

Gage

The annual trip that Eliza and I take to Darling Springs is one of my favorite things. We've been doing it for ten years—since it was just her and me. Since before she could remember.

I look forward to it every year.

I'm in the garage on Wednesday morning, tossing an overnight bag in the trunk for our one-night stay at The Ladybug Inn there when Eliza trudges out after me, sighing heavily. I'm still on cloud nine after last night and probably will be for the rest of my life, but it's dad time now.

My kid looks less than excited. As she drops a backpack in the back seat, she shoots me a slightly accusatory look—in the way that only an eleven-year-old can—and says, "Why aren't we taking them?"

I squeeze her little biceps. "Amanda has school. Then

she has ceramics class. You know how important that is to her. Especially now."

She heaves the deepest sigh in the world.

"Buck up, buttercup. You'll survive."

"What if we wait?"

I lift an eyebrow in question. "But we always take the trip this day," I say, confused. I thought she looked forward to our daddy-daughter trip too.

"Yeah we always *did*," she says, emphasis on the past tense. "We always took the trip the day after I got out of school."

"Right. And?"

She stares up at me, like she can't believe I'm not putting it together. "That's what we always did. But we don't have to do that *now*. It feels wrong to go without them. Why don't we just wait for Elodie and Amanda?"

I pinch the bridge of my nose and shake my head.

"Seriously? It's a no?"

I sigh now, but it's chased with laughter. How did I miss this? I open my eyes, then kneel so I'm closer to her height. "You're right. You're absolutely right."

She beams, that frown disappearing, stat. I shut the door to the garage and head back into the house, bounding up the steps to the kitchen, Eliza on my tail.

Elodie's in the kitchen, crunching into a piece of toast, reading something on her phone, wearing a pair of wide-legged jeans and a red blouse with black polka dots—her chocolatier costume, as she has said. Setting down her phone, she tilts her head and looks my way in question. "Did you forget something?"

She was adorable when I packed, reminding me not

to forget my charger, my toothpaste, and a book for Eliza to listen to on the drive even though it's less than a couple hours away and we usually talk the whole time.

"You and Amanda," I answer confidently. And once more, I don't want to wait a second longer. I don't want to figure things out after the trip. The future is *now*. "I don't want to take this trip without my wife. I don't want to spend Christmas without my wife. I don't want to go into the new year without my wife. We want to wait for Amanda to get out of school and take this trip with her and you. Today."

"Gage Archer, you keep surprising me," she says with a smile. Then she turns to Eliza. "Is that what you want?"

"Yes!" Then Eliza turns quiet, looks down at the floor, then back at Elodie. "I think I love you."

And that's it. I'm just done for.

I press the heel of my hand over my eyes, my throat tightening.

Elodie closes the distance to my daughter, sets her hands on her shoulders, and says, "And I love you."

Ah hell. My eyes are stinging now.

They hug and when Eliza breaks the hug, she shoots me a curious look. "Do you have something in your eye again?"

"Yes," I choke out.

"It's been a while since that happened," she says.

"I know," I say, my voice cracking. A long while.

"You can join in too."

And I do, hugging both of them like I don't want to let go—because I don't.

* * *

Eight hours later, Amanda has washed the clay from her hands and packed a bag, and she's tossing it into the trunk.

"Kenji will handle the shop tonight and tomorrow," Elodie says to me.

"That guy deserves a raise."

"Don't you worry. I already gave him one. I *might* have also suggested to the blond guy he's been crushing on at Samira's shop that he should stop by and pick up some free chocolate I left out for him."

"You little matchmaking sneak."

She shrugs proudly.

Then the four of us get into the car and set off for our first family trip. As the girls chat in the back, I reach for Elodie's hand, squeezing it across the console. "Got another room," I say quietly to her.

"Oh, you did?"

"Yeah. I figured newlyweds need it."

She tips her forehead toward the back seat. "And I bet they'll like sharing a room."

"I bet they will too."

As they chatter on, Elodie asks, "You're really not upset at all about not getting the second location?"

I shake my head with zero regret. "The thing is, I've never been happier not to get it," I say. I tell her about looking into the window last night. "I didn't see the location I thought I wanted. I saw Sticks and Stones. Sticks and Stones is busy and popular. I don't have to be greedy and get more. I have enough. And I love spending time with my family."

She glances back at the girls. "Yeah, you do."

"I don't want to work as much as I would have to if I had it," I say, driving along the winding hills toward the California coast. "But there is one thing I think I would like. Want to know what that is?"

"Me?" She bats her lashes.

"Yeah, I think I've made that clear," I tease, then turn serious. "I'd really like to keep doing the Sunday hot chocolate and cookies. All of us."

"I can picture that perfectly."

"So can I. And maybe the occasional cocktails and chocolates with you?"

"Hmm. Let me see if I can fit you into my calendar, Mr. Archer."

"You let me know, cupcake."

"I will."

But then I grip the wheel harder. Just because I want that doesn't mean it'll happen. "The question is whether Felix will ever want to work with us again when he finds out we tricked him," I say, heavily. "I'd have to tell him."

"You would."

"The place might not even be available."

"It might not," she seconds, then pauses. "But what if it is?"

I picture Sundays with my favorite people. "I'd like that."

Especially since nothing, not a damn thing, about

this moment and this romance and this time with her
has ever felt fake.

*   *   *

That night after we take the girls out to dinner at a cute
little sandwich shop next to a handmade soap and
lotions store, Elodie tugs on my hand, pulling me back
toward her as the girls wander inside.

We're standing under the sign for a shop named The
Slippery Dipper. "Thanks for bringing us here," she says.

"Anytime," I say, and I relax, knowing we'll have all
our anytimes. Well, as long as I do one more thing.
"You're my wife, after all. And you're staying my wife.
Just in case that wasn't clear."

She laughs. "It's very, very clear. And I like this order
a lot."

EPILOGUE

A SECOND TIME AROUND

Gage

Early next week, I trot up the steps that lead into the courtyard of The Escape, heading toward the lobby for Felix's office. I scheduled an appointment to meet with him, telling him I had two things to discuss.

I'd be lying if I said my muscles weren't tense. But a man's got to do what a man's got to do.

Own up.

In his office, with the door closed, seems as good a place as any to do it. But when I near the pop-up shop, I do a double take. Felix is there behind the counter, stocking more items. I peer. Are those our Special Edition T-shirts?

Yeah, they are.

He waves me over. So much for the privacy of the office, but at least the shop is closed.

"Gage," he says, when I push open the door and he

adds a new shirt to the stack. "We can't keep these in stock, but that's a good problem to have."

"Definitely," I say, and then I nod toward the shirts and other merch. I'm a goddamn bartender. I know how to talk to anyone. "Did you ever think you'd be selling merch for a hotel?"

He smiles. "I can honestly say never."

We shoot the breeze for a bit, but then he pauses, comes around the counter, and gives me a straight-shooter look that disarms me since I'm so used to his grandpa style. "But you're not here to make small talk. What's going on?"

I suppose that's no surprise. He runs a wildly successful business. He doesn't have time to dick around.

"Sir," I begin, since he feels like a sir right now.

"Yes?"

I swallow down my nerves. "I'd really like to keep doing this."

"Special Edition?" His voice pitches up with tempered hope.

"Elodie is pretty busy with her store, and honestly, I want to spend more time with her on weekends."

He smiles warmly. "That's great."

"But we'd love to do the cocktails and chocolates once a month, if that's of interest to you. And we all really enjoy the Sunday pop-up. Is there any way you'd consider extending the lease on Sundays for me? And my grandma and the kids?"

Now that I've said that out loud, it's a *big* ask.

He exhales, his face unreadable as he seems to give it

some thought. "I have to see what else I might do with the space. But I like the idea."

"Great," I say, but that was the easy bit of this two-part convo.

"And your other matter of business?"

No point dragging my feet. "And the other thing is… Elodie and I weren't actually engaged when we rented the place."

His brow knits. "Excuse me?"

Shit. I've offended him. But I soldier on. "We had the impression you wanted us to be engaged, so we pretended to be. You said you'd prefer to lease to a committed couple, so we decided to act like one."

When the ruse registers fully, his expression falters. "Oh." It's said with more disappointment than I expected.

"I'm sorry we lied to you."

He scrubs a hand over his beard. "And the wedding? Was that a lie too?"

"No, we really got married, even though it was a little impromptu," I say. His eyes stray to my ring, like he's checking the facts, so I keep going. "And we're staying married. But I wanted you to know the score."

A smile shifts the corner of his lips, but he seems to fight it off as he asks, "So you faked it, but got married for real, and fell in love?" He sounds too amused. That has to be a good thing.

"Yes, sir."

"I did have a good feeling about the two of you." He sighs contentedly. "I can just tell. It's a gift of mine."

He doesn't sound mad in the least.

But he also doesn't offer me the lease. "I'll let you know if it'll work out," he says.

* * *

After dinner that night, Elodie and I pore over real estate listings in San Francisco, scouring rentals. "We can't stay here much longer," I say, looking fondly at Zane's palace of a place.

"And neither one of our places is big enough for the four of us," she says heavily.

"But we'll keep looking," I add. "We'll find something."

And we do look, every night and every day until finally, we find a small three-bedroom outside of Hayes Valley that's available in two weeks.

I'm on that listing so fast.

A few days later, we sign the lease, then make plans to move in together.

And since my wife likes football, and Carter plays for the team, we say yes when Elodie's friend Rachel invites us to attend a game in a VIP suite to cheer on the star receiver. We pile into the chichi room above the field before the game. It's full of familiar faces and new ones too. Monroe's here, and so is Carter's brother, Axel. He's a thriller writer, and he's married to Elodie's friend Hazel, who's also a writer.

"And you write Elodie's favorite books," I say when I meet her.

Hazel smiles. "I've trained her well." Then she adds, "And Elodie makes my favorite chocolates."

Juliet's here too, and I thank her and Monroe for the bad sex challenge episode. "We took it," I tell them, then add, "But we made it the great sex challenge."

Elodie shoots me a naughty look. "And we take it every single day."

"And night," I add.

"Show-offs," Monroe mutters.

Then Elodie introduces me to her friend Fable, who's wearing a team jersey I've never seen before. It's sparkly with seventies vibes in the font. "Cool shirt," I say.

"Thank you. I designed it," she says, proudly. "And thank you for making my friend so damn happy. I'd be jealous if I didn't adore her so much." She squeezes Elodie's shoulder.

"You'll find your magic D soon," Elodie says, and a minute later, the door swings open.

A man in a sharp suit that can only be custom tailored strides in with the kind of confidence that says he owns the place.

Because, well, he does.

I'm not usually starstruck, but I don't bump into a lot of billionaires. That's Wilder Blaine and the dude just has charisma. Poise. "Fable," he says, in a deep, commanding voice.

She turns to him, flashing a smile. "Yes, boss?"

That surprises me. She doesn't seem fazed by his intensity.

"Do you have a second to discuss the proposal?"

She rolls her eyes his way. "Before kickoff? Do you ever stop working, boss man?"

Elodie whispers in my ear, "Someone is sassy with the boss."

I just nod.

Wilder glances at his watch, amused as he points out, "It's not kickoff yet."

"Fine, fine," she says, then heads up the steps in the suite.

The man with the dark eyes and chiseled jaw watches her closely as she walks. When she reaches him, he gives a crisp nod to the rest of us. "Go Renegades," he says, then leaves with Fable.

I turn to Elodie to ask what's up with that. But she's already grabbing Juliet's arm. "Did you get a vibe?"

"We all got a vibe," Juliet says.

"Every single one of them," Rachel adds.

"If they aren't banging in his office now I'm going to be really mad," Hazel says.

When Fable returns a few minutes later, the ladies pull her aside for a debrief, and I make a mental note to ask my wife for details after the game.

Then I settle in and root for the home team.

At the end of the year, Special Edition winds down, but Sticks and Stones keeps me busy. I promote Zoe, who's all too happy to take on more work, freeing me up some nights to come home to my girls.

Elodie's busier than ever since her store continues to reap the benefits of the buzz she so rightfully deserves.

But she's hired smart and capable employees, and she has Kenji, who's her right-hand man.

As for Sebastian, it's such a shame. It seems he's going out of business. Everything is ninety percent off as he's been forced to shut down his shops. I guess no one wanted his brand of small batch after all.

In early January, Elodie is at work and I'm at her place, packing up her kitchen cabinets, when Felix calls me. I answer it so fast.

"Hello, sir."

"I have an update."

"I'm ready," I say, steeling myself for whatever verdict he'll render. I took a big swing and there's a good chance I'll miss. "I leased it on Friday and Saturday evenings to a cake shop that makes the best flavors—Earl Grey, lemon cake with blackberry jam, chocolate cake with potato chip filling."

Damn, my mouth is watering while he's rejecting me. "Those all sound delicious."

"But wouldn't you know? The cake shop owners want one Friday night off a month, so I'd happily take cocktails and chocolate on the first Friday of each month. And the place is yours on Sundays too…on one condition."

I punch the air. "Anything."

"You should have a real wedding. At my hotel. It's on me."

I'm not saying no to that.

But there is something I have to do first.

* * *

Grams and I do a little shopping, heading to a certain jewelry store on Fillmore Street, owned by Rachel. It doesn't take long for me to find the perfect ring, bright and sparkling, like my wife.

"So this is her third engagement ring?" Grams asks when we leave.

"Yup."

"You should make it a thing. Give her one each year."

"Don't tempt me. I will."

She laughs. "Don't I know it."

Elodie's at work, so I head to the store, and it's teeming with customers. I go right up to the counter, like I did the first day I asked her out, with the blue velvet box in my hand.

"What can I do for you, handsome?" she asks.

I get down on one knee, flip open the box, and say, "Marry me again. So all our friends and family can come to our wedding."

When she races around the counter, saying *yes, yes, yes,* the whole store erupts into cheers.

A few days later, my brother and his partner return from their trip and take us out to dinner. Zane walks into the restaurant with a shopping bag from what looks like a men's store in London, Maddox by his side. When we make eye contact, he thrusts the bag at me. "Figured you'd need a wardrobe upgrade for all the dates you'll be taking your wife on." Then he turns to

Elodie and says, "Thank you for making my brother happy."

"Anytime."

* * *

One day in February, we invite all our friends and family to an intimate ceremony in the courtyard of The Escape near where we had our first kiss, and then our first official date. Maybe we did this whole romance a little out of order. Or a lot.

But as I wait at the fountain in the courtyard, my brother beside me, watching my wife walk up the steps while a string quartet plays "It Had to Be You," and Amanda and Eliza by her side, I'm pretty sure everything worked out exactly as it was meant to.

I say *I do* to Elodie for a second time, then I kiss my bride.

I loved writing Elodie's and Gage's romance so much that I wasn't ready to say goodbye! Scroll below for access to an exclusive bonus scene of their life together, but first be sure to find out how Rachel's and Carter's spicy, friends-to-lovers, sports romance unfolded in Plays Well With Others, FREE IN KU! You'll want to grab Hazel's and Axel's sexy enemies-to-lovers romance filled with dirty talk, banter, a feisty heroine, a grumpy hero, and only one bed in the room for free in KU too in My So-Called Sex Life.

Juliet's romance with her brother's best friend,
Monroe, comes next FREE to KU in JUNE!

* * *

Click here for the The Almost Romantic Bonus
Epilogue! Or scan the QR code!

Turn the page for a teaser!

EXCERPT - THE RSVP

Already read the other books in the How to Date series? Then you'll love The RSVP! Here's an excerpt below!
    -LB

* * *

Harlow

On the way to work on Tuesday, I spot a black rotary phone on the stoop of a brownstone. Odd. Is it headed for someone's vintage collection or destined for the trash? I snap a picture, then post it with the caption: ***Coming or going?***

Even though I've already finished my report, I want to read it over again and then send it at just the right time.

I wait till the end of the day, then email it to Bridger.

As closing time nears, Jules packs up. "Time to go," she says.

"I've got a little more to do."

She arches a brow. "Suit yourself."

I will, Jules. I fucking will.

Once everyone leaves, including Jules—*especially* Jules—I head to Bridger's office and rap twice.

"Come in," he says, and I stride inside and then shut the door with finality—a loud, declarative click.

"What did you think?" I ask.

He laughs. "You think I read it already?"

"I think you read it as soon as it landed twenty minutes ago," I say, feeling confident and powerful.

"I think your report is brilliant. And I think the phone is going." There's a sparkle in those blue eyes as he confesses he's looked up my photos—a confession that makes me feel bubbly.

"I think it's coming. Or staying, I should say," I add.

"I can see that too," he says, his eyes never leaving mine.

Now I feel more than bubbly. I feel...bold. I move closer, jutting out a hip against the side of his desk.

His eyes travel up and down my legs like he's fighting not to but can't resist. Good thing I like wearing skirts as much as he likes looking at my legs. "Did Carlos get you that intro to Fontaine?" I ask, prompting him.

"He's still working on it."

I smile, but it's a small one so I don't let on how thrilled I am that Carlos hasn't quite come through. "Then, what are you doing tomorrow night?" I ask.

For a second, he startles. I've surprised him. Good. He's most pliable when he's off-kilter. "I'm working," he answers.

I shake my head, then pop up onto his desk, perching my butt on the edge. "No, *we're* going to the Petra Gallery. There's an exhibit. Allison Tanaka-Fontaine is a silent partner in the business."

It's like watching a sunrise, the way his smile spreads, slow and unstoppable. "You're indispensable," he says as if amazed by me.

Good. I want to amaze him.

"I got us on the VIP list," I add.

"You did?"

"I sure did." I go for the kill, crossing my legs and leaning a little closer. "I wanted to do this for you."

"Harlow," he says, a low warning.

"We can go together," I say, pushing more. I'm not letting this chance pass me by.

"Together?" he asks, like he's never heard the word, never uttered it.

I slide my palm farther across his desk. I'm at a sharper angle now. The kind that shows off hips, and curves, and breasts. All the places he wants to touch me. "Yes, like a date," I say, and I should be nervous. But I'm not. I've been working up to this moment for the last year. I'm simply ready for my gift.

"This is a bad idea," he warns.

He's wrong. It's not a bad idea at all. "Are you sure about that?"

Another harsh breath. His eyes close. The man is at

war. Well, some men need to chase. I sit up, hop off the desk, head to the door.

The wheels of his chair squeak.

In no time he's up too, grabbing my wrist, yanking me around, and jerking me against him.

My wrist tingles. My body sings.

He glares at me, fire in his eyes. "You have done nothing but tempt me for the last few weeks," he hisses.

An accusation. And also the truth.

"Good," I whisper in a taunt.

"Why the fuck are you tempting me?" He bites it out, but it's not a question for me. It's for the universe. It's rhetorical.

Portrait of a man breaking. It's happening. Before my very eyes. This is art, and I love it.

My pulse beats wildly fast.

But I've been patient. I've waited for my chance. I stay patient.

He will bend. He will break. "Am I, Bridger? Am I that tempting?" I ask.

His nostrils flare. He exhales harshly. "You're destroying my self-control, Harlow."

I hum, like the wicked vixen I am with him. "Then… ruin it. Just ruin it."

He grabs my face, and he takes what he wants—my mouth in one hot kiss.

Read the rest of THE RSVP, a sexy, emotional, forbidden, age gap office romance FREE IN KU!

BE A LOVELY

Want to be the first to know of sales, new releases, special deals and giveaways? Sign up for my newsletter today!

Want to be part of a fun, feel-good place to talk about books and romance, and get sneak peeks of covers and advance copies of my books? Be a Lovely!

THANK YOU

Thank you so much for taking the time to read Gage's and Elodie's romance! I hope you loved them like I do! Reader reviews are the best way for others to discover new romance stories! I would be so grateful if you'd leave a review on the platform of your choice!

Xoxo

Lauren

MORE BOOKS BY LAUREN

I've written more than 100 books! **All of these titles below
are FREE in Kindle Unlimited**!

Double Pucked

A sexy, outrageous MFM hockey romantic comedy!

Puck Yes

A fake marriage, spicy MFM hockey rom com!

Thoroughly Pucked!

A brother's best friends +runaway bride, spicy MFM hockey
rom com!

The Virgin Society Series

Meet the Virgin Society – great friends who'd do anything for
each other. Indulge in these forbidden, emotionally-charged,
and wildly sexy age-gap romances!

The RSVP

The Tryst

The Tease

The Dating Games Series

A fun, sexy romantic comedy series about friends in the city
and their dating mishaps!

The Virgin Next Door

Two A Day

The Good Guy Challenge

How To Date Series (New and ongoing)

Friends who are like family. Chances to learn how to date again. Standalone romantic comedies full of love, sex and meet-cute shenanigans.

My So-Called Sex Life

Plays Well With Others

The Almost Romantic

Juliet's And Monroe's Romance (coming in June 2024)

Sawyer's Romance with Mystery Woman (August 2024)

Wilder's and Fable's Romance (November 2024)

Boyfriend Material

Four fabulous heroines. Four outrageous proposals. Four chances at love in this sexy rom-com series!

Asking For a Friend

Sex and Other Shiny Objects

One Night Stand-In

Overnight Service

Big Rock Series

My #1 New York Times Bestselling sexy as sin, irreverent, male-POV romantic comedy!

Big Rock

Mister O

Well Hung

Full Package

Joy Ride

Hard Wood

Happy Endings Series

Romance starts with a bang in this series of standalones following a group of friends seeking and avoiding love!

Come Again

Shut Up and Kiss Me

Kismet

My Single-Versary

Ballers And Babes

Sexy sports romance standalones guaranteed to make you hot!

Most Valuable Playboy

Most Likely to Score

A Wild Card Kiss

Rules of Love Series

Athlete, virgins and weddings!

The Virgin Rule Book

The Virgin Game Plan

The Virgin Replay

The Virgin Scorecard

The Extravagant Series

Bodyguards, billionaires and hoteliers in this sexy, high-stakes series of standalones!

One Night Only

One Exquisite Touch

My One-Week Husband

The Guys Who Got Away Series

Friends in New York City and California fall in love in this fun and hot rom-com series!

Birthday Suit

Dear Sexy Ex-Boyfriend

The What If Guy

Thanks for Last Night

The Dream Guy Next Door

Always Satisfied Series

A group of friends in New York City find love and laughter in this series of sexy standalones!

Satisfaction Guaranteed

Never Have I Ever

Instant Gratification

PS It's Always Been You

The Gift Series

An after dark series of standalones! Explore your fantasies!

The Engagement Gift

The Virgin Gift

The Decadent Gift

The Heartbreakers Series

Three brothers. Three rockers. Three standalone sexy romantic comedies.

Once Upon a Real Good Time

Once Upon a Sure Thing

Once Upon a Wild Fling

Sinful Men

A high-stakes, high-octane, sexy-as-sin romantic suspense series!

My Sinful Nights

My Sinful Desire

My Sinful Longing

My Sinful Love

My Sinful Temptation

From Paris With Love

Swoony, sweeping romances set in Paris!

Wanderlust

Part-Time Lover

One Love Series

A group of friends in New York falls in love one by one in this sexy rom-com series!

The Sexy One

The Hot One

The Knocked Up Plan

Come As You Are

Lucky In Love Series

A small town romance full of heat and blue collar heroes and sexy heroines!

Best Laid Plans

The Feel Good Factor

Nobody Does It Better

Unzipped

No Regrets

An angsty, sexy, emotional, new adult trilogy about one young couple fighting to break free of their pasts!

The Start of Us

The Thrill of It

Every Second With You

The Caught Up in Love Series

A group of friends finds love!

The Pretending Plot

The Dating Proposal

The Second Chance Plan

The Private Rehearsal

Seductive Nights Series

A high heat series full of danger and spice!

Night After Night

After This Night

One More Night

A Wildly Seductive Night

Joy Delivered Duet

A high-heat, wickedly sexy series of standalones that will set your sheets on fire!

Nights With Him

Forbidden Nights

Unbreak My Heart

A standalone second chance emotional roller coaster of a romance

The Muse

A magical realism romance set in Paris

Good Love Series of sexy rom-coms co-written with Lili Valente!

I also write MM romance under the name L. Blakely!

Hopelessly Bromantic Duet (MM)

Roomies to lovers to enemies to fake boyfriends

Hopelessly Bromantic

Here Comes My Man

Men of Summer Series (MM)

Two baseball players on the same team fall in love in a forbidden romance spanning five epic years

Scoring With Him

Winning With Him

All In With Him

MM Standalone Novels

A Guy Walks Into My Bar

The Bromance Zone

One Time Only

The Best Men (Co-written with Sarina Bowen)

Winner Takes All Series (MM)

A series of emotionally-charged and irresistibly sexy standalone MM sports romances!

The Boyfriend Comeback

Turn Me On

A Very Filthy Game

Limited Edition Husband

Manhandled

If you want a personalized recommendation, email me at laurenblakelybooks@gmail.com!

CONTACT

I love hearing from readers! You can find me on TikTok at LaurenBlakelyBooks, Instagram at LaurenBlakely-Books, Facebook at LaurenBlakelyBooks, or online at LaurenBlakely.com. You can also email me at lauren blakelybooks@gmail.com

Milton Keynes UK
Ingram Content Group UK Ltd.
UKHW020815080324
439029UK00015B/803